Praise for Chloe Harris

SECRETS OF SIN

"Obsession and passion sizzle on the pages of this mouth-watering debut."
—Kate Douglas, author of the Wolf Tales series

"Sensuality at its best!"
—Diana Cosby, author of *His Woman*

"Chloe Harris's debut novel is funny and slightly dark in a sensationally passionate way where jealousy, desire and love run wild. A great read!"
—Mandy Burns for *Fresh Fiction*

"Set in the Caribbean in 1745, this story is hot from page one, and the temperature just keeps rising. The characters are well wrought, and a clever subplot sets up the sequel."
—*Romantic Times Book Reviews*, Four Star

"These authors turned me into a believer, and made this book an enjoyable one . . . it touched me at a deep emotional level."
—Sarah Silversmith for *The Romance Readers Connection*

"A superheated erotic historical romance starring two delightful lead characters . . . Readers will relish this strong mid-eighteenth-century Caribbean erotica!"
—*Genre Go Round Reviews*

"Secrets of Sin . . . had me at hello. This book is erotic without being porny . . . really hot and descriptive . . . a compelling read!"
—Lynette Curtis for *The Season*—Historical Romance

Also by Chloe Harris

SECRETS OF SIN

In Deep

CHLOE HARRIS

APHRODISIA

KENSINGTON BOOKS

http://www.kensingtonbooks.com

APHRODISIA BOOKS are published by

Kensington Publishing Corp.
119 West 40th Street
New York, NY 10018

All Kensington Titles, Imprints, and Distributed Lines are available at special quantity discounts for bulk purchases for sales promotions, premiums, fund-raising, and educational or institutional use.

Special book excerpts or customized printings can also be created to fit specific needs. For details, write or phone the office of the Kensington special sales manager: Kensington Publishing Corp., 119 West 40th Street, New York, NY 10018, attn: Special Sales Department, Phone: 1-800-221-2647.

Aphrodisia and the A logo Reg. U.S. Pat & TM Off.

ISBN-13: 978-0-7582-3854-2
ISBN-10: 0-7582-3854-1

First Kensington Trade Paperback Printing: December 2010

10 9 8 7 6 5 4 3 2 1

Printed in the United States of America

In Deep

1

Jaidyn Donnelly heard the door open behind her. The unbearable task ahead was imminent. She tried not to cringe, but how on earth was she ever going to get through this?

She would because she had to. Wallowing in self-pity was not an option. Jaidyn had to keep telling herself it would be over soon enough. Then before too long she'd be off and it would have all been worth it. Yes, not only did she have to keep telling herself that, she had to keep convincing herself to believe it.

It was the only way to earn a passage north. Where she needed to be; where she was supposed to be. Yesterday wouldn't be too soon.

Madame Poivre, her hostess these past few weeks, had warned her she didn't think Jaidyn was cut out to be one of the girls. Well, she might not be, now or ever, but her body was all Jaidyn had. And she was determined to make use of it any way she could, period.

She steeled her spine just as Madame Poivre murmured, *"Amusez-vous, Messieurs,"* and let Jaidyn's first customers enter.

Customers—plural. She still couldn't quite wrap her head

around the idea of that. But when she saw them, her trepidation grew even more and her pulse leapt.

Contrary to what she expected, they were both reasonably tall and quite handsome. They both moved with an air of confidence that was more intimidating than she could have ever imagined. The man who absently threw his coat over the chair and began moving toward the bed was blond. The other man stood just inside the door and didn't move. He only stared at her. His hair was black. Not dark brown but shiny pitch-black. And his eyes looked like the sea she'd recently crossed and the sky above.

She knew that coloring.

Dear Lord! Not a fellow countryman. What were the odds of that in this remote corner of the wilds of the Caribbean?

The fact that this man might well be Irish caused a deeper shame and the comfort of kinship to battle for control within her.

She noticed that both men were now watching her and waiting. Jaidyn subconsciously looked away. Clearing her throat, she pulled the flimsy white dressing gown tighter over the matching corset that was scandalously cut below her breasts.

"Gentlemen," she began with a croaky voice barely over a whisper. "I have been instructed on what you expect. So, what would you have me do?"

The blond leaning on his elbows on the bed spoke first. "Patience. We have all afternoon and half of the night for this . . . At least I do. I believe my friend can stay even longer."

The lazy buoyancy in his voice shook her while his words confused her. What could possibly take so much time to do? Could they possibly want to more than once?

Surely not.

Jaidyn swallowed the building anxiety and studied a fascinating flower in the slightly worn carpet.

She looked up when she heard the soft rustle of fabric. The

dark-haired man had thrown his coat over the blond's and he was moving toward her.

Jaidyn stood as still as a statue as he walked slowly around her like he truly was examining a piece of sculpture. She could almost feel his cheek upon her hair and barely heard the words he spoke against it. "Tell us your name."

With a quiver, Jaidyn shook her head. She wouldn't give them her name. For one, she didn't feel as if she was still that woman who had left Ireland with happy expectations and dreams of a grand new life. And secondly, she just couldn't attach her disgrace to her birth name.

The black-haired man walked around her until he faced her. She shuddered once more.

"Are you cold?" He clasped her hands in his and she fought her first instinct to pull away.

"Come, sit down," he offered next.

This time Jaidyn didn't resist when he pulled her to the bed until she perched on the end of it between the two men. Heat began to seep into her whole body as the dark-haired man continued to warm her hands.

"I am Connor. And this is Reinier."

Connor. What a solid Irish name. She even had a cousin named Connor. There was no doubt in her mind now that he was her countryman. Her eyes moved to the floor. Once again she was torn between the solace and familiarity of home and the dishonor to her kin.

"Tell us something about you. Where are you from?"

She turned toward the blond man—Reinier, if she remembered correctly—and really looked at him for the first time. His eyes were amazing. She had never seen eyes like those before. Her own eyes were a deep emerald color but his were gold, mixed with the lightest, clearest shade of pale crisp green. They were so mesmerizing, she found she couldn't lie. "Éire. I was born and raised in Ireland."

Connor's hands on hers immediately stopped their caress.

Her heart sank. Had she said something wrong? Was he saddened that an Irishwoman had been brought so low? Somehow it hurt that this man might be disappointed in her.

"Born and raised?" Reinier questioned as Connor's hands tenderly moved up and down her upper arms.

She looked slightly away from Reinier's piercing gaze as she stuck to the story she'd concocted. "I am a maid's daughter. My father is unknown."

"You look like you loved to ride through the vast green fields bareback."

"Indeed, I did!" How did he know that? Bittersweet memories flooded her mind. Images of how she dashed through the lush countryside on the back of the filly that wouldn't let anybody close but her. Sadly, she'd never found the pleasure in "ladylike" entertainment such as needlework or fashion as the other girls her age did, elevated status or no. She'd much more enjoyed the rougher company of her outré cousins. "Much to my cousins' dismay, though." Jaidyn herself was surprised by the laughter that escaped when she thought back on the merry times then. "But was it my fault that their horses weren't as fast as mine?"

She caught Reinier looking over her shoulder at Connor with what she thought was an oddly knowing expression just before she felt Connor's warm breath on her ear. It was comforting to know he was here with her. It made her head—and her heart—suddenly light.

"You had a horse?" Connor's words catapulted her into the harsh reality of here and now. That jolly laughter died in her throat. What had she said! A grave mistake. Surely she would never last long enough at this to do what she needed to do if she couldn't even keep her story straight after ten minutes in the presence of two reasonably attractive clients.

Gathering her thoughts again, Jaidyn took the offensive as

she looked to Connor. "Of course not. I only helped the groom so often that he let me secretly ride a horse when the masters weren't home."

Seeing Connor's pupils dilate, Jaidyn instantly regretted her haughty tone. He was the customer. She should behave more like what was expected of her—only she'd never been good at that.

"You were grooming horses when you didn't work in your masters' household?" Reinier inquired.

Jaidyn wanted to reply; she was trying to think of another facet to her story, but when Reinier took her hand in his, all she could do was watch as he slowly raised it to his elegantly full lips. He placed a kiss so gentle on her palm. Connor's caress on her arms now felt like the light touch of butterfly wings.

Her mind stopped working for a moment. Jaidyn felt adrift in something she couldn't quite understand. Her skin heated under their touches and felt as if it was suddenly too tight.

Stunned at her own reaction, she met Reinier's unique gaze again. She let him guide her hand to his midsection.

Immediately the warmth of skin and lean muscle permeated her palm even through his clothing. Next, Connor's gentle touch brushed her hair aside. She wanted to linger in the amazement that so far this had been easy and gentle and not at all the quick roughness she'd expected, but she never had the chance. That moment both their lips rained kisses along her neck.

The sensation was so oddly pleasant, so . . . she wasn't sure what. Her fingers shuddered against Reinier's abdomen. Her head felt heavy and fell back against Connor's shoulder of its own volition. She was restless and sleepy all at the same time.

Their lips parted in unison to taste and lave even more. Jaidyn didn't even attempt to stop the sigh she knew she shouldn't have uttered.

She was drawn out of the fog she couldn't quite name when

she felt Connor's hands drifting down her sides to the small ribbon holding the flimsy gown that was her last pitiful shred of modesty. It glided off her shoulders as Connor gently prodded it off her arms, parting it to expose her breasts to both men. In her shock she let her arms fall and offered no resistance to Connor pulling the garment off.

The madness of it! She was going to—

It was the only way. Jaidyn had not been innocent when she'd come to Madame Poivre's, but she had also never experienced anything like this. She'd only imagined enduring quick pain, sacrificing her comfort and dignity to achieve her goals. Surely this was wicked beyond measure, and so now was she. Not only was there so far no pain and no quickness but—to her eternal damnation, she was certain—it felt good. And—Lord help her—she wanted it to continue.

Reinier sat back and gazed at her exposed breasts. Her nipples tightened in the cool air. His large hand was on her chin, easing her farther back onto Connor's chest as the Irishman's kisses moved down to her shoulder. Reinier's hand moved from her chin to subtly wander over her neck and then move down to cup one of her breasts.

The sweetness of the sensation barely registered before it was doubled as Connor caressed the other. Her pulse beat a jig when his rough thumb brushed against the hard peak. She sighed as his lips once again bathed her neck. When those soft kisses turned to gentle bites over her beating pulse, she arched, instinctively opening herself to their ministrations.

Jaidyn was lost in pleasures she hadn't known existed. Once again a restlessness she couldn't define crept into the enjoyment. She couldn't seem to stop her body from moving. Her hand reached out for something to hold and found the bedspread. Reinier intercepted it and brought it to the buttons of his shirt, whispering against her skin, "Undress me."

Without thought, her shaky hands worked the buttons of his shirt, inexplicably eager to feel what lay underneath. There was a slight tug behind her as Connor worked the laces of her corset. It fell away at the same time Reinier pulled the shirt over his head and tossed it aside. The next instant Reinier's mouth was tasting her skin again while he guided her hand back to his belly.

His skin was warm and soft and the muscles underneath were taut. Jaidyn was so wrapped up in the unique tactile sensations she did not realize her hand was being guided slowly downward. But when her fingertip skimmed the seam of his breeches, the actual magnitude of his enjoyment became glaringly clear.

She tensed and instantly felt ashamed of her virginal reaction. The next instant, Connor leaned in against her back as if to see what might be amiss. His broad chest against her back felt protective in a way.

But the reality that was now very clear was the matter. Their sweet kisses and balmy affection had lulled her into forgetting about what lay at the end of this business agreement—and that there were two to contend with. Yet she knew she must go on.

Right or wrong, there was pleasure for her in this. She had never thought there ever would be. And for whatever reason, she felt oddly safe with these men. She'd curse herself later if she was horribly mistaken, but with Connor there she somehow knew it would be all right.

When he began to gently suck her earlobe and his hands came around to lightly cupping, then squeezing her breasts, Jaidyn convinced herself that at least there was this pleasure now and she would enjoy as much of that as she could until it came to the humiliating act itself.

Everything else felt oh so nice, especially now as Reinier took the offering Connor held in his hands and began to suck and nip at her sensitive breasts until she gasped for more. Jaidyn leaned more fully onto Connor's strength while Reinier continued his assault.

The delicate fragrance of little white roses combined with something deeper, masculine and heady nudged her senses. Sandalwood. That was it. It wrapped itself over her tongue and stole into her nose. Tiny whiffs of it spread through her body and multiplied that strangely comforting feeling she had. Jaidyn gave a soft gasp and inhaled more of that fine aroma.

She didn't even notice that Reinier had untied her undergarment until Connor lifted her body slightly off the bed. The last bit of cloth between herself and what was to come slipped off.

Connor laid her down at the end of the bed and was gone. Jaidyn fought the urge to turn and find him, reach for him to come back, tell him that she needed him.

Before she could move, Reinier, with his tousled blond hair and piercing pale eyes, loomed above her. Instead of the sweet, light but slightly musky combination of roses and sandalwood, another bouquet filled her head. Deliciously sweet, like opium made from lilac poppies, yet there was something that made Jaidyn lick her lips and clear her throat as it slightly burned. Pepper, she thought and almost smiled at the contrast in Reinier's natural scent.

Jaidyn watched him as his beautiful lips drew a path of sweet, wet kisses down her body that set her shivering. But not with cold. His hand found the junction of her thighs and she allowed him to part them while his mouth continued to taste her heated skin.

Once more she couldn't fight the need to move, pushing both into his seeking fingers and then into the soft tick underneath her. Jaidyn's sigh held both delight and relief. Her eyes closed as she concentrated on the feel of Reinier's hand moving over her thigh to rest just above her mons.

On the bed above her she heard a low, favorable sound. The fact that Connor watched what she could not and reveled in what he saw sent a thrill through her veins and heightened each sensation tenfold.

Again Jaidyn gasped the instant Reinier's probing fingers opened her nether lips. His touch was delightful. His expert fingers stroked her with just the right pressure in just the right places. Each of his small movements sent delicious waves of welcome shudders through her body. A soft, appreciative sound escaped her when Reinier's deft fingers spread and explored some more.

That murmur turned into a keen and her back arched as he found her small erect nub and concentrated his attention there. A tickly, fiery feeling took hold and shook her whole being. She arched and moaned as funny stings sizzled through every muscle in her body. She pictured Connor watching, felt something akin to the warm glow of the sun just out of her reach. It was as if she was climbing too many stairs, only the strain in her muscles wasn't unpleasant.

Reinier stroked her folds and rotated his fingers on her sweetest spot until that sensation in her belly spread with a rush to her toes, her breasts, her fingertips, even to the roots of her hair. Then it was almost agonizing and she didn't know why, but she spread her legs more, a rough moan coming from deep inside her.

Abruptly, Reinier's touch stilled.

Jaidyn groaned with quick short breaths the very moment. She couldn't help it, but something like disappointment grew in her as every tingling wave of that sweet, heady rush through her body seemed to ebb and dwindle with every breath she took. Connor's wicked chuckle made her confusion and frustration that much more palpable.

But she was not abandoned for long. She soon felt Reinier

parting her slick folds again. He made short eye contact with her.

Jaidyn didn't quite know what to make of his lopsided, knowing grin. His fingers seated so intimately caused another wave of that delicious rush to flicker again. Then he was gone from her line of vision. Jaidyn lifted her head just a bit and saw him bend toward her—

What did he . . . ?

To her shock and surprise, his tongue set to work where his expert hand had left off.

No-ohh . . .

Was that . . . ?

Good. Lord!

His touch—hot, wet, wonderful—stoked a fire in her, raging and more eager than before. It moved through her, replacing her blood with molten syrup that licked at her, threatened to burn her from within. Jaidyn thought it impossible, but he was even more skillful with his mouth than with his fingers. She felt him spread her folds and he burrowed deep, his tongue swirling around her sweetest spot and licking over her in tiny, quick flicks in between. Jaidyn heaved off the bed even higher than before.

She quivered against his lips and writhed in desperation to reach whatever it was she'd been denied before, breathless, unable to do anything but moan. Something built in her, it swirled and pulsated in her.

Suddenly she knew. Suddenly Jaidyn realized there was a name for how she felt. It was pleasure, pure, simple, ecstatic pleasure that caused her to moan; relentless desire that lashed inside her and continued to build that pressure she knew from before. She was climbing toward something with every swirl and flick of his tongue. And she was almost, almost there. It was just out of reach—

But just like before, he halted and Jaidyn opened her eyes to stare at the plaster of the ceiling. He'd denied her again and she was torn between giving a frustrated harrumph or moaning at the exquisite shower of sparks raining on her.

Whatever it was he was doing, surely this torture was much worse than if it had been short and rough like she'd expected.

The bed moved under her and she saw Reinier knelt between her spread thighs, looking at her creamy folds. He tilted his head to the side and narrowed his eyes at her, but another movement caught his attention and his eyes flicked up above her.

Connor moved from the bed also. Just then Reinier used the flat of his hand to apply gentle pressure to her overly sensitized nub and her hips jerked against his hand and the small relief it brought.

Crouching down behind Reinier, Connor took her in. He bent his dark head toward her in a slow, seductive movement, never taking his intense eyes off her.

"Let me have a taste." Jaidyn shivered at the low rumble of his voice. "She smells so sweet."

When he spoke, his breath cooled her skin, making it pucker with goose bumps all over her. Reinier's hand moved just a little to make room. Her eyes fluttered shut in anticipation.

Then Connor's mouth was playing a symphony on her most sensitive spot, swirling light and fast. The longing in her built so fast she shivered once again and Jaidyn spread her legs even more, opening for him, silently asking him to end this marvelous torture for her somehow.

Passion steamed through her and Jaidyn gave herself up to it, to that familiar pressure, to the force of it that grew as his magical tongue twirled over her.

She released her death grip on the bed sheets and threaded her fingers into the thick, silky strands of Connor's black hair.

Her hands fisted in the soft mass, pulling him closer. The pleasure was almost pain now, but Jaidyn didn't think she could bear it if Connor also stopped right at that point.

"Please!" Her plea came out in a sob.

Connor's laugh vibrated though her. She writhed with every pass of his tongue. Something inside her coiled, tighter and tighter.

Finally, with one more sweet flick of his tongue, that something broke. She thought she'd shatter, every fiber of her exploding with bliss at once. Arching her spine off the bed, she felt as if she could fly. It was magnificent, breathtaking, miraculous, and filled her with so much joy she didn't want it to stop.

But it ended too soon and she was back in her body, tiny spasms raking it still. Small shudders of delight rolled through her as Connor continued lapping at her core with gentle caresses.

Left in an aftermath of shock and awe, Jaidyn watched Connor lazily crawl up the bed and lean on one elbow at her side. She marveled at the passion and admiration in his eyes. When he cupped her breast and placed a quick, warm kiss on her earlobe, she felt comforted.

She'd never expected this. She had only ever imagined giving herself. Never once had it entered her mind that she would receive anything more than coin in return. But they had shown her. Reinier might have started her on the path, but it was Connor who'd brought her to the end. She was glad it had been him. Now she wanted to give back, but she had so little experience she wasn't sure how.

Jaidyn turned to Connor as his arm came around her waist. Reinier lay on her other side. With her hands still slightly trembling, Jaidyn explored the solid planes of Connor's chest and marveled at the gooseflesh that rose under her fingertips as his eyes drifted shut. She felt a small rush of power at his reaction. It gave her the courage to explore lower still and glide over the prominence in his breeches.

She felt Reinier's balmy skin against her back and his breath at her ear as he watched her progress. As if he could sense what she wanted, Reinier entwined his finger in hers and together they worked the buttons for Connor's fly. As soon as there was room he guided her hand inside.

Her fingers instinctively wrapped around his hard length. Connor took a sharp breath between his teeth. Another rush of power set her body moving against Reinier's as he held her wrist, guiding her strokes.

Jaidyn shuddered anew when Reinier's tongue flicked over the skin just beneath her ear. "Slowly," he breathed. "But hard, lass. Squeeze the tip just a little before you let your hand slide down again."

Jaidyn followed Reinier's request as best as she could. The deep purr of satisfaction from Connor made her grateful for the instruction and eager for more. She moaned softly at the feel of Reinier's hard length at her cleft and Connor's under her hand. Unbelievable, but her body began to move in a restless rhythm once more.

Connor's arm came around, embracing them both. When Reinier sat up behind her and intertwined her free hand with Connor's, he guided Connor's fingers to her mouth. She wasn't quite sure what he wished her to do, but as he pressed them against her lower lip, she opened.

"Yes, sweet. Take his fingers into your mouth. Let them go a little, then suck at them again."

She did as he asked and the intimacy of suckling Connor's digits sent pinpricks of lightning through her skin. She continued her ministrations to Connor's fingers as Reinier laid her back. As he nudged her thighs farther apart, Jaidyn could feel the roughness of Reinier's breeches and his hardness straining against her sensitized tissues. He leaned in, bracing himself on his elbows. She knew another instruction was pending, and curiosity as well as yearning made her want it all the more.

"Now let your tongue run around his fingertips every time they almost slip from your lips."

Instantly she obeyed, rolling her tongue around the tips, then sucking his fingers in even deeper than before.

"Very good." Reinier's voice seemed rougher now. He moved off her as she continued to work as instructed. Each application of suction sent sparks to her core. She rejoiced in the hums of approval from Connor and delighted in the look his blue eyes held as he watched his fingers disappear into and slide out of her mouth.

She felt the bed move under her, and Reinier was now lying on his side beside her, farther up the bed than either she or Connor was. His large hand cupped the back of her head. "Wrap your hand around me and stroke me."

Reluctantly she let Connor's digits slip from her lips and turned to face Reinier—

There it was.

She didn't react with fear or hesitation as she thought she would. She was fascinated, perhaps a bit awed, and studied it. Hesitant, she wrapped her hand around Reinier's length.

As she slowly began to move her hand, testing the feel and shape of it, she felt the bed move again. This time, Jaidyn assumed, Connor was removing the rest of his clothing. In a very short time Connor's warmth covered her back and his arm snaked around her waist.

"Use your mouth on him," Connor whispered in her ear.

But how? she thought, eyeing Reinier's rod.

Then she understood. Connor's strong fingers in her mouth had been just a prelude to this. Walking before she ran.

Slowly Jaidyn bent, opening her mouth and letting her tongue taste the smooth skin. Just slightly salty and ever so soft. The experience was not at all unpleasant.

She wrapped her lips around the head, moving her jaw some

to take it all into her mouth. She let her lips move up and down, sucking, loosening and tasting.

While she felt Connor's hot length pressing against her cleft, he took her hand in his and guided it to Reinier's member. "Let your lips follow your hand."

After a few awkward caresses she found a rhythm. Her whole body hummed with each stroke. Jaidyn grew bolder, eager to show them both she was a quick learner.

"Open your throat." Connor's breath tickled the shell of her ear. "Don't swallow. You can take him deeper then."

She tried to relax her throat and as she began to suck harder she could indeed feel him at the very back of her throat. Emboldened by her success and the deep moans of approval from both men, she loosened her lips, letting him almost slip completely out before she started the deep slide all other again.

She could feel the vibration against the roof of her mouth as Reinier spoke. "Methinks we have just discovered her major talent, my friend."

"I expected as much." Connor let out a deep purring chuckle. "Her skill must be outstanding, having been blessed with lips as gorgeous as hers."

The bed dipped again as Connor moved and nudged her legs apart. Jaidyn gladly opened for him, needing his touch to ease the ache that was spreading once again. She moaned against Reinier's length and pushed into Connor's hand.

Connor entered her with one finger first and Jaidyn wanted to gasp, helpless against the quiver that raked her body. He pumped in and out of her so slowly, Jaidyn thought she was going to burst with delight.

Then Connor pressed two fingers into her and Jaidyn tried to swallow the moan at his intrusion. Stroking deep caresses teased her, aroused her. She felt her inner walls expanding, stretching to take them in.

Connor's fingers hit a spot deep in her that set her ablaze and had her eager for more. Passion enveloped her in a delicious bubble of want, fogging her mind so that all that counted was to feel more of that bliss his touch brought her. All of a sudden his fingers didn't seem to be enough.

Connor began to move her onto her forearms and her knees. Her mouth never left Reinier as he moved to lie farther down on his back. With a muffled moan, Jaidyn shivered as the front of Connor's thighs pressed against the back of her own. The head of his cock pushed at her slick entrance.

The moment she had dreaded before had come. She didn't understand what was happening to her, but she wanted it now. Not just it—but Connor. She wanted Connor inside her with everything she had.

His hand gripped her waist tightly and ever so slowly he entered her, just a little at a time, her secret muscles stretching to accommodate him.

There was no pain, only joy. Desire had sparks swirl and explode not only all over her body but in her mind also.

When he'd seated himself to the hilt, Jaidyn shuddered and moaned again long and low. He filled her perfectly.

Waves of pleasure, prickling and tingling at the same time, bathed her with each thrust. Jaidyn had never experienced anything quite like Connor's moving in and out of her in strokes so delicious and slow she thought she was on fire inside. A fire only he could quell. Obeying her instinct, she moved against him faster.

Soon she found a rhythm that gave her the most pleasure. Before long her mouth matched those movements as well.

Connor's maddening strokes became harder and she trembled and keened at the end of each thrust, her body rippling with pleasure until every limb felt like she'd strained her body for too long. She burned within, then the blaze combusted into a bone-deep inferno.

She was momentarily drawn out of her trembling haze as Reinier's hands cradled her head. He slipped from her lips and moved slightly away.

Now it was just she and Connor and his dizzying thrusts taking her higher and higher. Her nails dug into the tick beneath. Jaidyn enjoyed the titillating waves that rushed through her body at each of Connor's rougher strokes now.

Again that tickle in her belly started, spreading through her body. Again she felt something coil in her lower belly and Jaidyn moaned with bliss, knowing that relief would soon find her.

At last her climax came, rushed through her as blissful as before but somehow more intense, more complete this time. Her muscles contracted as if to hold on to Connor, as if to lock him tight. Connor's fingers dug into her hips. She was barely aware of anything as he pulled himself out, but still pushed against her back.

Hot and sticky liquid dribbled onto the small of her back and a little down her backside. Connor's seed.

Jaidyn had just begun to catch her breath when Connor sprawled next to her on the bed. Her heart had still not settled back into a normal beat when Reinier stepped behind her now.

His hand moved against the small of her back, rubbing Connor's seed into her skin. It was decadent and wicked, probably like everything else so far, but she couldn't quite form a thought clear enough to tell him to stop even if she wanted him to.

Next she felt his fingers enter her. Did she really want him? Somehow Jaidyn doubted it would feel as good as it had with Connor.

Then Reinier's hand moved slightly higher. The tip of his finger entered her puckered bud.

"What—" Jaidyn gasped, struck by a delicious tingling of the nerve endings there as he began to move slowly out and slightly deeper in, wiggling the tip as he went. She relaxed into a moan of pleasure.

"No."

Jaidyn tensed at Connor's growl.

"Why shouldn't I?"

They all seemed to freeze into a scandalous tableau for a moment.

"I see." It was Reinier who broke the silence as Jaidyn let her body slide onto the bed. "Seeing that she is out of the question, I might have to find someone else for it, though."

"You are charmingly incorrigible. Go ahead and tease me now," Connor replied, and it made even less sense to Jaidyn. "But you'll see. You'll soon see, my friend."

There was nothing about this that Jaidyn understood, and she thanked the stars she was too tired now to try.

2
_____

When Connor awoke, dusk had almost ended. Almost but not quite, judging by the pale gray light that streaked across the carpets. He rubbed a hand lazily across his face and into his hair, waking more fully and remembering where he was and with whom.

He propped himself up on an elbow and turned to the woman curled up beside him. She seemed so peaceful in her slumber, her lips slightly parted in a soft pout and her hair like a pale sunrise fanned out behind her. His gazed followed a line of tiny freckles down her shoulder to the curve of her breast. He couldn't help but trace its path with a fingertip. At that she snuggled closer and Connor felt his face crinkle into a smile. She really was an exquisite sight to wake to. He might actually not mind doing that again.

He wasn't surprised she still slept. Even in her sleep she looked so exhausted, Connor felt a strange protective streak slither to the surface of his mind. He and Reinier—

Where was the Dutchman? Reinier wasn't in the bed with

them. Connor sat up farther and, careful not to wake her, he tucked her into the crook of his shoulder.

His friend must have seen Connor moving because a candle was soon lit and Reinier was framed in its glow. He was sitting in the armchair where he'd thrown his coat when they'd first entered. Fully dressed, including the aforementioned coat, Reinier was sipping brandy. The look on Reinier's face was far too serious after such a pleasurable and fulfilling afternoon. And, Connor mused, drinking in the dark was never a good thing. "Leaving so soon?"

"Time and tide, my dear friend."

It wasn't hard for Connor to figure out what his friend's dark mood was about. Seeing one's spouse for the first time in four years might do that to anyone. "Time and tide and wayward wives, you mean?"

The grunt in reply followed by another long sip of his drink was not so much a response as avoidance. Connor left off his teasing.

They sat in silence for a long moment. Connor felt his gaze wander back to where Jaidyn lay snuggled up in the crook of his arm. Her upper lip was a bit fuller than her lower lip, giving her a constant pout. Connor would have loved to watch her some more, but a strangely derisive snort from Reinier made him look up just to see the Dutchman's eyes narrow at him.

"If that one was a downstairs maid," Reinier began, raising his glass to the woman Connor held. "Then I used to be an Arab sheikh."

Glancing down to make sure she was still sleeping, Connor tried to keep his voice low and even. "Fascinating, isn't it? She's a lady to be sure, a very passionate one, but a lady nonetheless."

"How in the world do you think she ended up here?"

Connor tamped down the urge to shrug. "No idea really."

Whatever it had been, it couldn't have been good. Not that he wasn't grateful for having had the pleasure of her company.

But it most likely would have been better for her if she hadn't ended up working for Madame Poivre. Connor wondered what it might take for her to give up a few of her secrets. He wasn't sure why, but he wanted badly to know her name.

"I have to give it to our hostess, though," Reinier said. "The whole idea of someone of her obvious birth refusing to give her name, spinning a tale that's so easily seen through, gives her a great air of mystery. Pair that with a pale beauty so rare here and her passionate enthusiasm. I wouldn't be at all surprised if it was all a ruse to attract more clients at higher prices."

Connor didn't like the idea that the lass might be a training doxy acting the part. It didn't sit well with him, and neither did Reinier for daring to suggest it. "There are other rare beauties, you know. Like those with more tawny skin and bright turquoise eyes," he snapped. Without thinking, Connor reached down and began stroking her hair.

Even in the dim light it was easy to see Reinier's lip curl in displeasure. "If I'd realized how possessive and ill-tempered you'd get from fucking a countrywoman of yours, I would have told Madame Poivre no and settled for watching you take the cat to one of the other girls' ample backsides before her taking both of us at once."

"I don't know what you mean." Connor grumbled and quickly pulled his hand away from the lady in question's glossy hair. He gently removed his arm, turning her away from him.

It seemed they were both ill-tempered. This was ridiculous, really. She held no special interest for Connor above newness, truly.

Reinier was his closest friend; Connor didn't want them parting on bad terms. Completely comfortable in his nakedness, he tossed off the sheet and sat on the end of the bed. "Pour me a glass of that, if you don't mind."

"Of course." Reinier rose and handed him his glass, then moved right back to his chair.

"I'm sorry," Connor began. "I should not have mentioned Emiline like that. It must be hard for you going home after all this time and after hearing she might be unfaithful." Granted, he'd heard it from Connor—and Connor had made the whole thing up after running into Emiline in town. But that didn't change how Reinier felt about the whole thing. "I don't envy you the task."

"Come with me, then." Reinier lifted his chin. "You can leave the *Coraal* in Mr. Parrish's capable hands and we can sail on the *Sirene* together. We've not sailed together in quite a long time. It might be pleasurable reliving those days."

The offer was tempting, but Connor's first instinct was to stay. Not just for the mysterious redhead sleeping peacefully behind him. Of course not. "Those are fond memories, and Maxfield would love nothing more than for me to put more into his very capable hands, but I think your wife might offer you a better reception if I stayed behind."

Reinier brushed Connor's last comment aside. "Don't worry for my wife. I can handle her."

Connor wrinkled his forehead. After having seen Reinier's wife just recently, he wasn't so sure. Besides, as much as he knew his friend wanted to avoid facing her alone, it was best. "I have no doubt, but I've things I've still to do here."

Reinier gave a disdainful snort and looked to the sleeping woman. "You're not ready to leave her, you mean."

"Purely for the mystery and another good fuck or two, I assure you. And a bit of gambling in town before leaving again. Why don't we stick to the plan and I'll follow in two days? We've done that before. One goes and the other one follows after. But it being your wife . . . if you'd rather not . . ."

"Don't be silly," Reinier retorted a little too quickly. "It's settled, then. In no less than two days I'll expect you on Ronde."

Connor nodded in acceptance, tilted his head slightly and

with a wink he tipped his forehead with his right index finger in a mock salute. "By your order, Captain Barhydt, I'll be there."

Reinier grunted with the hint of a chuckle and stood. After having pulled on his breeches, Connor saw his friend to the door.

Standing there long after Reinier had left, Connor watched the lass sleep. He had two more days with her until he'd leave. Just a couple more days to sate his lust for her body and unravel some of her mystery. Then he'd surely be ready to move on and see how Reinier fared with his wife—and if he might be of some assistance.

Yes, that was a good plan.

Making his way across the darkened room, he heard the lass stirring and stopped to move the candle closer before he settled back down on the bed.

"Is it morning?" She stretched lazily, wiggling the toes of her right foot, which had sneaked from beneath the sheet. Connor found the sight strangely endearing.

Just in time he managed to remember to reply. "No. You've only slept for a couple of hours."

"Oh." She sat up clutching the sheet tightly to her chest, squinting into the dark while her eyes adjusted. Connor smiled at her shyness. "Reinier has left?"

"He had an appointment to keep." Connor swallowed a sigh when he saw that her grip on the sheet didn't in any way allow him a small peek of that lovely, freckled bosom.

His grandmother used to call freckles like hers "fairy kisses." Come to think of it, she did look ethereal, like a fairy, with her skin so light her veins shone through. And that long, straight hair that cascaded down her back like a waterfall of liquid copper, her dazzling lips, her eyes that grew even rounder now—

Wrenching his attention away from her stunning beauty, Connor cleared his throat. "Are you hungry? I could go down and order up some food while you freshen up. Would you like that?"

She just looked at him for a moment and then back to her lap, biting her lower lip like she wasn't sure what to do or say. Her long lashes fanned the sudden blush on her cheeks. No doubt she was replaying the afternoon's events in her mind, not sure what to think of it all and not knowing quite how one was supposed to act in the aftermath.

Once again he felt oddly protective of her. His hand moved to rest on the coverlet over her thigh. "I know I could use a bite to eat and a bit of conversation with a fascinating and beautiful woman. You wouldn't mind indulging a poor sailor a little longer, would you?"

Her shoulders relaxed a little, but she didn't turn to him. Connor thought he caught the beginnings of a grin. "That might be nice, I suppose?"

He lightly squeezed her thigh and without thinking leaned in to peck her on the cheek. "Very nice, indeed."

He still wore his breeches, so he only needed to slide into his shirt. When he was about to close the door from the outside, his gaze lingered on her lying on the bed still unmoving, looking around the room and then out the windows.

Finally she scrambled to sit on the edge of the bed and he called to her, "Light a few more candles, if you please. I'll be back as quickly as I can."

There was definitely something about this woman that made her different from the others—at least for now.

In a very short time Connor sat in breeches and shirttails with bare feet on a blanket spread out on the thick Asian carpet. They feasted on a loaf of crusty bread, mango and papaya slices, pieces of roast chicken, a soft cheese made from goat's milk, and the best French wine Madame Poivre had on hand.

Three candles in their silver holders sat just off the rug to the left, illuminating the woman sprawled on her side before him in a hazy golden glow. She was wrapped in the sheet she'd clutched earlier, but that didn't lessen her appeal. Quite the contrary. The sheet parted slightly above her knees, allowing him a teasing glimpse of her calves.

Sipping her wine propped on one elbow, she seemed relaxed enough. Connor might catch her unaware. "You look completely decadent, lass, like Dionysus himself sent you to tempt me into his madness."

She took another long sip of her wine, then raised it as a toast to him. So she knew Dionysus was the Greek god of wine? Any lingering doubts about her upbringing or education were gone now.

Her tongue darted out to catch a stray drop. "My life has seemed like the height of insanity lately." Jaidyn smiled. "But that I actually found some pleasure in it, too, is almost ludicrous. Thank you for that."

Connor set his own drink down and reached for a slice of mango. "Don't thank me yet. The pleasures are not over." He held the fruit up for her. "Here, have a taste of this."

Obediently she opened. Connor took his time painting her lips with its juices, enjoying how they glistened in the candlelight, before placing the fruit in her mouth.

Watching her delicate throat work reminded him how good it felt when the tip of his cock touched the back of it as she sucked hard and laved him with her tongue. He wanted to watch her do it again—right there on the floor, caught in the glow of the candle's flicker. He wanted to twist his hands into her silken hair, guiding himself in and out of her warm, wet mouth.

Feeding her another piece, Connor tried to tamp down his eagerness for now.

"The height of insanity?" He didn't think confronting her with the obvious lapses in her story was a good idea. He wanted her to *want* to tell him the truth, which meant he had to coax it out of her somehow. "Indeed, you're as tempting as a maenad. And as beautiful."

She froze, holding the wine glass in midair. Her eyes darted toward him. Wariness flared in them like tinder, but then she shook her head slowly and relaxed again. Hitching one shoulder, she gave a mock sigh. "Poor sailor that you are, you might not be aware that you just offended me. The original maenads were hideous creatures. Not to mention extremely cruel and bloodthirsty."

Connor liked how her eyes lit up with mischief. "Forgive my slip, then. You as a mere downstairs maid would know better, I presume."

She had the astounding ability to lift only one eyebrow. It would make her appear lofty if it weren't for the lopsided grin that spread over her features. "Of course. I dusted the books once a day, you see."

"I see. Quite clearly." Bracing his elbow on his raised knee, he leaned back a little more. "So, tell me something about the maenads I don't know yet. What I know is give them something to drink and they'd lose all self-control . . . engage in wild sexual acts in their ecstatic frenzy . . . But wait." Connor cocked his head. "That sounds very much like you."

Laughing, she set her glass down, shaking her head. "Oh no. Not like me at all. Not typically me anyway. It seems I've only recently discovered that side of me. Hmm . . ." She drummed her fingers against her chin, deep in thought. "The maenads all have different names. That's something you as a simple seaman might not know."

Connor immensely enjoyed exchanging banter with her. Probably more than he should, but he couldn't care less right then. "They do? So, which one are you?"

She only gave him an airy flick of her wrist.

"Ambrosia? Agave?"

Now as she rubbed her toes against her ankle, a gesture born out of slight discomfort, Connor supposed, he couldn't help being drawn to the strangely erotic sight of her toes yet again. The movement had the sheet hitch up another notch, revealing a good part of her thighs. Connor let the tip of his tongue trace his upper lip.

"If you want to know my name, you only have to ask."

As if she could read his thoughts, she picked at the sheet until it covered her knees again, cutting through his thoughts, which were foggy with lust.

"What's your name?" Connor almost fell for it. Just in time he remembered to add, "But don't give me just any name. I want your real name."

She sucked in a breath and held it, her eyes round as plates for the fraction of a second. "Oh. That I won't tell you."

"You won't?"

She shook her head, her mouth a luscious slash of resolve. Well, then. There were other ways for him to cajole the truth out of her.

"No, I—" She gasped, watching horrified as Connor moved onto all fours, stalking around what was left of their dinner to stop near her feet. "What are you doing?"

He saw her breath catch as he wrapped one hand around a slim ankle. "All this time I was wondering whether you were shy or just a tease." He pulled her legs apart, slowly forcing her from her side to her back leaning on her forearms. "Now I know. But you should understand that two can play that game."

"What game?" She sounded confused.

Connor's seeking hands moved up her calves to caress her inner thighs.

"Oh," she breathed, her head wobbling.

He hummed at her willingness, so unspoiled and, in a way, innocent. If she'd been a doxy, she'd have faked more pleasure.

As it was, she was all the more exciting for him. Her reaction fueled his enthusiasm and he lay between her legs, nudging them farther apart with his shoulders.

His cheek rested just below her hip when he blew purposefully strong breaths across the nub of her sex.

"Ohh," she gasped again and rolled her hips once.

"Tell me your name," he whispered just loud enough for her to hear. His lower lip nudged her bud twice. He could smell her need, saw her hunger beading on those pretty ginger curls.

"Connor . . ." She had such an alluring, wanton sigh.

Two fingers delved into her already slick core, pressing down and stroking deep but slow, pushing in and sliding out just a little until she writhed and her sighs turned into soft moans.

Her breath became shallow pants when his thumb began tickling her tight rosebud. Connor's mouth watered for her sweet cream and he leaned down, his lips settling over her. Lapping slowly from her entrance up to her clit, he settled into tender strokes with the flat of his tongue. Back and forth it flicked, alternating gently sucking with light nips of his teeth while his fingers continued to push in and out.

Damn, she was tasty. "Your name," he whispered against her dewy folds. "Tell me."

He could feel her tighten around his fingers, her nether muscles flexing with her imminent release. Her head began thrashing from side to side. She licked her lips, her chest heaving with the quick breaths she took, her legs trembling.

Connor slowed, thinking he'd stop soon and tease her some more into revealing her name. But apparently she remembered that lesson only too well, because her hands delved in his hair, keeping his head just where it was.

When she fisted her fingers tightly in an ecstatic lock on his head, the small pinpricks in his scalp sizzled down to his toes. His body ignited with desire, a fiery blaze skittering down his spine and pooling in his cock. Connor felt his aching erection strain against the fly of his breeches and the hard floor.

He pushed the tip of his thumb inside her tight rosebud and wiggled it.

"Connor! Yes!" she screamed, threw her head back, and tensed, arching her body off the blanket as a moan ripped from her throat. She crested so hard he almost couldn't move his fingers inside her.

The deliberate brush of his tongue between her slick lips never ceased while his arms snaked around her thighs. Grasping her wrists tightly by her hips, he urged her legs farther apart, her thighs locked tight around his shoulders.

She writhed, completely at his mercy now. Her hips thrust up against his chin and Connor started another assault. Once more his tongue swirled over her core with playful licks and teasing nibbles. Faster and faster he flicked over her until his mouth closed to suck only her engorged pebble.

She jolted in surprise and his grip tightened in response, holding her in place.

"Connor! No, stop!" She breathed, a violent quiver shaking her body. When she stared at him, her eyes were dazed with lust.

In response, Connor lifted his head from between her thighs and gave her his most devilish smile. He could feel his lips wet with her honey and hoped they shone in the dim light like hers had earlier. "Tell me your name."

He set down to pleasuring her again until she twisted helplessly on the sheet. A hard tremor seized her. Feeling the motion, he smiled against her folds.

"Connor, please stop," she whimpered mindlessly despite pleasure lighting her face. "I can't—"

"Yes, you can. Tell me your name," he said with a low moan against her soft folds before he took her bud between his lips once again. His mouth was playing her body like a lyre.

"I won't stop unless you tell me your name," he said softly, compulsion barely hidden in the silvery tones of his voice. To emphasize his point, he let his tongue flick over her sensitized bud again. She shuddered with each pass of his tongue, her hips twitching frantically. Her legs tightened around his head, her heels dug into his back.

Gasping, then giving a deep groan, she heaved her upper body off the blanket. "Ohmygod . . . Connor . . . please . . . I beg you!" Her voice was rough, strained from her ecstatic moans that had turned into screams. It rang in his head like heavenly bells.

He chuckled but didn't let go of her. If she did as he asked of her, she wouldn't have to endure this.

Or maybe she would. Connor couldn't make up his mind about that right now.

Her body started to glisten with a fine sheen of perspiration. If Connor didn't know better, he'd think her musky fragrance had intensified. It was the most intoxicating, most exquisite aphrodisiac he'd ever tasted. He ravenously devoured her sex, his tongue spearing her lips just before his mouth leisurely closed around her clit one last time. He sucked gently and with a few quick passes of his tongue he took her over again.

"Oh . . . Connor . . . no!" Her gasp ended in a loud moan. "Jaidyn! My name's Jaidyn!"

"Is. That. Your. Real. Name?" Connor asked in between pleasuring her, accentuating each word with another quick, torturing flick of his tongue.

"Yes, oh God, I swear, yes, it is."

Straightening, he looked down at her as she sprawled, weak and stunned. Her eyes were closed, tears wetting her temples, but there was no mistaking the dreamy smile curving her lips for anything other than contentment.

Triumph had never tasted sweeter. "Next time you'd better do as I tell you right away."

The lass—*Jaidyn* snorted a defeated laugh.

"Come now, it wasn't so bad, was it?"

When her breaths became more even, she mumbled a disbelieving "uh-huh" as she opened one eye for him.

"Jaidyn . . . Jaidyn." Releasing his strong hold on her, he repeated her name as if testing it. He liked very much the sound and feel of it.

So now he had a name. He thought it meant something about an answered prayer, that she'd somehow been sent here just for him.

But that was ridiculous. Surely her name didn't really mean anything. No, what mattered was that he'd gotten a name and the rest of her mystery would soon follow.

Kneeling, Connor pulled his shirt over his head and let it fall to the floor. He could feel her eager eyes on him. Already he was rock hard and aching for her touch, but seeing her obvious desire now made him feel like he'd just risen another notch.

"Well then, Jaidyn." When he stood, he began to slowly unbutton his breeches. Suppressing a groan as his cock finally sprang free, he purred, "My turn."

Scrambling up, she knelt in front of him. She licked her lips and raised her hands to caress up and down his thighs. Connor could hardly stand, his knees having turned so weak just from watching her positioning herself to suck his cock.

When Jaidyn opened her mouth, he had to hold his breath not to moan. He was famished for her touch; a hunger he'd never felt before.

Her fingers trailed briefly over his cock and then her mouth was on him, eager and hot and sucking him with head-spinning strength. His fingers dove into her hair, whether for support or just to feel the silken mane. Throwing his head back, he released a gasp of pleasure, moving his hips forward to slide deeper into her throat. And as amazing as it already was, Jaidyn let him, taking in nearly all of him until her lips almost touched the base of his cock.

Something within him melted and ran hot as her lips and mouth and tongue, so wet, so delicious, drew him into her spell. His scalp rippled, his skin tickled, his breaths came in small groans as his body flushed to a fever pitch, passion raged within him, and his pleasure built with a force he'd never anticipated.

His hands fisted in her hair now, just like he'd wanted in the first place, and he took charge of the rhythm, of the intensity. He slid in deep only to glide out of her mouth faster. Scorching bolts ran up and down his spine, made him shiver and somehow at the same time burn. Desire swamped him, had him quiver and groan, and he thought the lust might drive him out of his mind.

His hips thrust forward, trying to make her mouth slide over him faster and harder. A tiny sizzling took form in his anus, coiled tight, and sprang free, rushing into his balls, then up his cock—

Jaidyn lifted her chin so she met his gaze, and their eyes locked. The world around them died and that was when Connor knew the only true reason why he'd wanted to know her name.

"Jaidyn!" he bellowed, shouting her name as he spilled his seed down her throat.

3

While Connor had dozed off next to her, Jaidyn couldn't find any sleep. It had been almost two days now. There was just too much going on in her mind, too many questions that required an answer, too many restless doubts. And there was also something else that wouldn't let her be; something pulsing and fluttering in her chest with every breath she took. Perhaps that's why she'd allowed herself the temporary luxury of just enjoying the moment. Now that Connor had opened the door to carnal delights, Jaidyn felt giddy and completely at ease, liberated. Just short of giggling in her euphoria. And all just because of him. Connor.

Strange, but all he needed to do was ask in that exciting commanding tone he sometimes used with her and she was eager to have him. It was like his voice reached deep into her then, echoed with a vibrating hum there and she found herself helpless to resist him, eager to forget everything but being with him.

She knew it was dangerous thinking, but still, she felt so . . . whole, so . . . understood. In a way she felt safe with him. Safe was something she hadn't felt in quite a while, and she wanted to hold on to that feeling, however fleeting.

Jaidyn didn't know if that reaction was customary, but she didn't want to think too deeply about it at the moment. Or of all the other things that should burden her. Later she would have to, but not now.

Jaidyn just knew that it wasn't just the pleasure. It was Connor. They fit each other so perfectly.

And to think she'd believed herself frigid. Those doubts gnawing at her had her almost think herself less of a woman. But Madame Poivre, with her strange French accent and asinine turban that wobbled like a newborn foal when she spoke, had known.

"Frigid, are ye?" The madame snorted a laugh. *"Don't you vorry, dear. There are no frigid vomen, only dilettante men. So 'ooever told you that vas a complete botcher!"*

Jaidyn wished she could place her accent, but it was odd and sounded even stranger when she murmured at her own reflection like she often did. However eccentric Madame Poivre was, she was wise as well.

Jaidyn turned to Connor. He looked so peaceful in his sleep. Fighting an absurd urge to trace the serene slashes of his eyebrows with her finger, she clasped both her hands and placed them firmly under her head.

My, but he was a ruggedly handsome devil. When he smiled at her, his eyes crinkled in the corners and his whole face lit up, the austere features softening. He wasn't just good-looking and passionate but also extremely clever. And when his smile flashed in the golden light of the candles, her heart stuttered.

The last couple of days had been a marvelous sensual blur. After lazy baths they'd fed each other fruit, cheese, bread, and roast beef, drunk wine . . . They'd slept in between just a little with their arms around each other. More than once, he'd slid his knee between her thighs when asleep to twist his limbs with hers more intimately. Then, when they were waiting for their exhausted bodies to recover, they told each other of incidents that had happened in their lives. She'd told him about the filly, strong-willed and haughty May Hem, whose name was her nature and that thought herself too good to be ridden by any other than Jaidyn. As a matter of fact, May Hem had rarely let anybody but her close.

They'd whispered when telling each other those stories as if they were secrets no one else was supposed to know. Or maybe they were shy with each other—and to bridge that shyness, Connor had taught her tricks in between that simply took her breath away. Cuddling, fondling, joining their bodies, sharing confidences—at least some of them. What they immersed in was perfectly normal in that small cocoon Jaidyn's world had become. Reality was shut out, suspended, not part of her for the moment.

She felt as if she'd become something new. Not even a new person, but a new kind of being. One that was wanton and decadent and free of all of her troubles. A fairy that could become anything for the beautiful mortal who had found her. With Connor guiding her, every one of those wicked things had taken her higher into a different world and new levels of passion she'd never known existed. What they did was removed from social mores. There was nobody to censure her. Certainly not in this remote part of the world. Or in this house. Surely not here in this room.

It was a fanciful notion, and part of the reality of it was that, unless Jaidyn was completely mistaken, an intimate bond had formed between them.

She'd done the one thing Madame Poivre had told her not to do—she'd developed feelings for Connor. As horribly wrong as that was, she was all but sure that he must have feelings for her too. Not only because he'd stayed so long. But in the way he held her when he slept, cherished her body when he seduced her. Even when he used that harsh tone with her. Always, what his body did to her was in complete opposition to his stern commands. And afterward, if she proved an obedient nymph, he'd give her that beautiful smile—the smile he always gave her that felt like an effulgent sunrise.

Connor stirred next to her, drawing Jaidyn out of her reverie. Eyes still a little puffy from the short nap he'd just taken, he curled a strand of her hair behind her ear with the fingers of his upper hand. Then he took hold of the nape of her neck and guided her closer, lifting her a little.

Picking her up as if she weighed nothing, Connor lay back completely when she straddled his thighs. He rolled his hips under her, letting her feel his swelling member, and her body answered with undulating hips, her core moistening and readying for him.

"Are you sore?" His voice was a sleepy croak.

Jaidyn bit her lower lip, loath to admit it. "A little."

"Perhaps we should do something else, then."

An unexpected pang of disappointment exploded in her stomach and Jaidyn fought not to pout. Was she just hallucinating or was he up and ready to go another round?

"Yes." He gave a dreamy sigh and buried the back of his head in the pillow. "Something else entirely. Show me again how you used to ride that filly of yours."

Leaning forward and stretching on him like a lazy cat, Jaidyn purred, "Are you sure?"

Connor cocked his head and searched her face, as he had done once or twice before already, without a doubt unsure of what to think of the mischief masked in her voice. She let him wonder for a heartbeat longer.

"I used to ride her hard. And if you're too sore . . . I wouldn't want to put you through such an ordeal."

There it was again, that lopsided grin of his. It made his midnight blue eyes sparkle, and it caused her heart to trip over itself yet again.

Rising a little off him, she braced her hands against his shoulders. Jaidyn sucked in her breath when Connor reached down to test her readiness. Then his fingers were gone and the fat plum of his member probed her entrance. Bit by bit she sank down on it, wincing once.

All the soreness was completely forgotten in the next moment. She moaned at the devastatingly slow advance. Connor gave a low rumble when he was up to the hilt in her.

Sliding herself up and down his hard member, Jaidyn began a measured, slow ride. She loved to be on top, loved to feel him thrust up against her. Simply seeing him lie beneath her had her blind with need, feeling his hard rod against her sex had still more pleasure rising within her with dizzying speed.

Connor bucked up against her. Jaidyn grabbed his shoulders for balance at his answering chuckle.

"I thought you used to give a hard ride."

He mocked her?

Circling her hips faster, she eased him out of her only to let her core swallow him again fully. The friction incensed her further, driving her to a mindless rhythm, whipping her with the sharp pleasure taking his width into her brought.

Leaning forward, Jaidyn let her tongue snake out and curl around his earlobe. "That's how I used to ride the chestnut filly," she whispered, grinding her hips on his thick member.

His strong hands clamped down on her thighs. She circled her hips, rose off him, sat down again, and delighted in watching his eyes rolling up, then shutter, his head pressing into the pillow. The tendons in his neck emerged, thick ropes of restraint showing how hard he tried in vain to hold back the guttural groans of bliss—evidence of the pleasure she gave him.

The world stopped spinning. It was just the two of them, the heat they created together, the passion that drove her—both of them mad with need, the desire to crest just once more in each other's arms.

His hands wandered up her thighs and captured her waist. His member seated so deeply, so fully in her felt divine. When he rolled his hips up to meet her halfway, she thrust back as hard as she could. He groaned every time she slid down the length of him. When he plunged into her, her own breaths were blissful moans.

The palms of his hands cupped her buttocks and Jaidyn moaned at his exploring fingers wandering down the cleft to where she ground against him. He let his fingers stay there, Jaidyn supposed, to feel her slick softness welcome his hard member only to release him, then capture him again completely.

Pausing, Jaidyn sat up completely, throwing her head back. When she began to move again, he opened his eyes. She loved the way he looked at her, his enigmatic dark blue eyes dilated with lust.

Jaidyn saw his gaze wander down to where he slid in and out of her. His hands caught her waist and held her in place, pumping his hips up against her faster. She struggled not to weep with pleasure, struggled not to crest too fast. The best she could do was hold on to him, to the pleasure, and pray that she'd last.

She gave a little yelp of surprise when Connor suddenly sat up and wrapped his arms all the way around her. His sweet mouth found the puckered pebble of one breast and engulfed it, eagerly sucking at it until a corkscrew of tiny, sizzling bolts slithered down her body and caused a fresh gush of moisture to coat him, easing his assault even more.

Jaidyn pulled him closer to her, shivering as his open teeth on her nipple added gentle abrasion to the sensation. She heard herself moan, low and deep, his thrusts coming even faster.

Before she knew what was happening, Connor flipped them around, taking charge but never leaving her warm embrace. She landed on her back, sprawled underneath him. He braced himself against the mattress and pumped into her hard, rolling his hips with long strokes that sent fire pulsing through her veins. Alive. She felt so alive with him.

Jaidyn was close. Her body tensed, her secret muscles fluttered as if holding on to him desperately. The tension in her body coiled until it was almost excruciating. She bit her lower lip and froze, waiting for the explosion that would come any moment now.

When it crashed over her, she sucked in her breath, then let it out in a scream, barely noticing how her nails raked his shoulders as the waves of pleasure washed over her.

Her orgasm ebbed by degrees and her body became pliant under his. The lust-induced blur around her cleared and Jaidyn saw Connor had once again watched her release as if it was a breathtaking spectacle, drawing out every last shiver with moderate thrusts. Now he wouldn't hold back any longer.

He left her and Jaidyn's right hand shot down to wrap around his hard flesh. His eyes closed as he pumped into the tunnel her fingers created for him. His climax wrenched her name from him in a coarse roar.

When his head fell forward and the haze of gratified pleasure vanished from his eyes, he looked down his body to see her milking every last drop out of him, his semen dripping over her fingers and onto her lower belly. Once he was completely spent, her hand retreated and she wiped it on the bed sheet.

Jaidyn met his stare and smiled at the utter amazement she found there. Her arms snaked up around his back, guiding him down to her. He fell into her embrace, burying his head in her hair. She stroked his broad back with loving caresses.

His strong heart was thumping in an erratic rhythm against

her sternum, his muscular shoulders heaving with the deep breaths he took. His weight on her, the way their bodies melded like they'd been made for each other . . . It felt so good. So right.

She wrapped her arms as much around him as she could. She dug her fingers deep into the powerful muscles in his back, suddenly overcome by an odd urge to hold on to him. In that moment, Jaidyn longed to be just a woman, *his* woman, and not struggle on her own with her secrets.

If only there was a way to turn the fantasy of her time with Connor into reality. She wanted so much to lay all her burdens at his feet and trust him to make everything right again. She was sorely tempted to share her secrets, *all* of her *real* secrets, with him.

But she couldn't. As close as they'd become, it had still been only a short time. Even if she confided in him and he agreed to help her, there was no future for them outside the dream he'd created for them in this room.

Bracing himself on his forearms, Connor took away most of his weight. His hands came up and he brushed a few wayward strands from her face.

His eyes flicked to her lips. Her heart jolted in her chest.

Would he kiss her? Finally kiss her?

He had not kissed her all this time. She longed to feel those wonderful, gentle lips that could do such amazing things to her body. She'd never yearned for a kiss. To her it had always been overrated, all that slobbering and that unpleasant feel of someone else's tongue roaming her mouth for her uvula. But with Connor, Jaidyn had a feeling that his kiss would be wonderful, just like the rest of what he did to her.

Jaidyn couldn't help wetting her lips. Her breath came shallow and fast. Her stomach gave an excited flutter when he brought his lips closer to hers.

They were just an inch apart.

Her own lips quivered in anticipation. He tilted his head a

little and Jaidyn lifted her head to close the distance, longing
for his lips to brush over hers, yearning to taste him . . .

Suddenly his supple mouth tensed to a displeased, pale line.
That gentle glow in his eyes froze over. He mumbled something under his breath and instead of kissing her, he was gone
from the bed so fast, Jaidyn shuddered with bewilderment. A
cool, empty foreboding settled where his warm body had been.

Connor stalked to the washstand, filling the china bowl with
water. Splashing his face a few times, dragging his wet fingers
through his shiny raven hair, he then let his head fall forward.
His shoulders slumped as if he was weary.

Jaidyn didn't understand what was happening or what had
his mood turn sour all of a sudden.

"Connor?" To her surprise, her own voice sounded unbear-
ably feeble in her confusion.

He didn't move. Neither did he answer. After taking two
more deep breaths, he reached for a small washcloth on the
stand beside the bowl, immersed it, and wrung it out. Tossing
the wet cloth at her without looking back, he growled, "Clean
up."

"Connor, what's wrong?" With shaky hands, she took the
washcloth that had landed next to her.

He still didn't talk to her. Her warm, teasing lover had become distant and cold.

This wasn't the man she'd just spent two glorious days with.

Neglecting to tie his hair back, he put on his clothes, still
draped over the chair, in a hurry.

Jaidyn sat stunned on the bed, helplessly watching the fantasy world of the last few days fade back into harsh reality so
swiftly and unexpectedly that her head and her heart both
ached.

He stalked to the door.

There he looked back at her. She could see the scorn and
contempt in his eyes. He was leaving her. Just like that.

Biting her lower lip, Jaidyn averted her eyes and reached blindly for the blanket, turning away from the door, away from him. She couldn't bear to watch him go. She thought her heart was smashed into a thousand pieces. She covered herself even more, hiding her face in the sheet, and blinked a lonely tear away. The stifling feeling of yet another betrayal made her heart howl and thud like a wounded beast against the bars in her chest.

The doorknob turned.

And the worst part of it all was, she couldn't even blame him. She'd fooled herself.

Jaidyn flinched when the door fell shut.

Then there was silence. Silence, confusion, and an ache in the soul so bad and abrupt she thought she'd go mad.

4

Looking out the window to the busy street below, Jaidyn sighed to herself. Here she was, right back in Madame Poivre's sitting room that was tucked away at the very back of the house. The room was different than the rest of the bawdy house or whatever fancy name the Madame preferred. Still, it was what it was. But in here friendly cream-colored wallpapers with golden fleurs-de-lis patterns welcomed her; a cream and burgundy striped settee invited her to sit.

Only a week before, Jaidyn had bravely declared she was willing to do anything to earn as much money as possible to get to Georgetown in the Carolinas. The Madame was reluctant, but Jaidyn had insisted.

And what did she have to show for it now? A broken heart and the knowledge that she couldn't continue to do this. After all she'd been through, she couldn't have imagined that it could have gotten any worse.

Jaidyn was hurt and angry. But at least this time it had been her own fault. She'd decided to go to work for the Madame.

She'd been a bloody fool, let herself get caught up in her own stupid fantasies and fall for Connor. She'd known it was wrong.

It couldn't have lasted anyway.

It was stupid, and there was really no one to blame but herself.

The sound of the door opening drew her out of her thoughts. Madame Poivre and her turban swept into the room and Jaidyn gave her a hesitant smile. Silently, they both took their seats at the small tea table. After a quick perusal, the knowing look in the Madame's eyes had Jaidyn ever more wary.

"Vell, my dear Jaidyn." The rouge on the older woman's lips was melting into the tiny wrinkles around her mouth as she frowned. "I 'ate to say it, but you look a little vorse for vear."

Jaidyn took the cup she offered, her mouth as dry as parched leather. The sleeves bit into her shoulders and upper arms. The stomacher was too wide and the skirts ended above her ankles, but what could you expect from a borrowed dress? "Actually, what I'd like to talk to you about has something to do with that."

"I can only imagine." Madame Poivre let out a grave sigh that sounded a bit too exaggerated. "And if you don't mind me asking, it vouldn't be because you 'ave fallen for Monsieur O'Driscole, vould it?"

Jaidyn's cup shook slightly in her hand, so she set it back down. "No, of course not," she retorted quickly.

"Tut-tut-tut!" Madame Poivre clucked her tongue. "I alvays tell my girls that is the number one rule!" She flicked her wrist and rolled her eyes, gasping, "But there you go vith your very first client."

"But I didn't!" Jaidyn protested. Perhaps if she denied it often enough, she'd believe it herself.

Madame Poivre waved her objection away and that blasted turban jiggled like flotsam, chiming in the Madame's disapproval. "Oh please, you think after all this time in the business I can't tell."

"Fine." Suppressing a grumble, Jaidyn crossed her arms on her chest and tapped a foot a few times. There was no point in contradicting her any more.

"So now maybe you'll agree vith me that this isn't the best vay to earn your passage north?"

Squaring her shoulders, Jaidyn thrust her chin up. "Yes. But what can I do?"

Madame Poivre patted her knee in a soothing manner. "There must be something else. Vat other skills do you 'ave?"

Jaidyn searched her brain for something else she could be of assistance with here. Sadly, nothing came to her mind. She wasn't even fit to clean carpets, never having done such chores before.

"As I said before . . ." Jaidyn hated that her voice sounded so meek. "I'm best with—"

"Yes, yes, 'orses, I know. I can't use that. And you don't make 'ats."

Jaidyn shook her head. "I never especially liked hats. Neither wearing nor embellishing them." In her frustration, Jaidyn picked up a currant cake and took a huge bite.

"Sew or embroider?"

Ridding the corner of her mouth of a few stray crumbs with the tip of her tongue, she gulped down the bun. "I kept pricking myself too much."

"Hmm." Madame Poivre tapped the side of the sugar cone with her teaspoon. "Maybe you could entertain clients in some vay vile they vait. Do you sing?"

"Not well, no." Jaidyn was tempted to reach for another roll of currant cake.

"Do you play the pianoforte?"

"I quit my lessons when I was ten. I couldn't stand the boredom," Jaidyn conceded and forced her uncommonly greedy gaze away from the plate of sweets.

Madame Poivre raised an eyebrow in disbelief. "The fiddle, then? Surely an Irish girl like you can—"

"Sorry." Jaidyn blushed.

"Vell, I can't imagine you vere on 'orseback your entire life. Is there not anything else you did to pass the time?"

"I did catch toads and hide them in my mother's bed." Was that a talent to be exploited here? Jaidyn wondered. "The maid making her bed always gave such a funny squeal."

Then Jaidyn thought of another thing she was good at. "My cousins taught me to use bow and arrow." It was still so painful thinking of what a wonderful life she'd had back in Ireland and how far away it all seemed now.

"*Non, non, non.*" Rolling her eyes, the Madame pulled a small flask from her pocket and added the contents to her tea. When she offered to add the liquor to Jaidyn's cup as well, Jaidyn held her hand up to say no.

"Did you never 'ave 'ouseguests or parties? Is there not anything you did for entertainments?"

Jaidyn stopped short. "Yes, of course we had parties."

"And?" Madame Poivre nodded with glee to encourage her to continue.

"Plays," Jaidyn stated. "We would stage plays or just collections of scenes people were familiar with, sometimes musicals—but I only helped with the scenery and costumes on those."

Madame Poivre rose from her seat. Teaspoon still in hand, she paced the room, tapping it on her chin while the turban bobbed in thoughtful unison.

"Scenery . . . and costumes . . . staging . . ." Jaidyn was convinced the Madame's mumbled soliloquy was actually a dialogue between her and her turban.

When Madame Poivre slapped the spoon loudly on the palm of her other hand, Jaidyn jumped in her seat.

"My dear, I think that's it!"

"What is?" Jaidyn narrowed a skeptical eye at her. "You want me to put on plays here?"

"Not the plays themselves, but the scenes." Madame Poivre looked triumphant. She obviously thought herself and her idea very clever.

Jaidyn was still confused. "The scenes? What do you mean?"

"Well, you see, there are always those clients who prefer a little drama with the love play. We 'ave an extensive variety of costumes and quite a few props for that matter, but vat if I could give them the 'ole fantasy?"

Seemingly enamored with her new idea, she was pacing faster now using her hands in grand gestures to illustrate her points. "Say there is a customer who wants to play a duke spanking a naughty maid. Or the sheep to a shepherdess. Or a majordomo in Macao . . ."

Now Jaidyn was getting the idea. "I think I know what you mean. So, instead of the room looking like a bedroom, it would look like a study, or a field, or the Orient?"

Cupping her chin, Madame Poivre muttered, "I wonder how much they would pay to not just 'ave the girl dolled up in their choice but the 'ole scene set for their personal fantasy experience."

Deep in her own thoughts already, Jaidyn didn't listen to the Madame's deliberation. There was one problem the Madame might have overlooked. "That might get rather expensive."

Madame Poivre wagged her finger at her in a friendly way as if to say she'd thought of it already. "So ven you staged these plays you spent a fortune each time?"

Now that Jaidyn thought about it . . . "No, we were clever about using what people had with them, what we had on hand in the house and what we might be able to paint or have the staff craft."

"You see, there is a talent I can use!" Madame Poivre threw both hands in the air. "Create a fantasy room for me at a reasonable price and if it's a 'it I will pay you vell for it. Not as much as you vould have made if you'd continued, but enough. Oh, and I almost forgot . . ."

Walking to the desk, she pulled out a pouch. "Here. That should be a good start toward your goal in addition to vat you'll make vith our grand new idea."

When Madame Poivre went back to her seat, she tossed the bag onto Jaidyn's lap. It felt rather heavy, so she pulled the drawstring and peeked inside. She was shocked with what she found. "What is this?"

The moment she'd spoken, she knew. It was Connor's money. Her heart sank while at the same time she fought the urge to toss the pouch into the cold fireplace or out the window.

"It's much more than we agreed on before." Jaidyn's voice broke. She didn't want it. But she needed to get to the Carolinas. And that was more important than that scoundrel Connor O'Driscoll.

"I know." The Madame looked highly amused with herself. "At the last minute, Monsieur O'Driscole saw fit to pay for 'is time 'ere plus ten more days."

"Ten more days? What? Why would he do that?"

Madame only shrugged. "Men. 'oo knows."

It just didn't make any sense. He obviously wanted nothing more to do with her. Even if he hadn't walked out without a word of why, the girls had already told her Connor never saw the same woman twice. "No, he couldn't have."

"Vy not? 'e seemed very adamant that you not take on any more clients in the near future."

What in the world . . . unless . . . Jaidyn felt queasy all of a sudden. "Pity? I don't want his pity." No, that was more than she could bear.

"Pity?" Madame Poivre snorted. "Oh no. That wasn't it at all. Mark my words." Again that finger waved in front of Jaidyn's nose, the turban underlining the Madame's statement. "Ve 'aven't seen the last of Monsieur O'Driscole."

"You may not have seen the last of him, but let me assure you, Madame, I have."

She tipped her cup to Jaidyn with a wink. "Vatever you say, my dear, of course."

Notwithstanding Madame Poivre's implication, Jaidyn swore she'd never again want to see Connor—even from afar. She just wanted to forget she'd ever met the man. And that was the end of it for her. "Good. Let's get back to what we were discussing before, my staging a room for you. Where should I start?"

"Let me think about who might be coming..." She was tapping her chin again. "Vere to start..."

The Madame's eyes glittered, her beam broadening until Jaidyn could see slightly yellowed teeth. "Rome! Someone is coming soon vith a taste for the classics. Give me ancient Rome and let's see vat it will bring."

Jaidyn grinned. "Consider it done."

Now she had something she was confident about to occupy her time and make the money she needed. After all, wasn't it similar to what she'd been doing all along—creating a character and acting the part? Now she'd switch to the much less dangerous part of set designer.

5

The ale wasn't what it used to be at the Admiral's Bones, Connor thought morosely while emptying another mug and setting it on the table with a loud clank. The Admiral, now reduced to a skanky old mongrel with an unpleasant smell, sat next to him, wagging his sad excuse for a tail and cocking his head. With a hesitant poke of one front paw, the Admiral begged Connor as his oldest friend for a friendly pat on the head.

Maybe he should visit another pub here on Grenada, like the White Rig, Connor thought as he obliged the ancient and blind dog. Or the Jolie Rouge, a dump only the lowest of low frequented. Even though the rum would only be more watered down the worse the company got. But Connor could definitely pick a fight there.

Yes, he needed to thrash somebody—or something; Connor wasn't particular on which of the two came first. He dropped some coins on the table and stood.

Maybe the rum and ale were finally working, because his knees were a bit shaky as he walked around the Admiral toward the door.

No, he could still remember why he'd wanted to drink himself to unconsciousness in the first place. Reinier's words rang in his ears like a clarion over the loud rumble in the pub.

You're thinking of her all the time and yearn to see her again. She'll be waiting for you.

Connor left the Admiral's Bones in search of trouble. A good brawl with some hard fists, a little breaking of ribs, and definitely the spattering of blood was what he needed. And he knew just where to get it.

The warm Caribbean breeze slapped him as he stepped outside and gulped in some fresh night air. Without thought, he started walking.

You were her first—technically speaking.

Technically. What the bloody hell was that supposed to mean anyway? There was no *technically* in that matter; she'd either had others or she hadn't.

Dammit. Connor's mood darkened even more at the thought of some other man's hands on her. Had she sucked in her breath and let it out in a gasp of pleasure when that bugger had touched her? Bowed her body to his with a moan and urged him on like she'd done with him?

Had she longed to kiss that bastard like Connor longed to kiss her—insanely, with every fiber of his being, with all his heart?

Connor hadn't been able to ban the image of her from his memory. Or her taste. Wild, syrupy honey. He'd never tasted something as seductive, as addictive as her.

Her scent was like the lush green forest he used to roam as a boy—a memory he thought he'd forgotten over the years. He'd almost been able to hear the birds of Erin chirping merrily when he'd inhaled her natural fragrance for the first time, then tasted her on his lips . . .

Her honor hadn't really been ruined before you seduced her.

Screw that. If she were a lady, she had no business being at Madame Poivre's. True, she was a gentlewoman. But Connor knew firsthand that she was no lady.

Not that he was pointing fingers.

Or complaining.

Firsthand was perhaps a poor choice of a word.

Even her eyes had the color of the woods right outside the village he grew up around in Ireland.

Everything about Jaidyn had felt like he'd come home, and that was why he was convinced he must be under some kind of spell—or maybe even cursed. That's why he mustn't see her again. He'd prove she had no power over him whatsoever.

"Good evening, Mr. O'Driscoll. How nice to see you again *so soon*." The blond whore's eyes wandered down his body once. Wetting her lips, she fluttered her eyes reluctantly up to his again. "Let me know if I can be of any assistance to you. I'd gladly . . . submit to your every wish."

The lass batted her eyelashes invitingly. Normally, he'd mentally rub his hands in glee at such an offer. But tonight—

Connor jolted out of his thoughts, blinked a few times, and looked around. He'd come here? To Madame Poivre's? The one place he didn't want to be? The one place he, in fact, wished—just this once—didn't exist?

As if strings were attached to his limbs, he crossed the threshold and tried to give the blond whore a smile that didn't reach his eyes.

After a quick survey of the room, he knew Madame Poivre would be in her private quarters at the far back of the bawdy house. Connor found himself stomping toward her rooms, determined to tell her that . . . What exactly?

That she could do whatever she wanted with Jaidyn; he wasn't interested in her any longer.

Indeed, that was exactly what he'd do. Then he'd leave and

not come back here for a very long time. If ever. Never mind that he once again felt that peculiar shortness of breath and those cold talons wrapping around his heart.

He didn't knock more than once; he didn't wait for permission to enter. The more time he lost, the more—

The sight that greeted him stole his breath. And not in a good way.

Madame Poivre was sitting there, smiling extremely foolishly, watching as right that moment Jaidyn, with an exuberant cheerful laugh, embraced a young, bulky man and mumbled something that sounded suspiciously like, "Yes! Oh, yes!"

Something indefinably, inexplicably dark roiled inside of Connor. He let out a scathing snort, kicking the door behind him shut with his boot.

"Well, well, well," he scoffed and all three pairs of eyes settled on him. His lips quirked. "Obviously, she took to her new profession. Who would have thought?"

Madame Poivre stood as if that had been her cue. "O'Driscoll." She sounded so taken aback that she'd even let her fake French accent fall. "This isn't what it looks like."

Connor brushed her comment aside with a casualness he didn't feel. "Of course. It never is. I, more than anyone, would know."

The older woman's eyes narrowed and she hitched herself up, hands on her hips. "Watch your tongue. I won't have you insult anyone's professional integrity here, or how I run my business."

Another movement caught his eyes. Jaidyn had left the young man Connor was going to beat into a pulp any moment now, and was sauntering toward him, one proud eyebrow higher than the other. "Oh, look what the cat dragged in. What are you doing here?"

"I could ask the same of you," Connor drawled, meeting Jaidyn's hard stare straight on.

"Miss Donnelly? Auntie Polly?" The young man showed guts to interfere, Connor had to grant him that.

"Winston, that's none of your business," Madame Poivre mumbled in a calming voice.

Connor now noticed the man had some nasty bruises along the left side of his face. It didn't take much to put two and two together. Madame Poivre had told Connor about a young buccaneer, nephew to a certain Auntie Polly, and he'd already suspected then she'd been talking about herself.

Ignoring the women shielding the young man, Connor's lips twitched into a vicious grin full of teeth. "And you'd be who? Black Eye Winston, the hangman's next meal?"

At that insult, Winston was about to rush toward Connor, but sadly he was held back by both women.

Madame Poivre murmured, "Perhaps it's better you leave."

Jaidyn gave Winston an encouraging nod as she patted him on the shoulder. "Don't forget what we talked about."

Winston's face, distorted in outrage a second before, now softened to an imbecile's vacant expression. "Never, Miss Donnelly."

Connor was sure Winston was going to start salivating any moment, so he was resolved to not only break Winston's nose. Before he was through with him, Connor would castrate him as well.

With a last cunning look at Connor that said "this isn't over yet," Winston gave a curt bow. Then he left the room through a hidden door at the rear.

"Captain O'Driscoll, I will not tolerate such brutish behavior here." Madame Poivre crossed her arms on her ample chest.

Connor's head turned from the door through which that bugger Winston had left toward the Madame until the full impact of his scowl settled on her.

"Squeamish, *Auntie Polly*?" Connor sneered.

Madame Poivre's face turned a deep crimson. She narrowed

her eyes at him and puffed in agitation. "Preposterous! I must ask you to leave."

Connor ignored her. "I do believe we had a certain business arrangement that I blindly trusted you to keep."

"Of course we did. And no one has touched her ever since."

"Yes? But what about her touching others?" Connor's vision dimmed with the bloodred rage coursing through his veins.

"Yes?" Jaidyn spoke up. "What about it?"

That drew Connor's attention away from Madame Poivre and his glare focused solely on Jaidyn. His patience was taut and, Connor was certain, it would snap soon.

"Well." His voice was low, the words pressed out from between clenched teeth. "If you're into it so much now, and as I do believe I've paid them all, I will have my share now too."

Stepping up to him until their noses almost touched, Jaidyn gave another snort. "If you think that I'd disappear into a room with you once more, think again." Her smoky voice was low and dripping anger. Connor felt himself harden like a randy stud.

"I'd pay handsomely."

"Oh? Well, that changes everything, of course." Jaidyn sniffed, shaking her head.

Connor gave her a devious smile. "Spoken like a true harlot."

One dark green eye narrowed considerably at him, and that was when Connor knew he couldn't wait much longer, knew what he'd do to her to punish her for her willfulness, knew he had to have her—*now*. Reaching for one of her wrists, he tugged her behind him, and recalcitrant, she scuttled along.

In no time at all they were upstairs with Connor trying various doors to see which room was available. When he finally found one empty and gaily waiting for customers with candles lit all over the place, he entered with Jaidyn in tow, closing and locking the door behind him.

Jaidyn turned and they both glared at each other again. Her cheeks were flushed in anger, her eyes narrowed, spitting hateful daggers at him. Her mouth was pressed into a fine, pale line.

Connor would have swallowed hard, only his mouth had become as dry as sandpaper at the breathtaking sight. God, she was beautiful. He could see the rage simmering right beneath her skin. When he saw her hands ball into fists by her side, he knew she itched to scratch his eyes out.

Oh, their lovemaking would be fantastic. Hard, sweaty, dirty, just the way he liked it. She'd rake her claws down his back until she drew blood. He'd fuck her even harder for it, stuff her with his cock until she never wanted nor thought of anybody else again.

Someone was banging on the door from outside, wrenching him from his reverie. Connor realized it was Madame Poivre, screaming at the top of her lungs. "I won't let you do this. Leave at once!"

Without breaking eye contact with him, Jaidyn answered her. "Not to worry, Madame Poivre. He won't enjoy this. Actually, I believe he'll never frequent this place again. After this night he won't be able to use the sad scraps of what is going to remain of his manly parts."

The banging stopped all of a sudden. Connor thought he heard Madame Poivre's unexpected snicker turn into a full-blown laugh as she left them.

Tilting his head, Connor felt a smile flick over his face. "Those are your plans, then?"

Jaidyn thrust her chin up in defiance, her scowl spitting poisoned daggers.

"Maybe I should tie you to the bed, then."

She licked her pouty lips and gave him another of those

deliciously arrogant glares, her eyes sparkling like emeralds in the sun. "We both know you'd like that too much, *Captain O'Driscoll*."

She spat out the title. So she'd reverted to cool distance as she'd probably been taught all her life? That was fine with him. But Connor didn't miss the breathy undertone either. No doubt she enjoyed their butting heads as much as he did.

"True." He stated the obvious without remorse, turning to shed his frock and loosen his necktie. "Why don't you get rid of your dress and make yourself comfortable on the bed on all fours?"

Jaidyn didn't move. Of course she didn't. He could bloody well go to hell; she wouldn't move one finger for him even if he begged her on his knees. This farce was over. Chin up and shoulders proudly square, she stomped around him toward the door.

Captain O'Driscoll gripped her upper arm tightly, wrenching her around to meet his glare. Her breath rushed out as her back connected with the door.

"Take your hands off me," she hissed.

"No. Do what I say."

Just as another slight was about to tumble from her lips, she caught a teasing glimpse of his immaculately defined torso through his halfway open shirt. That instant she remembered what his suntanned skin felt like, the hard muscle underneath . . . The memory became more vivid as he stepped even closer and his musky rose scent flooded her senses.

Jaidyn reeled in her wayward thoughts. That kind of thinking only led to trouble, and she was through with Captain O'Driscoll's kind of trouble. "Now, why would I do that?"

His teeth were clenched. The muscles in his jaw jumped with fury.

Good. Apparently it hadn't occurred to the conceited bastard that she might protest.

He inhaled deeply, probably to calm himself. Unexpectedly, a toothy grin spread over his infuriatingly handsome features. "Because, my darling, you want to do it just as much as I want you to."

His eyes bored into her. Her selfish body reacted to his hot and demanding stare. It wasn't going to work. Not this time. "I don't want you!"

She tried to break free and he only held her tighter. Howling with frustration, she pummeled his shoulders. "Why in Hades did you come back here?"

"That is my business." He stepped closer, pinning her wrists to the door and crushing his body to hers. He was hard and ready. Her knees threatened to give out.

"All that matters is that I'm here . . ." The tip of his nose almost touched hers. "And I will not leave until I get what I want." His voice was low, dangerously low. And throaty. She tried to shake off the sensation of desire, but her secret muscles clenched in anticipation. "If you don't remove your dress, I'll rip it off."

"You wouldn't dare," she hissed, but a hidden, despicably traitorous part of her was wondering why he held back.

"Try me." His eyes burned with need, their rich color darkening to heated sapphires as his pupils dilated even more. Jaidyn felt luscious slivers warm her body in places that only he had seen.

"N—" Jaidyn hadn't even voiced half of her refusal when he yanked at her dress. The next moment a ripping sound exploded.

His raw strength shook her. The bodice of her dress, shift and all, tore away. A gap down to her belly button exposed her. As if that wasn't enough, her treacherous garments slowly slipped from her shoulders, leaving her completely exposed to Captain O'Driscoll's sweeping gaze, which wandered up and down, lingering here or there.

When the remains of what once was her clothing pooled around her ankles, a faint smile flitted across the hard planes of his face. "Now get on the bed. On all fours. Show me your ass."

She thrust her chin up. "No. We can stay here like this all day but I will never lie down for you again."

His hands captured her arms again and once more his body pressed into hers. "I will stay as long as it takes. But be warned, my patience is almost at an end."

Jaidyn struggled against the heat it brought, her body and mind in complete opposition.

"You? Will stay? Ha!" She saw his lashes flutter with the force of her breath. "Now you will stay. Well, now it's too late! You left and I moved on to other things." Let him think what he wanted about those "other things."

"You moved on? Well, Jaidyn . . . *Donnelly,* I believe it is, isn't it? Let me make one thing perfectly clear, Miss Donnelly: you moved on while still on my coin, and I will have what I've paid for."

His gaze locked on her lower lip. A shiver of longing whispered over her, then spiked to full-blown desire as she watched him lower his head. But instead of kissing her lips, he leaned in, trailing hot, ravenous kisses up and down her pulse.

Tears of pain and frustration stained her cheeks while her body quivered in response. "I hate you!"

"No, you don't." He breathed against her skin and it immediately tightened with ripples of gooseflesh.

"Yes, I *do!*" She twisted her body. How dared he think she didn't know her own thoughts? He knew nothing of her. Jerking with all her might, she freed one hand and smacked it across his cheek with as much force as she could muster.

His only reaction was a triumphant chuckle as he licked a drop of blood from the inside of his lip. "No, you don't. You want me as much as I want you."

Suddenly he freed her arms and cupped her backside, his fingertips digging in as he lifted her up. Her back hit the door again, forcing all air from her lungs. Jaidyn wrapped her arms around him to find her balance, tearing his shirt in the process. When he thrust his engorged member, still confined in his breeches, against her moist core, her nails raked hard into his shoulders. Satisfied, she watched the welts rising and a small amount of blood filling those little wounds.

Jaidyn looked up into his eyes—

And time stopped. The world seemed to fall away and they were frozen in a sea of longing. His eyelids lowered to her mouth. She bit her lower lip hard when her gaze settled on his lips also.

Before she could even blink, his mouth took hers. His lips were almost brutal, crushing hers as his tongue forced its way in, demanding surrender.

It wasn't as much of a kiss as it was a conquering. Jaidyn fought back with equal force, pouring all her hurt, anger, and lust into the kiss. She bit his lower lip and thrust her own tongue into a duel with his.

The strength of his longing rolled off him in crushing waves. He stroked his tongue even deeper. Heart thundering in her ears, her body was ablaze with passion, seeking to be filled. Her legs wrapped around his waist, her hips grinding against the hardness hidden beneath the fly of his breeches.

It was just a kiss, Jaidyn told herself. She at least deserved to finally be kissed.

But it was . . . too much. Jaidyn capitulated, giving in to his demanding kiss with a moan of surrender, and let him take her as he willed.

His kiss changed, slowed and calmed. He gently took her

bottom lip between his in a soft sucking. She responded to the new gentleness, turning her head to the side in an invitation to continue. Connor's mouth molded to hers lightly, letting his tongue ease inside in a languid exploration. Jaidyn shivered at the hum he couldn't suppress as she tasted him back. Their tongues danced, eager for each new delicious sensation.

When he broke their kiss, she whimpered.

He let her go. Her feet slid to the floor on legs barely able to stand while his hands fell to his sides. Panting, Jaidyn fought hard to breathe, awash in conflicting emotions.

"Now." His voice wasn't more than a hoarse croak. "Do as I say."

"No!" She crossed her arms in front of her. This had to stop here. She couldn't afford to give in to him again. "I'm not that weak."

"Weak?" Connor turned on his heel, astonishment written all over his face. "No, of course you're not weak. You're strong."

He came closer, cupping her chin between thumb and forefinger, lifting her gaze up to meet his. "We both know that we fit each other. In bed. A perfect match. I felt it the first time you shuddered in my embrace and even more distinctly when I buried my cock in your cunt. It was like a zing shooting up and down my spine." His voice was low and even. Monotonous, but sweet in a way. Jaidyn felt herself drawn into it. "I knew you felt it too. But you didn't know what to make of it. You still don't know what it means, do you?"

At home she'd heard the unbelievable story of men in the Orient, so-called snake charmers. As described by the distant friend of her late parents, those snake charmers played the flute so skillfully that they could even hypnotize deadly poisonous snakes. Why Connor's voice reminded her of that now, Jaidyn couldn't say, though.

Leaning in, Connor braced himself against the door. "Reason tells you something's not right about what you crave. Let me help you open your eyes. Stop questioning and just give in to what you really want."

Her breath seesawed out of her. Jaidyn felt dizzy. His words echoed what she felt inside.

No, it was nonsense. All of it. She wasn't really like that. It was a part she'd been playing. It was not who she was. None of this was real.

She respected herself too much to let the scoundrel humiliate her. Jaidyn shook herself out of the trance and derision chilled her glare as she looked at Connor still crowding her.

A strange, dark glitter flitted through his eyes. "Get on the bed on all fours and present your backside to me."

He turned and walked toward a chair, pulling his shirt over his head while toeing his shoes off. "And make it quick."

Jaidyn almost cringed at the harsh tone. His unyielding eyes bored into her. Was it just her imagination or had he suddenly become taller?

Her reason was screaming in outrage, but another part of her wanted to obey his command, wanted to be his siren once again. She was shocked at how fast she found herself on the bed like he'd ordered.

Just when Jaidyn was about to protest, she looked back over her shoulder at him. Instead of hissing something truly offending, the words died in her throat. She could only stare with her mouth agape.

He was standing there in all his naked glory, his dark eyes roaming her body. His gaze felt like velvet rubbing up and down her spine and Jaidyn fought hard to suppress the visible proof of the pleasant shiver that tickled over and through her.

Then his head tilted a little to the side and he fixed his eyes on her core. Jaidyn caught her breath. Every joint in her body started to turn into wobbly custard. Her sex was pulsing for him, starved for his touch. It seemed her body instinctually recognized him, creaming, readying and aching for him with a fresh gush of welcoming moisture.

Her face flamed at her wanton reaction. If she could feel it, could he see it?

It was a long time until he finally broke the silence, and when he did, his lids lowered, his nostrils flared and his voice was mesmerizingly deep. "Spread your legs more. I want to see your glistening cunny."

There was no use denying she wanted this. Not just the character she told herself she was playing. All of who she was wanted this man.

Damn him.

She tried one last time to hold on to her anger. When she finally found her voice again, she snapped a demeaning, "Well?"

His gaze seemed glued to her wetness. He didn't react.

"What are you waiting for? Let's get it over with."

That got his attention. His dreamy smile traveled up her back and shoulders until his unsettling gaze focused on her. "You don't know me that well after all."

Even his whisper was a velvet rumble. In response, the tension in her body escalated. The tingling along her sides turned into blistering sparks showering on her until Jaidyn thought she couldn't take any more.

But her affronted reason wasn't silenced yet. "Or maybe you were just too easy to forget."

One corner of his graceful mouth kicked up. "Let me remind you, then," he said, his voice laden with seduction, the promise of hot, elemental and fierce sex buzzing underneath. Jaidyn gasped and gooseflesh washed over her.

Finally he moved. He took a step forward and, as he did so, he lifted his hand to his mouth. Jaidyn was mesmerized by the sight of him licking the pad of his thumb, recalling only too well what that swirling expert tongue could do to her body and mind.

When he knelt right behind her, he reached with his other hand for her nape, squeezing it lightly. "Look at the wall. Not at me."

Licking her lips, she reluctantly complied as the pressure on her nape intensified.

She jolted in surprise as his moist thumb touched her wet clit, brushing over it once. Sizzling waves echoed in its wake and slowly abated to a constant hum, making her gasp and close her eyes. She couldn't help but thrust her hips up like an offering, bumping against his rigid member.

Her head started spinning at another gentle and intimate caress of her sensitized nub. Jaidyn ceased struggling against him and what he did to her.

One last time, she told herself. *One last time before it has to be over.*

Keeping her eyes closed, she reveled in his touch, gasped as he brushed over her pulsing clit once more. Her elbows buckled when she was sucked into a void of carnal pleasures again.

He must have felt her body become pliant because his hand left the back of her neck, drew an intimate path down her spine until it came to rest on her right buttock.

The time in between those delicious strokes of his thumb tickling her nub seemed too long. She moaned in anticipation of the next scrap of ecstasy he'd throw her way. When it came, she felt not only the delicious pulsing of her hungry sex increase for a moment, but at the same time heard a loud smack. A strangely tingling, biting pain on her right cheek spread, adding to the delicious feeling of lust coursing through her, intensifying it tenfold.

Had he just slapped her?

Jaidyn didn't have time to make up her mind about what she

thought of it, because again his thumb flicked over her hard nub and at the same time he slapped her backside once more.

The passion spreading through her veins spiked and another hard shiver shook her body. Jaidyn opened her eyes with a gasp.

"What . . . are you doing?"

Connor gave a knowing chuckle. "You like that, don't you?"

His thumb found her drenched nub again. The sharp pain of another slap turned into a hot, erotic tingling sneaking all over her body and under her skin.

"N—no?"

Jaidyn could have wept when his hand left her right buttock and touched the apex of her thighs, slowly rubbing down.

"You're lying." The hot air in the room cooled the moisture he spread over the soft skin of her inner thighs and Jaidyn knew she was so aroused, she was dripping.

"Stop all the pretense. Just feel. Just enjoy." He slapped her again and his thumb worked that magic on her clit. She sucked in a loud, high-pitched breath that turned into a soft moan.

He slapped her harder and faster. Jaidyn anticipated each bite of his hand. It speared her sex and had her body go up in flames of deep, intense lust like she'd never felt before.

And that's when her reason whispered something she hadn't been able to grasp before.

This was his true nature. He reveled in this. His lust grew with her succumbing to him. The pain he inflicted upon her and that she could absorb and change into pleasure was what gave him pure pleasure. It was a constant giving and taking, an abyss of passion she'd thought she'd never desire.

It was so simple. Like the answer had always been there—just out of her reach. Until he'd helped her open her eyes. Like he'd promised he would.

With that epiphany, she gladly leapt over the lip of the crater of this new kind of sexual bliss, longing for the next slap and dreading its force at the same time.

He didn't use his thumb anymore to stimulate her. He didn't have to. The next slap had her wince, then groan, then writhe with white-hot ribbons of lust slithering through her body.

The skin on her right backside must have already been an angry red, but she didn't care. She yearned for that next slap—and when it came, she felt her sex clench and flutter in pre-orgasmic shudders.

He stopped and Jaidyn was torn between relief and frustration. With a tight grip on her waist, Connor bent forward, whispering another husky command. "Hold tight, Jaidyn. And don't let go."

Blindly groping for whatever was handy, she wrapped one hand around the bedpost until her knuckles turned white. Her other hand found the head of the bed, which she held on to for dear life.

The next moment he thrust into her, rough and deliciously ruthless, and Jaidyn whimpered in delight. He didn't wait for her delicate flesh to accommodate his thick member. Instead, he instantly pumped in and out of her, each thrust accentuated by another hard slap on her cheek. Each retreat felt as if it would suck all the air out of her lungs.

Sweat covered her from the heat he brought. Thrusting back, she ground her hips against him. She moaned and groaned and even cried a few times.

Their coupling was furious and wild. Hard thrusts, even harder slaps—and Jaidyn wanted it to never end. All her consciousness, every fiber of her body longed for and centered on those recklessly fierce strokes of his thick member together with those biting, pricking, painfully delicious slaps he delivered.

She couldn't get enough of it, of the friction, the heat. The pleasure was threatening to drown her.

And then she hit the burning lava. It splashed, cascaded around her, and spat her out again in a climax so violent, so blinding, so soul-shattering that she shouted his name against the ceiling as she came in nearly never-ending ripples.

6

Connor dug his fingers into the soft flesh of her hips, fighting for breath, struggling to control the erotic ecstasy simmering beneath his skin. Her secret muscles convulsed in so many spasms that their hard grip felt like she was strangling him.

When he heard her crying his name as she came, it sent him over the edge with her. He drove his cock in even deeper, wanting to fill her with his seed, to mark her as his. With the last shreds of his conscience, he pushed her hips away from him. He couldn't muster the strength to pull out.

He spat his seed on the coverlet, shivering so hard he groaned. Scorching sparks lit every cell of his body, drowning him in a contented peacefulness he'd never experienced—until he'd met her.

His breath came in hard and heavy gasps. He sank down on her, his torso resting on her back. Their mingled scent and the musk of wild lovemaking caused a blissful sigh. With trembling hands, Connor caressed her sides, fingers splayed to feel more of her. Too weak to move much, he kissed every inch he could easily reach.

"Jaidyn . . . What have you done to me?"

Right then, in the murky depths in his soul, he already knew. All those foreign thoughts running through his head, why he craved her touch so much, why he never wanted to leave her again . . . It all suddenly connected, made sense.

He felt her body quiver and thought he heard a sound, something akin to a soft sob. She was moving and Connor gave her enough room to maneuver out from underneath him.

Contented, he lay on his side, propping himself up on one elbow. He watched her absolutely delicious backside as she slowly scrambled from him on wobbly limbs—and he knew what he had to do.

That proposal was just a formality, yet he had to do the honorable thing and ask. Of course, there was no doubt she'd jump at the offer. A woman in her position . . .

"Stay. I—"

"No."

Connor frowned. She wasn't still angry at him, was she?

He rolled his eyes. Well, if she wanted it like that, after such a good fuck he had more than enough patience. "Why not?"

"Because I don't want to. That's why." Sitting on the edge of the bed, she straightened her back.

"I want to ask you something." Reaching for her, he let the tips of his fingers tickle down the small of her back to her cleft. What he could see of her right buttock was furiously red. A stirring sight. It clashed with her copper hair. Connor had to fight the temptation to fondle, kiss, nibble, and lick away those angry marks on her skin.

He made a mental note to exclusively use her left cheek next time. And the time after that he'd . . . or he'd just knead her buttocks, spread them so wide he could see her tight entrance where he'd—

She turned a little to speak over her shoulder, her back even more unbending. "Do you expect an answer also?"

Her open hostility was rather trying. In the face of such willfulness, Connor couldn't lie there any longer. Sitting up, he scrambled off the bed, walking toward where his breeches had fallen in his haste. "You're as stubborn as a mule!"

"Really?" She gave him that haughty eyebrow again, wrapping the bedspread around her. "I believe it takes one to know one."

With that she leaned back against the headboard, pretending to be completely mesmerized by her fingernails.

Connor took a calming breath. Why did she have to be so . . . headstrong! His fingers dove into his hair and he inhaled slowly once more until he was sure he was composed enough.

"Look, Jaidyn. I . . . I care for you."

"Oh?" She slapped her thigh. "You do have a rather peculiar way of showing your affection. I didn't know I was supposed to grow fonder—*fond* of you in your absence."

Abruptly, Connor brought his hands down. "I had to leave! I had an appointment to keep."

Jaidyn flicked a dismissive wrist, staring out the window. "I'm sure it's none of my business."

"Damn right, it isn't!"

"My thoughts exactly."

Somehow he had pictured this moment entirely differently, not her antagonizing him every chance she got. Well, he'd be damned if he let her provoke him into doing or saying something he might regret later.

Bracing himself against whatever was next to him, he tamped down his ire. What was that anyway? A statue?

"Careful," she mumbled. "The paint isn't dry yet."

Connor jerked his hand away from the papier-mâché, leaving a dent. Damned if it didn't look like Venus holding a blasted apple. Well, it wasn't Venus any longer, maybe Hippolyta or another Amazon queen with just one breast left.

His palm was full of white paint. Cursing under his breath,

Connor stalked toward the washing bowl, trying to rub it off while the water furiously splashed.

What the hell was a freshly painted papier-mâché statue doing here? And there was a table that almost groaned with the weight of fresh fruit displayed. Actually taking in the room for the first time, he noticed that behind Jaidyn over the bed was a canvas, a nude couple decadently coupling.

Oh, that picture was inspiring. He might try just that with Jaidyn later. Delicate chains lay in an earthenware bowl next to him. They might be quite helpful with that too. And a riding crop next to that bowl . . .

Where the hell was he? A travesty of Ancient Rome?

"You were saying?" Jaidyn inquired.

"Can we call a truce?" Reaching for a towel, he caught her haughty stare. If she didn't lower that arrogant eyebrow right now, Connor would have to kiss it down. "I mean . . . I want to ask . . ."

Dammit. Connor hastily threw the towel to the floor. He was acting like a stupid, lovesick lad. "I want to try to see where this leads."

Frowning, she shook her head slowly. "Where what leads?"

Connor already had a feeling she'd act a little dim-witted about it. "The two of us."

Her mouth stood agape. "There's no such thing as 'the two of us.'"

"But there could be." Was she being obtuse on purpose?

He took a step closer to her, explaining with his palms up. "I want to take care of you, Jaidyn. I could provide for you, buy a house here on Grenada. A house you could live in, with a huge garden. An estate with more than enough room for . . . knowing your fondness for horses, my brother's neighbor breeds horses. Finest horseflesh far and wide, believe me. We could go north and you could choose one, or two, or if you like even—"

Adamantly shaking her head, she cut him off. "I don't need

a horse. I have my own." Suddenly her eyes widened and she gasped. "Now, wait a moment—"

Clearly he must have heard her wrong. "What do you mean, you *have your own*—"

"Are you asking me to become your mistress?"

"Your own *horse*?"

Connor had never seen Jaidyn's eyes as wide as they were right now. She clapped her mouth shut and blinked once. "Yes."

Now it was his turn to be confused. "Yes, what? Horse or mistress?"

Rolling her eyes, she took a deep breath and spoke slowly, as if he were a brainless dolt. "Yes to the former, no to the latter."

Was she serious? Did she think she'd get a better offer than that? "Why?"

He wanted her with him. What was wrong with that?

"Why what? Horse or mistress?" Jaidyn seemed as confused as he was a moment ago.

"I'd appreciate it if we kept to one of the two only." He saw her nod. "How did you suddenly get a horse?"

"Well, Winston—"

With a roar, Connor started pacing the room, stretching his fingers until his knuckles cracked. Then he balled his hands into fists, waving them in front of him. "I knew it. You beguiled him . . . I'll kill that bastard!"

"Pah!" Jaidyn sputtered. "I did no such thing. He's a . . . friend."

Halting in mid-step, Connor let his hands sink. "And this just keeps getting better."

"Oh," Jaidyn gasped, flicking her wrist as if chasing a gnat away. "Think what you will!" Crossing her arms, she scowled out the window.

"It's not that I have a choice because *you* won't tell me!"

Smacking the mattress right and left of her thighs, she glared at him, frothing fury bubbling in her wonderful emerald eyes. "I would if you stopped being so pigheaded!"

"Pigheaded?" Connor blurted, his stance wide, his hands braced on his hips. "Give me some credit and at least call me bullheaded."

Jaidyn snorted deprecatingly.

"Well?" Connor was making an effort not to growl.

"If you truly want to know . . . Winston saved me. I was on a ship due north, but we were attacked by pirates. They took me prisoner, but Winston managed to smuggle me out in the dead of night and brought me here. Madame Poivre promised she'd take good care of me."

Connor couldn't believe what he'd just heard. "By selling you the first chance she got?"

"No."

No? Connor resumed pacing. As far as he knew, she was a doxy the first time they'd met.

"She was strictly against it. I insisted, telling her I needed the money and I needed it fast—and that I was willing to do whatever it took. You know the rest."

That stopped him. Connor turned around to face her. "Do I?"

"Yes." She nodded quickly.

"How many men have you had before me?"

"What?"

"You heard me."

She sucked in her breath and pursed her lips before she answered him. "I don't see what difference it makes."

Shrugging with a casualness he didn't feel, Connor attempted a smile that probably showed too much teeth. "Then tell me."

"Why do you care?"

"How. Many," he pressed out from between clenched jaws.

"One!" Jaidyn was back to hissing at him, leaning forward, her hands balling into fists. "Just one."

Something in Connor's chest suddenly expanded until it burst with a deafening pang, leaving a strange kind of queasiness in its wake.

"Did you love him?" Was that why she didn't want to be with him?

"At the time I thought I did. But it all happened so fast I didn't really have a say in the matter."

There it was. So it was true after all. *Technically*, he had been her first. Knowing that had his heart beat heavy in his chest, although Connor didn't really know why. Something rolled around in his mind, something he couldn't grasp, and that almost made him miss the rest of what she revealed.

". . . turned out he was a very dishonorable man despite his sweet countenance. So I had to leave. However, instead of starting a new life in the New World . . ."

"Your ship was attacked and now you're stranded here," Connor murmured as he paced the room like a wild horse trapped in a small paddock. The room was filled to the brim with his alluring natural scent. The nightly sea breeze whispering shyly toward Jaidyn through the open window did nothing to alleviate the emotional whirl in her.

Jaidyn wished she could do the same, pace agitatedly to free her roiling thoughts, but she forced herself to appear calm and detached. Like the businesswoman she needed to be now.

A savvy businesswoman wouldn't feel as confused as she was with Connor—Captain O'Driscoll. She had to stop making those slips. Jaidyn needed to keep reminding herself not to call him by his given name, not even in her mind. For the sake of her heart she had no choice but to uphold a professional distance and focus on her real mission. She had to get to the Colonies.

Becoming Captain O'Driscoll's mistress wasn't an option. Any hope of that was as fragile as a soap bubble. No, it had to be this way. They'd keep things strictly business and she'd make him see they both benefited from that freedom. Before long she'd be gone. Just looking at him made it perfectly clear he wasn't made for commitments—as small as they might be. Taking her on as mistress meant just that, and they both certainly needed no attachments.

Connor stopped his vigorous strides so fast, Jaidyn almost jumped. "And what was that about a horse?"

Oh, he was curious. Well, she'd give him just one more scrap of part of the whole ugly truth, hoping he'd be content with it.

"May Hem." Jaidyn didn't like her filly being called a "horse." It sounded much too common for such a special animal. "Her name's May Hem. Tonight Winston came to tell me he'd finally been able to smuggle her out as well. He said she was waiting for me at the Admiral's Bones where he knows the hostler."

Rubbing his temples with his thumb and forefinger as if it would help him think, Captain O'Driscoll scoffed. "So. Let me make sure I understood you and your situation correctly. You're stranded here, robbed of everything but your horse."

"That sums it up nicely, yes."

His hand snapped from his forehead as fast as a whip and, with an awkward shrug, he flicked his wrist, palm up. "But you don't want to become my mistress." His eyes were literally glittering with animosity. "Why? I seem to be missing something."

"Not at all." It seemed Captain O'Driscoll didn't like taking no for an answer. "I just think it wouldn't be proper," Jaidyn said, letting her eyes wander to the fruit bowl. Her upbringing had taught her not to blush when lying. But she'd never mastered the fine art of looking somebody in the eye when doing so.

"Proper?" Sputtering and snorting a laugh at the same time, he pointed an accusing finger at her. "You're . . . well, suffice it to say that I believe you're in no position to lecture anybody on what's good and proper."

Oh! That insufferable, tenacious, mulish man! "Why, thank you. Let me return that compliment. What I meant is that I won't be here for long. If you insist, we can keep the arrangements we have now for a while longer, but as soon as I can afford it, I'll book a passage to the Colonies."

"You need to get north?"

He could be awfully dim at times. "Yes. Didn't I just say that?"

"Hmm." With one hand on his hip, he rubbed the back of his neck with the other. "I've got a ship."

Yes, she knew that. "And?"

"I could get you wherever you need to go."

"You could." It wasn't a question; Jaidyn made no pretense to hide the doubt in her voice.

"Mm-hmm." He nodded, the bud of a small smile forming on his lips. Why did Jaidyn suddenly feel like a mouse staring at a snake?

"The catch?"

"What?" His reply came too quick to show genuine surprise.

"Captain O'Driscoll." She tried to sound patient but she wanted to make it clear that he shouldn't regard her as completely naïve. "I'm fairly certain you don't offer that passage out of the goodness of your heart."

"Well," he drawled, fingering those strange chains in that transparent glass bowl that the Madame had insisted be there. Their use Jaidyn could only imagine.

"I suppose I'd take you north if we kept to the same arrangement but exchanged our bed sport for passage instead of coin." He flicked his wrist as if it were nothing. "To keep things strictly *business*."

That cunning man dangled that passage like a carrot in front of a donkey's nose. Picking at a lint on the thick, square embroidery of the Roman-style bedspread wrapped around her, Jaidyn considered it.

He'd take her north and he'd have his fun with her on the way there. No strings attached ever. When they finally parted, she supposed it wouldn't take long for him to move on. It was an ideal solution for him.

And for her? Oh, she'd enjoy the ride. No pun intended. He'd make sure. No doubt about that.

But she had to be very careful. She couldn't let her feelings for him grow any deeper. She'd have to keep her distance even when he'd try to lure her in with his sensuality—which, to be honest, was a great experience every time. But at what cost?

True, she'd get to the Carolinas sooner than expected, but she'd spend more time with him along the way. She knew she couldn't tell him any more of the whole truth. Part of her still found it hard to trust anyone after having been betrayed so badly. And part of her knew that if he did care for her like he said, the whole truth would just be too painful.

Could she resist the temptation to finally be on her way and still continue her arrangement with him?

He was obnoxious and infuriating, and she should say no and end it here and now.

But how much longer would it take to make it to her new home if she did that?

When they parted in Georgetown, could she readily move on and not waste one more thought on him? Could she put that dark chapter in her life behind her? Go back to a mundane existence, just enjoy having tea in her own parlor and not look back? Or perhaps she'd look back and smile upon the fading memories of Captain O'Driscoll and Grenada, secrets she'd take to her grave.

If she could do that, it could be an ideal situation for her as well.

"We have a deal, Captain O'Driscoll."

On the other hand, spinning such an enormous cobweb of lies could become enormously tricky.

The smile on his face grew into a full-blown grin. "Capital!" He reached for his shirt and coat so fast, her forehead wrinkled in confusion.

"Stay here and rest. I'm afraid the bed in the captain's cabin isn't as spacious or comfortable as this one. I need to get everything ready. We can set sail with the morning tide if you want— or if that's too soon . . ."

Once again Jaidyn had an inkling her life was being pushed into a different direction; a feeling she'd had too often lately for her taste.

"No." Jaidyn cut off the strange sentiment with a curt shake of her head. "Tomorrow will be fine."

"I'll be back later," he promised and was out the door, his coat sloppily dangling from one arm.

Rolling up on the bed, Jaidyn was sure she wouldn't be able to fall asleep any time soon. The uncertainty of what was to come, admonishing dread mingled with tentative joy, was unsettling.

But she was wrong. As soon as her head hit the pillow, she was adrift in hazy dreams.

Sometime later, she felt the coverlet being lifted. The gentle fragrance of small roses and sandalwood lulled her back into sleep. Connor had come back, she thought with a smile. He smelled a little of the cool night sea. Underneath that fresh, salty scent the heavy aroma of burnt pipe tobacco hummed.

The last thing she noticed was that he wrapped his arm around her, his hand cupping her naked breast. Then he kissed the crown of her head and Jaidyn was sucked into the abyssal void of obscure dreams.

7

Like most days in the port of St. George's, the day dawned fair with a good breeze. The sailing should be swift. Connor couldn't wait to get started; Jaidyn seemed to be just as eager. She'd dressed quickly and had her few belongings gathered in a satchel and one small trunk equally fast.

Madame Poivre hadn't protested when he'd told her he was taking Jaidyn with him. Quite the contrary. She'd smiled effulgently, dabbing a stray tear from the corner of one eye with her white handkerchief—the same one she'd used to wave at them as they ascended the coach that would take them to the Carenage, the inner harbor area of St. George's.

She'd also thanked him repeatedly. Not for wrenching Jaidyn out of her grasp, Connor assumed, but more for what he'd accomplished last night at the Jolie Rouge.

Now Connor and Jaidyn were on their way to the port and he couldn't have felt better. Soon they'd be aboard *his* ship, the place where he felt most at home. That was just the upper hand he needed. It wouldn't be long now until Jaidyn was clay in his hands and all her thoughts of keeping it strictly business washed overboard.

Jaidyn was eerily silent, but Connor was content that he'd found the perfect way to keep her by his side, however temporary it might be. But the temporary part would be remedied soon enough. Whether she was here or someplace north, she would eventually agree. There were many subtle ways in which he meant to persuade her into giving in.

The *Coraal* was a merchant's ship, and as risky as it was, he'd agreed to take the northern routes henceforth so that Reinier could spend as much time as possible with his wife Emiline. So it didn't really make any difference whether Jaidyn would welcome him here on Grenada, or en route—where?

What was wrong with him? How could he have overlooked something so crucial? In his haste to grab at the chance to gain the advantage over Jaidyn, he'd forgotten to ask her exactly where in the Colonies he was taking her. What was she doing to his common sense!

"Jaidyn, darling." His voice was a smooth drawl. "To which Colonial port am I taking you?" Connor was hoping for New York or perhaps Boston. The farther north, the longer the journey, the better as far as he was concerned.

Turning her head from the hustle and bustle of the port, Jaidyn blinked at him as if seeing him for the first time. "Georgetown in the Carolinas. Do you know it?"

"Pardon?" He must have heard her wrong. There was no way.

"I'm told it's a small port just north of Charleston. Surely you've been to Charleston if you've not been to Georgetown."

Steely claws slashed into his chest. "Are you sure that was it?"

"What do you mean, am I sure? I think I remember where I was going." She lifted her chin, every bit the slighted lady.

Still, he had to ask one more time so he would believe it. "So you expect me to take you to Georgetown in the Carolinas?"

"Has your hearing gone all of a sudden? Yes, Georgetown. Is there a problem?"

There might be a slight problem, yes. He'd been to Charleston, of course, and he'd been to Georgetown too. He'd barely gotten out alive.

"No, of course not," Connor assured her, never letting his voice betray his concern. "Your wish is my command, given the price is right."

The price, however, for landing in Georgetown was his neck, but Connor wasn't going to tell her that. Good God! How stupidly lovesick had he been agreeing to take her without knowing where they were going?

Jaidyn wasn't worth his head on a pike—not yet at least. Then again, who knew what might happen in a week or so with her in his cabin every night?

They arrived dockside in no time at all. The coach jerked to a halt. Connor jumped down, giving her a slight bow and a quick wink to cover his apprehension. Jaidyn didn't really respond, just raised that damned sexy eyebrow again before accepting his proffered hand to help her descend from the vehicle. One of his deckhands scurried to get her things while he and Jaidyn boarded the *Coraal*.

The all hands on deck whistle sounded and sailors scrambled to gather in neat rows on the deck in anticipation of the captain boarding. Under different circumstances it was all Connor needed to feel at ease.

Maxfield Parrish, his first mate, and the new pilot, Winston Matthews, stood by the plank to greet them. The surprise in Jaidyn's eyes when she saw Winston was almost enough to make Connor forget they were sailing to his doom. Almost.

"Mr. Parrish." He tipped his hat to the younger man, who responded in kind. "Has everything been made ready?"

"Yes, sir. All is ready to sail north. We're just waiting for you to inform us of the exact course."

"Soon, Mr. Parrish." His first mate knew about his past, and Connor couldn't chance his reaction giving away that anything was amiss. "It'll be nor by noreast to start with."

"Aye, sir."

Connor turned to Jaidyn, then back to Maxfield, making introductions. "Miss Donnelly, this is Mr. Maxfield Parrish, first mate of the *Coraal*. Mr. Parrish, may I present Miss Donnelly."

"Pleased to meet you, Mr. Parrish." Jaidyn gave a small curtsy.

"Likewise, Miss Donnelly." Maxfield responded with a small bow.

Next, Connor looked at Winston to find him and Jaidyn shyly smiling at each other. "I believe you know Mr. Matthews."

They both nodded to each other and Connor added, "Mr. Matthews, why don't you show our guest that special piece of cargo we have on board."

Winston beamed, which looked a little awkward with his fading black eye. He'd hidden his long white-blond hair under a bandana that looked very much like the cloth that his aunt had worn as a turban the evening before. "My pleasure, sir."

Jaidyn eyed Connor with a certain suspicion but followed Black Eye Winston Matthews all the same.

The instant they disappeared below deck, Connor barked, "Mr. Parrish, give your orders and follow me, please."

Maxfield turned to the crew, cupping his hands around his mouth to carry his voice. "Hands to quarters, look lively now, boys! Finch, make ready to pull the anchor. Stiles, sling the topsail yard, and Coleridge, haul out the foresail. It's nor by noreast."

As soon as Maxfield finished, Connor made his way below deck to the captain's cabin at the stern. Maxfield entered on his heel, remaining standing by the table that served for both dining and charting. Connor moved through the open set of folding doors that separated his sleeping quarters from the rest of the cabin. He hung his hat and coat on a hook behind the washstand before joining Mr. Parrish at the table. Reluctantly, Connor sat down.

"We sail for Georgetown."

Maxfield's eyes bulged. "Pardon me for saying so, but is that wise?"

With a low harrumph, Connor set one elbow on the table while his other hand ran through his hair. "No, I am positive it is not."

"May I speak freely, sir?" Maxfield's expression was now more worried than shocked. Connor knew the feeling.

"You usually do." He waved at Maxfield, who sat down next to him.

His whole body tense, Maxfield wiggled a little on the edge of the seat. "What were you thinking?" His voice was a razor-sharp hiss. "You could be killed if you return."

"I am aware of that." Connor stared at the map on the table next to him, his gaze unblinking until his vision blurred.

The mate's voice rose in frustration. "Then why do it?"

"The lady paid for passage north and I agreed." Technically, she was still going to pay—and pay dearly, much to his enjoyment—but Maxfield didn't need to know that.

"You agreed to sail into the one port where they want to hang you?" Maxfield was bold enough to bring his fist down onto the table, shaking the instruments out of place.

"No." Connor gave him a stern look of warning. "I agreed to take her to the Colonies. I didn't realize it was Georgetown at the time." Of all the large seaports she could want to go, how was he supposed to know it was the one small spot he needed to avoid?

Maxfield folded his arms over his chest. "You should have asked."

"I am aware of that." Connor made sure his glare conveyed that Maxfield was close to pushing him too far. "I wasn't thinking all that clearly at the time."

"I wonder what could have had you so distracted that you didn't think *all that clearly*." Maxfield sniffed. "It's not like you to be so careless."

After a pause, his first mate searched his face. "It's the woman, isn't it?" At least his tone was quieter now and less impertinent.

"Yes."

"What is she to you, then?"

"That, Mr. Parrish, is my business." Connor looked down his nose at Maxfield. It was his own fault he'd indulged Maxfield too much. "Careful, now. She is a guest on my ship and a lady. That is all you need to know."

Still, Maxfield persisted. "You can't expect me to sit back and let her sail us into your death."

"I have not lost all my senses yet." Connor narrowed his eyes at Maxfield. "I will think of something. I do not plan to go to the devil any time soon, even if we are sailing toward hell."

At that, Maxfield sat back, avoiding Connor's glare in a sign of defeat. Silence stretched between them; silence so charged with unspoken words and hidden import that Connor could almost touch it, cut it into slices, and feast on it.

"I would not want to lose you, sir," the young man whispered at last.

There was more meaning in that than Connor wanted to deal with at the moment. He had too much on his mind to worry about Maxfield's moodiness right now. In Maxfield he'd found a complementary spirit. Connor had helped him understand who he was, and in the process their relationship went beyond what was normal for a captain and his closest officer. The young man was nosing around where he shouldn't be. Hell, those were recesses of Connor's mind even he himself didn't dare to tread right now.

"And how is Drusilla? Did you have a letter while we've been docked?" At the mention of his fiancée, Maxfield blushed. Connor knew the guilt associated with what she didn't know about her would-be husband served to stop the mate's previous thoughts in their tracks.

"She is well."

"Good. Well, back to your duties, Mr. Parrish. I don't want one bad word about our guest and our destination from you or the crew. Is that clear?"

Maxfield rose from the table and bowed his head. "Yes, sir."

Connor also stood and they made their way back to the deck.

As they walked past Black, one of the older crew members checking the rigging to the mizzenmast, Connor heard a slightly disgruntled murmur. He couldn't make it all out, but the words "woman," "bode ill," and "you'll see" were clear.

Connor just shook his head. He should be stern with him. But the man was in his last years and still refused to leave the sea. So Connor tried another tack first. "Mr. Black, a word, if you please."

"Yes, Capt'n." The older sailor turned and stepped closer.

"Did you see my guest come aboard?"

"Aye, Capt'n. May I say, she's very lovely, sir."

Connor waved that aside and instead wrapped his arm around the wiry older man as if he was imparting a great confidence. "Keep an eye out for me, will you? She is so lovely that I think she might just be a selkie. I've a mind to find her seal skin and keep her." Acting surprised now, Connor leaned back, regarding Black with exaggerated suspicion. "Now don't you go trying to beat me to it."

The wizened sailor looked at him as if he'd gone insane.

"What? You don't believe in legends like selkies, Mr. Black?"

The old man stepped from one foot to the other, reluctantly shaking his head in the end.

"Well, I do suppose selkies and all those other superstitions about women and the sea are really just rubbish to talented, dedicated sailors like us." Connor gave him a friendly slap on the back as he stepped away.

"Aye, Capt'n." Black nodded quickly and went back to work.

Mr. Parrish was standing by the wheel when Connor joined him. Watching the flurry of activity, he followed Maxfield's gaze and saw both Winston and Jaidyn walking their way. "How is Mr. Matthews fitting in?"

"Very well, sir. He seems to be an able seaman."

"Good." He turned to Mr. Matthews as they arrived. "I trust our cargo is secure and safe?"

Jaidyn piped in before Winston had a chance to answer. "Yes, May Hem is well as can be aboard ship again after what she suffered the last time."

With a curt nod Connor dismissed both Mr. Matthews and Maxfield. "Back to work, gentlemen." They both headed off to their duties.

Jaidyn turned to watch the harbor as it grew smaller. Connor joined her, covering her hand on the railing with his own. "It must be hard for you too?"

"I'll be fine, truly." She eased her hand from under his. "Thank you for bringing May Hem. I don't know what to say. I had planned on trying to send for her as soon as I could."

"It was my pleasure."

"It was a surprise to see Winston on board also." She spoke hesitantly like she wasn't sure if he'd object to her mentioning their friendship.

But now that he knew that truth of how Winston had saved her, he only felt gratitude toward him. "It's nothing, really. When I spoke to him at the Jolie Rouge last night to talk about your horse, I may have mentioned that my pilot had recently retired. And he may have mentioned he was available." He shrugged his shoulders in a dismissive gesture.

"Just as well. It's nice to see another familiar face." No matter what she said, Connor knew this couldn't be easy for her.

If she only knew just how hard their destination made it for him. But Connor knew just what he was going to do to distract them both from their worries. If they were sailing to his possible destruction, he was damn sure going to make sure they both enjoyed the ride. Those figure-eight coils of thin twisted rope and the set of unused leather straps he'd asked Maxfield to find him last night and that were now resting on the rolltop desk in his cabin would be just the beginning.

The world shifted hard to one side, groaning in pain. Then the awful sound of splitting wood woke Jaidyn seconds before Annie burst into the room. Still groggy, Jaidyn couldn't understand what the maid was screaming about or why she'd grabbed her and was shaking her with so much force.

"They'll take you! They'll take you! We must do something!"

There were shouts overhead Jaidyn couldn't understand. And fireworks.

Fireworks?

"Please, miss, please! Wake up! We must do this quickly."

The ship lurched again. Jaidyn was on her feet but stumbled, falling hard into her trunk. Things were so loud and jumbled, she had to cover her ears.

Forcing Jaidyn's hands away from protecting herself, the maid dragged her back up on her feet. "Don't you understand, we've been boarded by the French and they will take you if they know you're a lady! You must put my spare dress on so they don't know who you are. Quickly, now!"

Jaidyn struggled to understand. Why wouldn't the fog in her mind lift?

"Damn the laudanum," the maid cursed. "Please, miss, listen! Put this dress on and hurry!"

The world spun in loud, crashing circles. The next thing she knew, Jaidyn was dressed as her maid and Annie pushed her out of her cabin into the blood-covered hands that grabbed her and dragged her on deck.

She sat with some others, she didn't know who, huddled against the biting wind on the aft deck. Her eyes fell on the captain. He lay there, not five feet in front of them. A growing bloodred blotch over his chest colored his pristine shirt. His eyes were staring, unblinking, empty. Dead. Jaidyn's stomach lurched.

A well-dressed woman appeared, looking regal and obscenely out of place. It took much longer than it should have for Jaidyn to recognize her own new emerald day dress and ermine-lined traveling cape. What was happening?

"My lady." A man bowed to place a slobbering kiss on the woman's knuckles. "Rest assured you have nothing to fear from us. I will personally guarantee you safe passage to your father." His thin lips split into a lecherous grin.

Still petrified, Jaidyn shook her head. What was this? They were under the impression . . . mistaking Annie for her! Jaidyn stood on shaking legs, determined to right the wrong and to wipe that disgusting grin off the man's face in the process. "Annie? What is this?"

Turning around, the maid stared down her aquiline nose at Jaidyn. The look in her eyes was unlike anything Jaidyn had ever seen before on her. It was foaming with icy contempt. Loathing so strong it felt like a physical punch to Jaidyn's stomach.

"Why are you wearing—" Sudden agony numbed Jaidyn's mind, crimson dots scuttling around blindingly white stars. She fell to the deck. The whole side of her face exploded in pain as her own mother's ruby ring broke her skin.

"You bitch," her maid hissed, small droplets of spittle showering Jaidyn's face. "What a lousy maid you are to see to your own safety and leave your mistress behind." Pivoting on her heel, she stomped away but not without one last snarl. "Set her adrift with the rest."

The disgusting man wearing that awful tricorn stepped up to her, his dirty hands cupping Jaidyn's chin, turning her head from side to side for closer inspection. His face was pock-marked, his breath foul, his touch revolting. Jaidyn slapped his hand away.

"Feisty little thing. Pretty, too. We'll find a better use for you." Jaidyn fought not to gag. He let her hear his nasty cackle then looked up at his minions. "Take her and what other belongings we might use."

Fighting with all her might against those hands coming at her from all sides, Jaidyn tried to fill her lungs with enough air to let out an ear-splitting scream. But to no avail. Those hands made it impossible for her to move, to breathe, to—

With a start, Jaidyn woke. Her limbs were entangled in the blanket, her body covered with a sheen of cold sweat. She was back on the *Brightstar*, her mind howled, her instincts screeching for her to get up and take flight.

Finally, she woke enough to realize where she was. She was vastly grateful she hadn't found her voice and screamed. It wouldn't do for anyone to come running, thinking she was hurt. It would be too hard to explain.

Jaidyn rubbed her face to help her weary mind scatter that appalling memory.

Connor had insisted she take the time to rest and refresh herself. But she hadn't wanted to leave the deck. Somehow she'd felt calmer above where she could see everything that was happening and scan the horizon for other ships.

It was silly, really. She was so much wiser now than she'd been on her first journey.

Connor had nearly dragged her down here earlier. She'd sat on the bed only to appease him, but when he was gone, her lids became heavier by the minute. Rising so early that morning coupled with the emotional whirlwind of late, Jaidyn hadn't realized how tired she'd really been.

Sitting up on Connor's bed now, Jaidyn stared out of the large bank of windows at the ship's stern. She was on board the *Coraal* and she was safe. Connor wouldn't let anything happen to her.

Well, not anything that he didn't do himself, but that was a whole different set of worries.

Rising, Jaidyn went to the washstand. She splashed her face with water to dilute the last remains of that recurring nightmare. When reaching for a towel, her gaze fell on the tiny knob in the wall right next to her.

It wasn't just a knob, it was attached to a door. She'd nearly missed it because it was almost completely hidden by Connor's coat hanging from a hook. Jaidyn couldn't help but give in to the urge to see what that door hid. When she turned the doorknob, a small alcove opened, and to her surprise she saw

that tiny space set into the wall boasted a small copper bath-
tub.

Well, she might not have more to wear than those three old-
fashioned dresses Madame Poivre had kindly provided her
with, but now she knew she could at least take a bath whenever
she wanted to. Like now.

The tub wasn't very big, so Jaidyn used what water she had
in the washstand pitcher. She shed her garments and took a
quick sponge bath that left her feeling refreshed and more in
command of her senses. After donning a fresh chemise and a
pale green gown with lace the color of salmon around the neck
and petticoats, she set out to brush her hair until it was shiny.

Leaving the recess of the captain's dormitory through the
opening in the folding doors, which Connor had drawn to give
her some privacy, she now stood in the middle of the captain's
cabin.

It might not be huge, but that was understandable. The
Coraal wasn't a huge, cumbersome ship either. To her left she
saw a rolltop desk and wondered if that was where all his sailing instruments were kept. To her right was a table with nautical charts neatly rolled and secured.

Jaidyn sat down, tracing the outlines of islands and other
strange markings on the open sea map in front of her with one
finger.

It was a strange feeling to be finally on her way to Georgetown. She could almost sense her new home getting closer with
each passing minute. Jaidyn understood now more than ever
that she mustn't let her feelings for Connor grow. They were
too deep already as it was.

She felt protected—something she hadn't experienced in a
long time. Jaidyn also felt . . . *treasured*, she supposed was the
word that fit best, in a way. Somehow Connor had discerned

her secret wish and had brought May Hem here. Before that she'd learned he'd hired Winston away from those thuggish buccaneers. His actions . . .

Yes, well, perhaps he was a good man, but that didn't change anything. She had wrongs to right and obligations to fulfill once they landed. If circumstances were different, maybe—

There were too many ifs in that thought. Things were as they were. The situation guaranteed there was no future for them after that. Feelings would only hurt them both. Her guilty conscience wouldn't allow her to view their relationship as anything but a business agreement, regardless of any affectionate emotion she might develop or already have for him.

A quiet rap on the door tore her out of her musings. Once the door opened, Jaidyn saw a young lad enter, scrawny, pimpled, and blushing when he saw her. He looked down and shuffled his feet. "I'm supposed to get the table ready, miss. Dinner is on its way here."

Jaidyn jolted, immediately turning in her seat to look out the huge windows. Good Lord, how long had she been sitting here? The boy scurried to light a few lanterns and Jaidyn grimaced. She'd been so lost in her thoughts she hadn't noticed dusk settle.

Now she remembered Connor mentioning something about their first dinner aboard the *Coraal* as he'd reached for those leather straps on the desk. He'd said Mr. Parrish would join them. She was glad the first mate would be there with them; it meant she wouldn't yet be alone with Connor.

Mr. Parrish seemed to be a pleasant enough young gentleman. He was slightly shorter than Connor, and his brown hair was lightened to blond in places by the sun. She liked the way the small bend in his nose from what she assumed had been wild younger days took him from boyish good looks to a more mature attractiveness.

She was looking forward to getting to know him better. There had been something a little hesitant in his soft hazel eyes when they'd met, but Jaidyn couldn't blame him for being a little wary of the captain's sudden change in plans.

Plastering a smile on her face, Jaidyn rose to let the boy set the table.

8

After dinner, Connor was impatient to be alone with Jaidyn. Maxfield wasn't welcome here in the captain's cabin now or in the next few hours.

The first mate turned in the doorway, throwing one last glance at Connor. "Shall I help pull the folding doors, sir?"

Connor shook his head. "Thank you, Mr. Parrish, but that'll be all."

Jaidyn rose from her chair with a genuine smile. "Thank you for having joined us for dinner, Mr. Parrish. I enjoyed our lively conversation very much."

Maxfield returned the friendly gesture, bowing to her. "My pleasure, Miss Donnelly. Good night."

The quiet click of the door's lock told Connor they were finally alone. He unlatched the folding doors while Jaidyn stood by the cushioned chests under the windows.

She seemed to freeze in place as he pulled back the door to reveal the dormitory. He didn't miss the sudden stiffness in her shoulders or the bobbing of her throat when she swallowed hard. If Connor didn't know better, Jaidyn wanted to be any-where but here with him.

Was she scared of her own wants?

Walking toward the coat hooks, he carefully hung his frock. Maybe he should stop thinking so much and just seduce her.

Except that pushing her skittishness aside wasn't an option. For the games he had in mind, he needed her trust, which meant he first had to earn it and then ease her into his favorite brand of depravity, show her there was nothing wrong with it despite it being . . . *nontraditional.*

With a few quick flicks of his fingers the necktie came un-done. He let it fall on the bed. It might come in handy later. Then he tugged at his shirt while kicking his shoes off. Sitting on the bed, he rid himself of his silk stockings before pulling the shirt over his head. When that was done, he slid back on the bed just far enough for his shoulders and head to be braced against the timbers.

A strange stillness spread through him again. He exhaled slowly. It was like a steady glow, or more like an unwavering hum in his body. He became attuned to her every move and each nuance of her body that would clue him in on her feelings.

She was fussing with a fold in her skirts, trying to avoid eye contact. Connor assumed it wasn't shyness but something else entirely. Something she didn't tell him. He'd known from the start she was a woman with secrets, but some obviously weighed heavier on her mind than others. Whatever those se-crets were, he'd get them out of her eventually. At least for the moment, time was on his side.

Time was actually the only thing on his side.

And if he really thought about it, even time wasn't on his side. He had just about a week with her—and then some very hard decisions would have to be made.

But until then he'd stick to his course. If this was the trip to his personal doom, he'd make it as wickedly pleasurable as his green-eyed goddess could make it. And what he'd shown her so far was just the tip of the iceberg. There were many more pleasurable things he'd introduce her to step by step in the days to come.

Jaidyn appeared to be absolutely fascinated by the tips of her shoes peeking out from under the hem of her moss green day dress.

A smile tugged at the corners of his mouth and he half expected her to announce once again that she'd been instructed on what he expected and to ask him what he'd have her do, like she did when he first met her. She'd been temptingly innocent then, and in a way, she still was.

Hitching back her shoulders, Jaidyn threw her head up and plodded toward him. Her steps were hesitant, but she put one foot in front of the other until the folds of her skirts brushed against his kneecaps.

Connor let his eyes explore her, leisurely traveling up and down those wrappings that hid her delicious body. His fingers itched to take off each layer, revealing the gift that was her. Jaidyn must have seen the desire in his eyes, because the pulse in her throat leapt.

"You're staring at me."

Leaning his head to the side a little, he looked his fill before answering, "I'm staring, Jaidyn, because you're ravishing."

Slowly he lifted his upper body off the bed, like a predator ready to pounce. "I'm staring because . . ." Connor heard his own voice had become low and husky. "I'm thinking of the wickedest ways to make you come again and again once you're out of those garments. In fact, I haven't thought of much else all day."

His gaze latched onto hers and locked her in place. Her breath caught and her eyes widened. Then, as the air left her lungs slowly, she nervously chewed on her lower lip.

"Why don't you pin up your hair?" His suggestion apparently took her by surprise, because she furrowed those elegant ginger eyebrows.

"I'm sorry?"

"Pin up your hair, Jaidyn. There—" He indicated with his chin that she should sit at the rolltop desk.

Half turning there, she halted. "I . . . I don't want to."

"You don't want to? Or you can't?"

Anger flared in her eyes for an instant.

"Well," he said and stood, reaching for the brush on the washstand. "Just sit down and I'll do it for you."

"You?" she sputtered, looking down to his hands wide-eyed.

"Yes."

In spite of wrinkling her nose, she padded toward the desk. Once seated, she turned on the stool. Connor felt her gaze tickling the skin on his back as he walked toward one of the heavy chests by the windows. He promptly found the small box with pins and a few small leather bands.

Setting the box down on the top of the desk in front of her, he began to brush her hair in long, deliberate strokes until he felt her melt into the seat.

"I—" Her voice croaked as she began, so she cleared her throat and started again. "It seems like ages since I've had my hair put up properly. I've hardly gone out since I arrived in the Caribbean. And then it's too much effort and I'm not very good at doing it right on my own, I'm afraid. Most of the time it only comes down again as soon as I move my head."

Connor hummed, totally absorbed with brushing those beautiful, straight copper strands. He'd need to plait it tightly so it would hold.

"Why do you want my hair up anyway?" Tilting her head back, she looked up at him.

Parting her hair, he began plaiting the first thick wisp of hair.

"I want to have an unobstructed view of your body . . ." He stopped to lock his eyes with hers. "When you strip for me."

For a moment Connor saw her pupils dilate, nearly swallowing all of her amazing emerald green irises.

"Hand me that leather band, will you?" He reached for it and when Jaidyn held it up for him, he wrapped his fingers around it. A visible shiver started at the contact point and skittered down her body.

Wrapping the leather around the braid, he started plaiting the second strand of hair.

"I enjoyed dinner." She was fiddling with another small leather band. "Mr. Parrish seems to be a nice fellow. The ladies must think a roguish young man like him infinitely charming."

"Perhaps, but remember Mr. Parrish has a fiancée waiting for him in Boston." Connor had a feeling Maxfield was engaged to the wrong woman, but that wasn't really any of his business. Maxfield was his first mate. He was reliable. He was inquisitive. He was devoted. He was submissive. That's all Connor needed to know.

"Oh?" Again she looked up at him working on her hair. "Has he met his spouse yet?"

"What? Of course he has!"

"Yes, *of course*," she murmured.

Connor halted in mid-motion. "In this modern age you don't buy a pig in a poke anymore without seeing it. Proxies are barbaric. But I know some still make use of them. To each his own, I always say, but I'd never sign a proxy in my life. Hand me another leather band, if you please."

She held it out for him over her head. "You do have deft hands."

Connor smiled to himself. If Jaidyn only knew what else he could plait—even swifter than her hair. "Surprised?"

Tilting her head back, she grinned up at him. "Astonished is more like it."

Playfully, Connor nudged her head forward and set out to braid the last strand of hair. He noticed she started opening the desk drawers, one after the other, peeking inside.

Oh, she was curious. Connor liked that. He hoped her curiosity would get the better of her in other situations as well.

"What's that?" She was pointing at the brass disk in one drawer.

She wasn't just curious, she was genuinely interested in his nautical instruments. Connor liked that—a lot. "This is an astrolabe. I use it to determine local time by the positions of the sun, moon, and stars."

He reached for another leather band and tied the third braid. "Fascinating . . ." The rough slide of another drawer could be heard. "And what's that? Looks like a pair of compasses."

"And that's exactly what it is," he said as he plaited all three braids at the back of her head, then rolled the braid up. While reaching for several pins to secure the bun at the back of her head, he explained, "It's used to measure distances on the map."

"I see." Wood screeching on wood told Connor she was trying the skewed drawer that held the magnetic compass. Once she had it open, she closed it. Apparently she knew about compasses enough to go on.

"And this?" Jaidyn pointed at the wooden octant with ivory scales and a brass index arm that lay tied and secured under the drawers.

"I use the octant to determine our location during the day." Connor reached forward and opened the wooden box right next to it. He carefully took out the brass sextant. "Now this is a sextant. I don't use it as often as the octant and mainly during the night. This instrument is very sensitive. One tiny shake and the mirrors are out of adjustment." Connor held the brass sextant up for her inspection. "Both the octant and the sextant are used for navigation."

"By the looks of it, that sextant must also have cost a fortune. I see why you'd rather use the wooden octant."

Connor smiled at her practicality. "Yes, but it's more accurate than the octant. When we have bad weather and I can't see the sun, the octant is useless, so I use the sextant instead."

He placed the instrument back into the box and closed it, opening a drawer she hadn't tried yet. Reaching in, Connor took out the marine chronometer. "And do you know what that is?"

Jaidyn leaned forward, giving the chronometer a cautious perusal. "It looks like a very large pocket watch."

"It does, doesn't it? But it's really a chronometer, helping me to determine the longitude at sea."

"That tiny thing is a chronometer?" Jaidyn leaned closer to look at it from all sides. "I've seen one before, but that was nothing like this. It was big and heavy and . . . well, it looked more like a samovar."

Connor smirked. "Actually there's a bit of a funny story there. Last time I was in London, I spent the night playing cards. A young man joined our table. He introduced himself as William Harrison. Soon he had no money left, but he was so convinced of his next hand that he placed the chronometer in the betting box. Will piped," Connor raised his voice to imitate the young man's way of talking, "*This chronometer is actually my father's. It's a prototype. Once I've tested it at sea, my father will win the twenty thousand pounds the Board of Longitude offers.*" Connor cleared his throat and continued with his usual voice. "What more can I say?"

Shaking her head, Jaidyn laughed. The sound had Connor's heart speed up.

"He lost."

"Aye." Connor beamed with pride. "He lost. I found out this chronometer is remarkably accurate. If only Will's father knew."

"Well," Jaidyn suggested, "you could tell him in a letter."

Connor chuckled. "I already did."

Jaidyn laughed some more, and the endearing jingle was what heavenly harps must sound like. Connor cupped her cheek. "I've never heard you laugh before."

Her eyes widened at that. The next instant, all merriness in them died. She looked down, her eyelids fluttering as if she'd just now realized he was standing there with nothing on but his breeches. Her pale cheeks flushed a little.

Connor grabbed the small box with pins and stored it away in the chest he'd taken it from. Aware of Jaidyn watching him once again, he closed it and lay on his side on top of the padded lid, one knee up, braced on his elbow.

He remained still, feeling that purring calmness settle over him again. When he looked back at her, he willed her to come to him with his gaze only. "Tease me, Jaidyn. You know you want to."

Slowly, Jaidyn rose and took an undecided step toward him, then another. When she was in the middle of the cabin and still out of his reach, a slight blush crept up her décolletage.

Connor saw her reach back. Her hands must be working the laces. The gown gradually loosened at her shoulders and she wiggled a little until the dress fell down half her upper arms.

Holding his breath, Connor suppressed a groan. She must have seen it, because a shrewd smile tugged at her gorgeous lips.

Turning her back, she showed him how the corset gapped open and allowed him a teasing glimpse down to the dimples at her lower back. Looking at him over one shoulder, she tugged the gown farther down her shoulders.

Her gaze spoke of her desire. There was nothing impetuous about her boldness, she was teasing him as deliberately as she dared, instinctively recognizing what would be too hasty. Her sensuality wafted off her, wrapping itself like silk ribbons around him. This woman drew him in like a puppet on strings.

Helpless to resist her allure, Connor got up and strolled to-ward her, walking around her once. He was close, so very close, but still not touching, taking her scent deep into his lungs. Her fresh, grassy scent was now sweetened by the tentative musk of her beginning arousal. That steady hum in his mind became more urgent.

Leaning forward, he balled his hands into fists by his thighs to keep himself from touching her. He placed a gentle kiss on the back of her neck and felt her body give a longing quiver in reply. His lips explored her right shoulder down to her upper arm where her dress still refused to fall. He gave it a soft nudge with his nose until it loosened and fell to her elbow. Tiny kisses marked the trail he took, straight to her other shoulder, where he repeated nudging her dress down.

Now all that was left for the dress to fall was her opening her elbows. Connor kissed his way back up, and when he reached the back of her neck, he gently bit into it.

She gasped and shuddered, gooseflesh rippling her skin. Her hands lowered automatically and her clothes finally fell to the floor, pooling in a heap around her ankles.

Walking around until he faced her, Connor squatted to pick up the discarded garments she stepped out of obediently. He threw them in the direction of the table. Maybe they landed there; Connor didn't know. His gaze was locked with hers.

Her intent look darted down to his mouth and back up again. She bit her lower lip like she'd done before, but this time, Connor knew, she wasn't worried; she silently asked to be kissed.

Yearning to do just that also made his lips tingle. He moved forward until their lips were a whisper apart, no more. He could feel her breath on his skin, could taste it on his lips.

Jaidyn closed the distance between them, gently stroking her tongue between his lips, then tilting her head a little to allow him better access. With a shaky whimper, her whole body melted into him as he kissed her. Greedily he drank the sound, lapped it all up as his tongue thrust forward.

Her boldness triggered his hunger faster than he would have thought. If it was possible, he grew even harder. His skin tingled with awareness. That dark roiling in him went right on building. It was familiar, but usually it peaked at some point much later. That she brought it out so early, that his unconventional passion rose as fast as a bush fire raging through his body, took him by surprise. She was hazardous to his senses and his reason.

Desire slammed into him like a bolt of lightning into the mainmast of a ship. It left him equally devastated, but he steeled himself against his hunger, telling himself he'd need to be patient . . . still . . . just a little longer. Damned if he couldn't wait to have her spread and wet and aching for him.

Connor broke the kiss and took a step back, trying to get his ragged breathing back under control. Her delicious lips were glistening and swollen. The image of her luscious lips wrapped tight around his cock, that mouth taking him in deeper and deeper, that throat working around him was enough to make him catch his breath. God, he wanted her on her knees and sucking him hard until he came down her throat and he felt her swallow it all.

It took all the strength in him to tamp down his desire. This wasn't about instant gratification. It also wasn't about him, Connor reminded himself; this was first and foremost for her. That he got rewarded in the end also was a very pleasurable side effect.

"Stay put," he uttered, but his voice was no more than a breathless croak.

Connor went to retrieve the necktie he'd placed on the bed earlier. Swinging it in his hands until it was rolled tightly, he walked back to her.

Jaidyn was watching him handle the cloth, wariness written all over her. "What's that for?"

"I'm going to blindfold you," he said matter-of-factly, try-ing not to let the anticipation show.

When another visible shiver raked her body, she looked away. Connor felt the ghost of a smile brush his lips.

"Is that . . . I mean . . . do we really need to?" At the edgy pitch in her voice, Connor paused.

The tension was back in her shoulders, yet at the same time she eyed the necktie with barely concealed curiosity. Again she bit that sweet lower lip, her chest heaving with quick gulps of air. Her eyes were dilated and she pressed her thighs together.

Oh, she wanted it, but she was afraid of her desires. Connor swallowed the lump of lust so thick in his throat it almost choked him. He felt his cock jump in its confinement as if that keen lump had just dived straight to his groin.

"Jaidyn. Do you trust me?"

Staring at him, she blinked, obviously confused. Connor could almost see her mind slogging through that question and all the possible answers to it. Her reply took longer than it should, but he knew that didn't mean she questioned him or what they were doing here, just that she was thinking carefully about it.

Her face showed her honesty, but also her vulnerability. "I do, yes."

In his mind, he purred. "Then close your eyes."

He felt protective, yet at the same time his gut clenched with lust. Oh, he would protect his woman. Nothing would happen to her that she didn't want to.

After one more moment of hesitation, Jaidyn obeyed and Connor slung the cloth over her eyes, securing it at the back of her head with a knot. She instinctively leaned into him, press-ing her back against his chest for reassurance.

His hands caressed down her arms. Then he embraced her, placing another soft kiss on her earlobe. He waited to feel that iron rod that had replaced her spine melt away, lending her his strength to fight the sudden darkness, the instinctual panic that came with one of her senses being taken away.

Jaidyn leaned her head back against his shoulder, her hands traveling along his lower arms until her fingers entwined with his, showing him she'd pushed all her worries and doubts aside and was ready to move on. Such a brave woman. A fighter. God, he liked that about her.

Connor opened his arms and took a step back. "Now," he rumbled, the stern tone in his voice in complete contrast to what he felt inside. "Don't move. I'll be right back."

Her breathing quickened again and she made a visible effort to remain calm. As soon as she succeeded, Connor turned to his desk, opened one drawer to retrieve the leather pouch with a clip, and fastened it to his breeches. In it was a sharp jackknife. Then he grabbed one coil of rope.

Turning to her again, he reached with his free hand for one arm, his fingers wrapping around her wrist. His mouth rained tiny kisses onto the soft porcelain skin from her shoulder up to her neck. "Tell me, which one of the instruments hidden in my desk do you remember?"

Her mouth opened and closed, but she didn't answer.

"Pick one," Connor encouraged her. "Just one. Don't think. Just tell me the first one that comes to your mind."

"The chronometer," she whispered.

"The chronometer?"

Jaidyn gave a small nod.

"Now, Jaidyn. Listen carefully." Lowering his voice, Connor spoke intently. "What's going to come will push your limits. If you say 'chronometer,' everything will stop immediately."

Jaidyn cocked her head, then shook it. "But—"

"No 'but.' Be certain you only say the word when something's beyond your bearing. If you say 'chronometer,' the games end here and now. Do you understand?"

Her breath caught again as probably her mind tried to come to terms with what was to come. Connor was going to strip her of her will, intent on tearing down her defenses, but with that safety net he'd put some of the power back in her hands.

Her reply was at first too low a whisper to be heard, but before Connor could ask if he'd heard her right, she breathed in deep and repeated a now firm "Yes."

The word seared him with a fresh blaze of lust, the dark hunger in him cresting to a mindless ache. *Patience*, he repeated in his mind over and over again, even though he wasn't sure he could muster enough self-control to get through this *slowly*.

"Such a sweet, tempting lass," Connor drawled, setting out to bind her hands. He wrapped the rope several times around her wrist so that it would hold her without biting into her skin later. Looking up, he measured the distance to that hook in the ceiling right above her head and left enough rope before he cut it and started on her other wrist. Swiftly he worked, so completely absorbed in the task he fell into reverent silence.

"Connor," Jaidyn whispered, a quiver in her voice.

Connor halted. "Hm?"

"I—I'm scared."

He cupped her cheek, his thumb caressing the elegant slope of her cheekbone. "There's no need to be. You know that."

Jaidyn leaned into his touch, her lips curling tentatively. "Yes, I do. But still . . ."

"Shh, now. Stop thinking." Connor dipped her head back and settled his mouth over that almost-smile. She welcomed him, opening her lips for him.

That hunger was back with its full force and, groaning, he devoured her mouth. His tongue delved deep and tangled with hers, sucking it, claiming her—all at the same time as if his kiss was meant to keep her too aroused and too busy to ever think of wanting to stop this.

The fire in him turned into a conflagration. Wrenching his

lips away, he took a reluctant step back. Gulping air into his lungs, Connor sought to gather the last shreds of his sanity for this. Knowing she'd soon be spread wide for him helped him drive the need back. A little.

Kneeling, he bound her ankles as well, leaving more than enough spare rope for further use. Then he picked up the four loose ends of the ropes around her wrists and ankles, his hand clutching them like a vise. He got up again, looking at her.

Connor had thought her beautiful before, but now, as she was prepared for what he'd thought up, she was truly breathtaking. Her skin was slightly flushed, making those gorgeous freckles that were so lavishly strewn over her body appear alluringly darker. Especially her breasts, those lovely small breasts that begged for his touch, his flicking tongue. A small but delicious tremor began to rake her body.

"I saw the way you looked at Mr. Parrish at dinner." Connor let his voice sound cold on purpose. "Did you imagine what his hands would feel like on you?"

Before she could shake her head or react in any way, he traced the trail of a few freckles around one nipple with the ropes in his hand. Her breathing pitched at the contact. At first she winced, but then her chest heaved so much it almost looked like she sought the caress.

"When he cupped your breasts?" With his free hand, he cupped her other breast, his thumb circling the areola until her nipple popped up shamelessly.

"Pinched your nipples?" Rolling the erect pebble between his thumb and forefinger, he lightly pinched it. Jaidyn threw her head back, panting.

"Did you wonder what his lips would feel like?" Connor dipped his head, his tongue snaking out to wet the erect nipple. He saw goose bumps ripple her skin, and a soft moan escaped her lips.

Her arms whipped up to his head, but he stopped her instantly. "No. Leave your hands down."

She stretched her fingers, then balled her hands into fists. Her chin inched higher as her instinct fought her stubbornness.

"Is it so hard to obey?" Connor drawled, taking one of the two ends of the ropes that bound her wrists. "We'll have to remedy that."

Reaching up, Connor threaded the rope through one of the hooks fastened to the rafters in the ceiling. He took the end of the other rope and threaded it to the hook a little farther away, then pulled on the ends until her arms were high up in the air and she was standing on the balls of her feet. He fastened the ropes so that they would hold her and walked back to her.

She looked strikingly beautiful bound there and at his mercy. The position of her arms thrust her breasts out like a present for him to devour and do with as he pleased. Leaning down, he latched onto one. His tongue swirled over her nipple, his lips nipping it, pinching it lightly. Then his mouth settled over her neglected hard peak, sucking it into his mouth until he felt her squirm against him, panting little whimpers.

Those keening sounds she made drove him to the brink of control. He smelled her body exuding that mouthwatering, tempting musk and it drove him down on his knees. He squeezed his hand between her legs.

"Open your legs," he suggested, his voice a feral rasp. Spreading her legs would force her to stand on tiptoe, and she must have realized it, for she remained standing securely on the balls of her feet.

Gathering the remaining ends of the ropes again, Connor slapped the insides of her lower thighs. "Wider. Let me see all of you."

Her fingers wrapped around the ropes holding her arms up at her wrists and she teetered a little as she obeyed, balancing on the tips of her toes.

When she opened completely for him, he saw she was drenched with want. Connor tilted his head back a little and raised his mouth, kissing and nibbling every inch of her nether lips. He drank every tear of pleasure she wept. Not lingering too long on one spot, he opened his mouth and let his tongue snake out. With an agonizingly slow stroke he licked over her once, then stopped and watched as his breath cooled the hot path his tongue had drawn. Her sensitized button seemed to swell and pop up even higher as if impatient and begging for more stimulation.

And that was exactly what he gave her. Another long, languid stroke of his tongue, then he waited again. After inhaling twice, he licked over her once more. She tilted her hips, her core instinctually seeking his mouth, but when he didn't react, she grumbled with frustration.

"Faster, Connor. Please. Don't stop."

He denied her with an instinctive shake of his head even though she couldn't see him. "You don't demand, Jaidyn. The only thing you do is wait for what I give you when I think it is the right time."

She sucked in a deep breath. Connor thought he caught a whiff of anxiety when she gave a little shiver.

"Do you understand?"

Jaidyn swallowed hard. Then she gave a curt nod only.

"A gesture isn't good enough," Connor growled.

"Y-yes." The word trembled from her lips and it rained tiny, sizzling sparks over him.

"Yes, what?"

Jaidyn was about to shake her head, confusion written on her face. Then suddenly she halted—as if a candle had been lit in her mind.

"Yes . . . *s-sir*?"

Pleasure so searing, so ruthless slammed into his gut like a white-hot poker. His cock was straining against the fly of his breeches, debating with his wits the use of waiting longer still.

"Good. Now don't move."

If he were completely honest to himself, he'd been hoping for something like a lapse. Now he would get that wonderful, exquisite item out of his trunk filled with all sorts of toys. What he was looking for in the padded chest by the windows he'd lain on earlier was a tiny gold chain that connected two small flat clamps. When he found them, he paced back to where Jaidyn stood, breast clamps tucked away in one hand.

With his free hand, he cupped her chin and tilted her head back, fingers digging into her cheeks until she opened her mouth. His heart thundered in his ears. Her lips were soft and inviting when his tongue traced their shape. Her breath was warm against his lips, but the trembling had seized her body without pity now. He knew the reaction was normal under the circumstances; nevertheless, he asked himself if he didn't push her limits too far.

All his doubts were swept aside when she let the tip of her tongue meet his in a brief, hesitant touch. His whole body clenched, then roared with the pleasure that once again snaked through his veins, heat and need licking at him from the inside out.

Connor nipped and sucked. His tongue swirled around hers and his body caught fire, greedy lust scorching his mind, rendering him helpless against the hunger hissing down his back right to his pulsing cock.

He leaned down and closed his lips around one puckered nipple again. Jaidyn gasped and arched her body, trying to get closer, silently begging him for more. He bit into her nipple and she answered with a high-pitched moan, her hips twitching wantonly against him. His tongue swirled some more, his teeth went on provoking her already hard peak, and then he brought one clamp up, opening it with his thumb and forefinger. He sucked her nipple hard until it sprang from his lips with a soft pop. Then he let the clamp bite into it and screwed it close, adjusting it just one turn before it was too tight.

A gasp tore from her. "Oh God!" Jaidyn swallowed several times against that new sensation. "No," she breathed over and over, shaking her head.

Connor nuzzled her throat up to her ear, the fingers of one hand snaking around to hold her at the back of her neck, massaging gently. "Take a deep breath, Jaidyn," he whispered into her ear. "I know you can take it."

Her breathing pitched and she licked her lips a few times. Suddenly she threw her head back and a moan shoved past those pain-filled gasps.

Oh, he'd known she'd like the result. He licked over her other nipple, sucking it, playing with it, nibbling it until it, too, was wet and hard enough for the second clamp. When it latched onto her hard peak, she panted, biting her lower lip hard. But the throaty groan she'd tried to hold back came out anyway.

Connor saw her body started to glisten with a fine sheen of perspiration. Reaching down, he found her swollen nether lips wonderfully creamy. She gave a loud moan when two of his fingers thrust into her and steadily, but oh so slowly pumped in and out of her.

"You're wet. Can you feel it? Can you feel the juices running down your thighs?" Her secret muscles contracted around his fingers. "I love that you're slick and hungry so fast."

The fluttering in her core increased until she seemed to frantically hold on to him. She held her breath and stilled completely.

"Oh, no," Connor hissed and slid his fingers out of her. "You won't come. Not yet."

Jaidyn gave a groan of protest that ended in a sob.

Careful to always let her feel him next to her, he picked up the remaining rope ends again. He twisted them in his hand until they formed a nice flogger. Then he gently whipped her left cheek once. Her moans pitched and she swayed. Connor put one hand between her shoulder blades to anchor her. Then he flogged her some more, a little harder each time, each stroke coming faster until her every breath came as a mixture between a gasp and a groan.

Seven or eight? He lost count of how many blows he'd delivered because his gaze was riveted on the trickle of milky, wet heat crawling down the inside of her thigh just past her knee.

Connor stopped. He parted the ropes and threaded each one through hooks in the ceiling. He pulled the ropes tight. And tighter still. Jaidyn was completely suspended in the air, her limbs spread, her head back, her breathing ragged groans.

Panting and moaning, her nipples flushed and her pussy drenched. Pleasure was written all over her. Connor felt his heart doing a funny somersault.

Leaning forward between her spread legs, he took the tiny gold chain connecting the two clamps on her breasts into his mouth. His tongue wrapped around it and he tugged at it a few times, just a little, not too much, but he heard her suck in a deep breath, letting it out slowly with another low, throaty moan.

Her moist heat wet his breeches. With one quick motion, he freed his cock and positioned himself. Her welcoming moistness trickled down his shaft, but before he gave in to the urge to thrust into her, he reached for the clamps with both hands.

The moment he opened them, he shoved his cock into her in one hard stroke.

Jaidyn gripped the rope holding her up tightly, letting out a scream. Her muscles constricted around him, eager to finally welcome him in. His self-discipline faltered when he felt her hot, tight sheath surround him. Connor groaned, clenching her waist as much for his own support as for keeping her in place for his thrusts.

Only when he was seated up to the hilt in her did he pull out again, but he took his time with it.

Rolling his hips again, he sank deeper into her slickness. Burning, prickling waves of pleasure rippled through him, searing his body and mind alike.

Tiny, orgasmic tremors were raking through her. Each time he eased out of her wet sex then slid back inside, those quivers deepened. Oh, when she came, it would probably be like an earthquake.

He began to fuck her in the rhythm her breath dictated, his gaze locked on her, on the sight of those beautiful, angry red breasts swaying with the force of his thrusts.

Long, hard strokes jolted her. He pushed into her, left her completely only to pump into her again and again, harder and faster still. She would burst with the next stroke, and he felt his own instinctive response to her pleasure sling through his veins.

Connor retreated. Ecstasy raged in tiny sparks through his body, centering in his lower back.

"Come, Jaidyn. Come now."

Then he thrust into her again.

Her climax started. It was hard, it was violent, shaking Connor probably as much as her. Wave after wave of those spasms made her quim grip him even tighter until he could barely move. Her orgasm seemed endless. His head spun when Jaidyn screamed against the ceiling until her voice failed her. And Connor rode her through it.

Then he felt it too. That tiny spark that would burn him alive. Connor knew he'd never come harder in his life.

He couldn't pull out. Not now.

He wanted her to be his. Now. Always.

But he knew he mustn't take the choice away from her.

Letting his head fall back, he thrust deep into her one last time. Hot as lava and blinding as the sun, ecstasy coursed through his veins down his body, into his cock, and burst out of him.

All reason fled. Only pleasure remained.

He came with a loud groan, grinding the root of his cock hard against her core as he filled her with his seed.

As if from far away, Jaidyn registered that Connor let her down. When her feet touched the ground, her knees, as wobbly as jelly, gave out. But before a gasp of surprise could escape her, he was there and caught her.

She couldn't think. Her mind was too dazed. So Jaidyn let herself sink into his strong chest, feeling it ripple as one of his arms supported her shoulders while the other hooked into the hollow at her knees. He lifted her up into his arms and carried her.

His heartbeat was fast and met the erratic drumming of hers. With a sigh, Jaidyn snuggled even closer.

She felt the soft mattress of the bed touch her bottom. He laid her down completely, pulling his arms from beneath her. Placing a quick kiss on her forehead, he whispered, "I'll be right back."

And he was. He must move as quick as lightning, or maybe Jaidyn's sense of time was jumbled. His fingers worked to loosen the knot of the blindfold at the back of her head and Jaidyn felt it being tugged from her eyes.

She didn't want to open them. She felt so sleepy without being tired. That was confusing. Much too confusing for her mind, which couldn't find its way out of the fog that blurred each and every thought she had.

His hands cupped her breasts, kneading them slowly, spreading something like oil over them. She moaned at the pleasurable sting in her sore tips, her legs folding on their own accord. She'd thought after what she'd just experienced she'd be too exhausted to feel anything, but, clearly, she'd been wrong. A fresh wave of scorching desire spiked her body. Arching her chest into his touch, Jaidyn rolled on the bed like a lazy cat, rubbing her thighs together.

But despite her response, he left her. It didn't upset her, though. She knew he'd be back in no time at all.

There he was again, nudging her thighs apart with one hand. She let him do it, sighing with pleasure.

Jaidyn blinked her eyes open. The room wasn't as bright as she thought it was. He must have put out all but one light at some point.

Connor stood by the bed, bending over her, a cloth in one hand. She feasted on his body with her gaze, his wonderful, muscular body that gave her so much pleasure. Her eyes settled on his semi-erect member and Jaidyn licked her lips. How she yearned to feel it in her mouth, swelling and rising to every sucking caress, hardening even more with every little flick of her tongue around its head . . . but he was too far away for that and she felt too drowsy to lift off the bed and obey her instinct.

Jaidyn wheezed in a deep breath as he wiped her swollen, throbbing core with that cold, wet cloth in his hand. Her body bent to his touch, though.

He straightened and threw the washcloth into the general direction of the washstand. Then he settled in next to her, wrapping his arms and legs around her. His sweet, playful scent filled her senses and Jaidyn melted into the cocoon of his body, drifting in and out of consciousness.

Stretching her muscles, she felt her body was a bit sore, but amazingly that sticky blurriness in her mind had faded.

And with that, she felt her breasts sting cruelly and her left buttock throbbing mercilessly. Thank goodness she didn't lie on that side or else—

Connor was staring at her, taking in each and every reaction from her. "How do you feel?"

What a question. She felt good, which was probably understating facts, but she also felt as if her strength was depleted. "Sore, but good."

Jaidyn saw the glimmer of pride in him, his lips curling into a tiny smile. "Good."

"And you?" she asked.

"I feel contented."

Contented? What just happened between them—

Did Jaidyn really want to explore that? Was she amazed or stunned that Connor had pushed her to experience things she hadn't thought possible, or normal, or pleasurable? Yet she'd enjoyed it all. She had handed herself over to him and he had shown her new heights she hadn't even imagined existed.

But he'd always seen what she wanted, what she needed. It shouldn't surprise her. Still, she was a bit confused about it all.

"Connor?"

"Hm?" He brushed a strand of hair behind her ear and met her searching gaze.

"What you said . . . I mean . . ." Her voice, or her courage, or both left her.

"It was just role playing, Jaidyn."

She nodded absentmindedly. "Because . . . it is a bit at odds with—"

He pressed his lips to hers, immediately silencing her and all those dizzying thoughts that suddenly came tumbling into her brain, filling it to the brim until it was ready to burst. His lips always seemed to have that effect on her.

"I'm not really jealous," he whispered just loud enough for her to hear.

"You're not?" Even if she wanted Mr. Parrish? That sounded so illogical.

Connor shook his head, caressing her hair. "I'm not, as long as you don't feel the need to hide something from me."

Jaidyn winced inwardly.

"So, if you want Maxfield, you'll have him, regardless of what he might have to say about it. I only have to order him."

"I don't want—" *He only has to . . . ?* "You mean, since you're his captain, he'll obey you?"

"That too. But it's a bit more than that."

A bit more than that? What did that mean? "You mean, he joins you sometimes, like Reinier?"

"On a rare occasion, yes. But what I mean to say is if you want Maxfield, you can have him, because he enjoys being under my command in every way." Connor's hand circled her neck almost possessively, then began a slow caressing down her side. "And like you, he enjoys the punishment when he disobeys."

To emphasize his point, Connor kneaded her still sore cheek ever so lightly, sending a bolt of heat to her core. "I'd even say he enjoys it a bit more when he doesn't really deserve it at all."

Her eyes bulged at the realization. What he was saying jolted her just a bit out of the sensual haze.

Connor chuckled, the rumble vibrating deep in his chest, tingling into her. "Are you shocked?"

She couldn't lie. She was shocked. If she thought a little more about it, maybe it was her turn to be jealous. But in her current state, curiosity won out over all.

Jaidyn bit her lower lip to hide a grin. "But I thought you said he had a fiancée?"

"He does. He cares for her deeply, in his way. She's far away in Boston and doesn't know about that side of him."

"But you do?"

"Yes, I do."

She hesitated, not knowing if she wanted to know more, or if he'd even be willing to tell her.

"It's all right, Jaidyn." He trailed soft, almost tickling kisses across her neck as his fingers played the same teasing game along her hip. "Ask anything you like."

"How . . . how did you know he would . . . that he wanted . . ." She really didn't know how to phrase it. Jaidyn still couldn't believe they were talking about this and that it wasn't dampening her mood. Far from it.

"Doxies talk sometimes. The sailors they're with talk sometimes too. So I think he must have known discipline was something I indulged in. And once he joined the *Coraal*, I began to see signs he might enjoy it as well."

All the while Connor continued to tantalize her skin with his featherlike touches. Jaidyn's next question came out in a whispered moan. "Like what?"

Connor gave a lazy shrug and lay back on his back, his gaze directed at the rafters in the ceiling. Rolling onto her stomach, Jaidyn propped her chin on a fist atop his chest.

"Like how when we were alone he always kept his head slightly bowed, never quite looking me in the eyes. And how he would always refer to me as 'sir,' never 'Captain' or my proper name. Just 'sir.' "

He squeezed her stinging bottom, a purely possessive gesture. Jaidyn's pulse skittered. "Yes," was all she could manage as goose bumps covered every inch of her body.

"So, one day after we'd been sailing together for a while and had become closer as friends as well as captain and first mate, I tested him. We were charting and I told him that his work was shoddy. He was sitting at the table and I stood beside him with my hand on his shoulder and told him that maybe he needed to be punished for it. The work was fine, really. He's very good at charting. But instead of balking at the accusation, he bowed his head even more and said 'Yes, sir'—and, of course, his britches told the rest of the story."

She tried to picture the scene between the two men; Maxfield bent over the table or tied like she'd just been. Jaidyn's skin was ablaze and her center pulsed.

But then a chill ran through her. Maybe she was intruding? Jaidyn wanted so much not to care, but she did. Sitting up, she pulled the coverlet up to her chin. "If I'm in the way . . . if you'd rather be with—"

"Jaidyn, stop it." Connor shook his head and all but ripped the coverlet from her grip, exposing her once again. "As I told you, Maxfield loves Drusilla best he can. For now I give him something he craves that she can't. In time he'll have to find someone who can give him what he needs or he'll have to learn to live without it. I hope for his sake it's Drusilla. But—" Connor gently pressed her down onto the bed. His head dipped to take one tender nipple into his mouth. "Can we not talk about them any longer? I'd much rather wrap my arms around you and feel you close to me while we talk some more, if you like."

Jaidyn didn't understand who anyone was anymore. Not Connor, or herself, or the now enigmatic Mr. Parrish. Connor's lips laving and soothing the ache from her throbbing peak wasn't helping.

His mouth moved toward her other breast, giving it equal attention. When his gaze found hers again, his mouth curved upward. "Is there anything else you'd like to ask?"

Did Jaidyn want to know any more? Or did she just want to feel? Just live in the moment and forget about what was past—and what was to come.

His dark blue eyes dawdled here and there as they slid down her body, starting anew the keen tingle.

"So before, you said you felt contented?"

"Yes." For the fraction of a second, Connor narrowed his eyes. "Why?"

Wrapping one leg around his waist, Jaidyn straddled him.

"Pity." The word came out a bit muffled as she leaned down,

mimicking his earlier actions and sucking the delicious pebble of one of his nipples.

"Because . . ." Trailing wet kisses across his chest to his other nipple, she let her tongue dart out and flick over it quickly. "I thought if you felt . . ." Gyrating her hips against his crotch, he hardened in response. ". . . up to it, I could see to your pleasure now."

Connor smirked. "You are insatiable. You may be the death of me."

"What a way to go," Jaidyn whispered, scrambling down his body. "Don't you think?" She dragged the flat of her tongue in one slow stroke up his member.

"But if you don't want to," Jaidyn said and sat up, her thumb swiping over his weeping head. She brought her hand up and sucked the wet digit, her eyes half closed as she savored the seductive taste.

Connor's hand snaked around her head and pulled her back down. "Woman," he growled, his handsome, calmly smiling countenance darkening. He used that steely tone on her again. "Finish what you started. Now."

Aye, sir, Jaidyn thought with a grin as she set to pleasuring him.

9

The smell of the apple tarts surrounding her, Jaidyn sat at a small, rough-hewn table in the undersized galley, busily cutting carrots. It was nice of the cook, a Mr. McCutcheon, to let her pass some time pretending to be of assistance in the clean and serviceable ship's galley. Even she could see she wasn't doing a very good job, although it helped some to keep her mind off things. The poor carrot was mauled rather than diced, so distracted was Jaidyn by her growing feelings for Connor and how they spent their nights together. Cook just shook his bald, wrinkled head at the mess but didn't complain.

In the last few days she would wander in from time to time and Mr. McCutcheon would give her something small to keep her hands busy, like cutting vegetables or kneading dough. He was trying to teach her a few things here and there. She was willing to learn, but it was going as badly as her chopping was.

The sailing had been fair, the winds brisk enough to keep them moving at a steady pace. She often found herself with time on her hands while Connor went about his duties as captain. At times she was glad for the distance to be alone with her thoughts. But other times, like today, the last place Jaidyn wanted to be was alone with her thoughts.

Sometimes she would stroll on the deck or stay in the cabin and read. Connor had a nice collection, and they weren't even all about ships. She wished she had the patience to sit and read more. But either the subject matter didn't engage her enough to keep her thoughts from straying, or she'd start something like a book of sonnets that reminded her too much of the man whose room she occupied. It was better when she was busier and didn't have as much time to worry about what would happen when they reached their destination and she had to leave Connor.

Despite that, her favorite thing had become watching Connor as he worked. She told herself it was another way to try to figure out what about him intrigued her so much. He was quick to help out with a snarled line or a torn sail. That he wasn't afraid to get his hands dirty was admirable.

Thinking of how the small calluses on his hands from such hard work felt when he touched her sent a pleasant shiver down her spine.

Jaidyn refused to let her mind veer in that direction. Shaking the memory off, she thought of how much she enjoyed listening while he instructed some of the more educated members of the crew. He taught the coxswain and boatswain the business of reading charts and working with the instruments, so that they'd be fit to be first and second mates one day.

Jaidyn finished one carrot and picked up another. She'd already had a feeling that she wasn't the only one hiding something. She'd seen those furtive glances some sailors threw her way. She'd also picked up on the way some, Connor included, avoided talking about their destination. She wondered about what else Connor might be hiding.

One thing at least was obvious. Earlier today she'd seen Connor working on something again that he quickly stashed away when he'd seen her. Jaidyn had no idea why he didn't want her to see it. As far as she could tell, it looked like something for the ship. From what she'd seen, all it was were strips of leather.

But, she sighed, moving the knife haphazardly through the orange flesh, what was one more vexing thing on top of everything else?

It was quite apparent Connor was wooing her, seducing her into giving in. He'd made no secret about it in St. George's. Everything he did now was screaming it louder than words ever could. He wanted her to become his mistress.

With each day that passed, Jaidyn found it more difficult to not imagine what it would be like to continue to fall asleep in his arms and wake up in the same arms that made her feel safe, cared for. And in a way . . . loved. In those hazy moments between deep sleep and almost wakening, she knew whatever happened, in his arms everything would be fine.

It was tempting. *He* was tempting. And that was exactly what he was counting on. That sneaky man.

It could never be. And soon she'd have to tell him why, but like a coward she continued to put it off. The reminder of what was awaiting her was like a splash of ice-cold water.

"There you are!"

At the sound of Connor's voice, Jaidyn yelped in surprise, nicking her finger with the knife. She quickly set it down and brought her finger to her lips, trying to stop the flow of blood with her tongue. The look she gave him should have chided him sufficiently, but he proved impervious to it. Connor sat down on the bench beside her, pulling her finger from her mouth.

"Here, let me see that." He examined the cut, which was very small and the bleeding had almost stopped already. Connor quickly pressed his lips to it and then held her hand in his lap. "See? All better."

He gave her that boyish grin again that always made her

pulse pitch. Vexing indeed. Of course he would think it was his little kiss and not her own swift action that fixed things. And why wouldn't he be so cocky? The whole crew practically fawned over him.

Well, she wasn't going to let herself fall for it. "Did you need something, Connor?"

"I thought you might want to come up on deck to watch the drills." He seemed much too excited about drills.

"What kind of drills?"

"When the sailing is fair like it is now, I don't like the crew to get too idle. So we often do foul-weather drills or gun drills." Connor shrugged and leaned back, waving his hand as he explained, "We haven't done a gun drill in a while. I thought it might be good for them. We all enjoy a good loud run with the cannons."

"A gun drill?" Jaidyn didn't like the idea of hearing the guns at all. "Do you expect trouble?"

Connor calmly caressed her hand. "No, of course not. There will be no trouble while you're aboard my ship." He leaned in closer, brushing her shoulder with his other hand. "You must trust me when I say, what happened to you was out of the ordinary. With so few pirates nowadays, merchant ships rarely have trouble beyond Mother Nature. Especially those from a Dutch-based company not involved with the French and English troubles."

"Yet you have guns on board." Jaidyn didn't need to be coddled. She tried to pull her hand away, but he held it fast.

Bringing her fingers to his lips again, Connor kissed each knuckle lightly. "Pfft. They're mostly just for show these days. Makes owners of the cargo feel better about our services."

And it helped her feel more protected too. He didn't have to say it; Jaidyn was smart enough to figure it out herself. She wrinkled her nose.

Last night she'd had the nightmare again, and he'd woken

her out of it. She hadn't told him what it'd been about, but he'd probably guessed. The last thing she needed was for him to be overly kind and attentive.

With the bright smile of a man who seemed to think he'd picked the right card, Connor pulled her to her feet. "The crew enjoys playing at war every now and then. We make a friendly competition about it. You'll see."

Wonderful. They were all going to have a blast; she, on the other hand, wouldn't.

Although, and there was no denying it, Connor thinking of her and working to make her feel better did feel good. Yes, it felt very good—and that was bad for many reasons.

Maybe the drill was much better distraction than mangling helpless vegetables. Cook would probably be relieved too that she was nowhere near his kitchen. So Jaidyn let Connor pull her along without resistance.

While all the crew took their positions, Jaidyn stood to one side at the forward end of the deck. The youngest of the crew were acting as powder monkeys, running back and forth with black powder and wadding. She guessed there was no sense wasting actual balls on a drill.

Two or three men manned each gun. The *Coraal* boasted four nine-pounders and half a dozen six-pounders. A coxswain or boatswain directed each crew, and they all raced to have the best time in aiming, loading, and firing. They went through several rounds with the leader of each crew shouting orders and each gun crew racing to win the extra mug of rum apiece promised to the most efficient team.

There was so much going on, Jaidyn hardly knew where to look. One man got his foot tangled up in a coil of rope and fell, sending black powder everywhere, followed by the shouts of his whole team voicing their annoyance. Another team screamed encouragements to cajole their powder monkey to a faster pace. A member of a third crew blew out the wick of the team closest to him, but Connor didn't miss a thing and quickly barked they'd be disqualified that round.

It all seemed like more of a sport than a chore. And once again, as much as she wished it wasn't happening, Jaidyn was in awe of Connor's leadership and his command of his crew. He knew when to be stern, when to be congenial, when to punish, and when to praise. It was obvious just how much his crew respected and cared for their captain.

Damn him for being such a good man! Things would be so much easier if she could find him more lacking.

After four rounds, the scores were tallied and the drills ended. Connor announced the winning team. The crew took a short break for food and rest before the ship went back to its normal daily routine.

Jaidyn decided to check on May Hem. She spent time with May Hem every day, not only because the horse appreciated her company, but also because May Hem was a wonderful listener. She walked May Hem as much as she could up and down the length of the hold, groomed her, and taught Georgie, one of the younger boys, how to help with her.

When she reached the hold, her would-be groom, a thin lad around fourteen with shaggy brown hair and eyes the same color, was spreading fresh hay in the stall. "Hello, Georgie. How's our girl today?"

"She's good, miss. I stayed with her during the whole drill. She got a little skittish, but I talked her through it." His chest puffed with pride.

"You've been a great help, Georgie, or Mr. Jones, I should say."

"Thank you, miss." He looked at the ground and shuffled his feet, not quite comfortable with the praise. Once, the boy had confided in her that he was hoping Connor would help him secure a position as a groom on a large estate up north. As far as Jaidyn was concerned, he was more than qualified.

"Go on to your other duties now. I'll brush her down."

Smiling, Georgie handed over the reins and skipped away even before Jaidyn had led May Hem to the stall.

"How are you today, girl?" Jaidyn moved the brush in long, soothing strokes down the horse's flank. "Things are so simple for you, aren't they?"

Wouldn't it be nice to have such simple needs? Jaidyn could hardly imagine how her life could be much more complicated—or infuriating, for that matter.

At her father's death, Jaidyn's mother had fallen into a deep lethargy she'd never recovered from, and she'd followed him soon after, but not without revealing what Jaidyn would have never believed: that Randal Alexander Donnelly wasn't Jaidyn's real father; instead, a certain Neil Flaherty, a mere commoner who had been transported for smuggling weapons and other banned goods into Scotland, was her father.

He had built a new life in the Colonies vowing to send for Jaidyn's mother, but her growing belly could not be hidden any longer and she accepted Donnelly's courtship.

With both parents gone, Jaidyn was easy prey. Before that, Jaidyn really had had a pleasant life that wasn't tainted by worries graver than how to avoid a tea party in order to spend time with her horses. All of a sudden she'd become the rich, albeit eccentric heiress, and fortune hunters were running down her door. That's when things started to deteriorate.

In a weak moment she'd sought shelter in the arms of an unworthy man. To escape him and all those stifling rules society pressed upon a lady like her, she'd mustered the courage to write to Neil Flaherty—who had come up with a brilliant plan, in Jaidyn's opinion.

But then things had gone from bad to worse.

And now things were not just adverse, they were infuriatingly complicated and tangled. It felt like a knot in her belly, a knot so thick she feared she couldn't sort it out.

And the reason for it all was that Irish devil on deck!

Oh, she'd thought it would be so simple spending some time with Connor while on her way to meeting her real father. Theoretically, it would have been simple, but Jaidyn hadn't taken into account that despite her efforts, she'd developed feelings for Connor. Strong feelings. She liked him. Very much. Perhaps too much.

"What should I do, girl?" she asked May Hem with another stroke to her chestnut coat before she moved to the horse's left side and began again.

After all they'd shared, after having spent all those nights in Connor's bed and enjoying all the wicked things they did, she couldn't deny her feelings any longer. But the more she cared, the more it hurt to think of leaving him. She didn't really have a choice in the matter because she had to keep her commitment once they docked.

Trapped in a damned vicious circle, that's what Jaidyn was. She had to focus on things she didn't like about Connor, which were innumerable, she was sure, if she could find any.

Oh, yes. He was overbearing. A little. All he did was pursue one goal, trying to convince her that she should become his mistress, showing her what would await her once she agreed. But that was totally out of the question, because—

"Do you want to hear something funny?" Jaidyn stood on tiptoe to whisper in May Hem's ear. "Connor thinks the idea of a proxy marriage is barbaric."

The laughter died in her throat. Jaidyn set down the brush and wrapped her arms around May Hem's neck, trying her best to hold back the tears. "He's here," Jaidyn made a small fist and thumped her chest right over her heart. "I don't know how or when he'd gotten there. I tried so hard to keep him outside. But somehow he's forced his way in."

Now all she could think of was him. She wanted him there, in her heart, but it was tearing her apart at the same time.

Sooner rather than later, she had to let him go. Connor would always be a precious memory in all those cold nights that awaited her.

How was she going to be able to walk away?

Finally, the tears couldn't be stopped, hushed sobs obscured by May Hem's withers. "My sweet girl, what in the world am I to do?"

How could she tell Connor that she belonged to another man?

And how could she tell her husband that her heart belonged to Connor?

For all she knew, she could even be carrying Connor's child. What would her husband say to that?

Shuffling along the coast as they did now under the present weather conditions, the *Coraal* would make it into Georgetown in three days. Connor let the pair of compasses drop on the map, rolling his shoulders to ease the tension.

Three more days he could spend with Jaidyn.

Three days left to come up with a solution to the problem of not being hanged as soon as he landed in Georgetown.

His fingers dove into his hair. Had he been seriously thinking of a plan to avoid his untimely demise?

No, unfortunately not. He'd been sure that by now Jaidyn would have opened up to him completely and would have agreed to permanently become his mistress. If she had, it wouldn't be a problem to sail into Charleston, send a letter to his brother Kieran to tell him to meet him there. But it wasn't meant to be that easy.

In the last few years he'd sailed undercover to ports close by, but never directly home. None of those trips had ever been comfortable. Each time he took a huge risk to keep in touch with his twin brother. Most often they met in Charleston, the crowded port there providing additional cover. Although their relationship was strained, Connor felt he still owed his brother the courtesy of keeping in touch as best he could and doing what little he could for the family business under the circumstances.

Being a rich merchant, and his neighbor a breeder of horses who was willing to lend him a mount whenever the fancy struck him, Kier didn't have a problem with traveling to Charleston and back. Very few people outside of Georgetown knew that Connor O'Driscoll and Kieran O'Connor's wanted brother were one and the same. As long as his visit to the Carolinas was brief and well planned, it stayed that way.

Georgetown. It was still hard to believe that's where they were headed. Whether or not she'd agree to be his mistress was moot if the authorities in Georgetown got hold of him.

With Kieran's aid, they'd create a diversion and Connor would accompany Jaidyn to Georgetown disguised as his brother. He'd assist her in doing whatever she obviously needed to do there and get out with her as soon as possible. Then Connor would start a new life with Jaidyn by his side. Provided his brother was in the mood to help Connor, which he never was these days. Usually, blood was thicker than water—just not in this case.

Stretching, Connor leaned back in his chair, crossing his fingers at the back of his head and leaning it into the cradle of his palms.

Now here he was, mere days away from home where everyone knew him and certain people wanted him hanged. If he could make it into port, the only logical thing to do—the only choice he really had—would be to stick her in the ship's boat with a few of his crew and sail away as fast as the wind could take them.

Too bad there was no way he was going to do that.

Jaidyn held something back, and time was running out. He

was still no closer to keeping her after they reached George-town. And for the life of him, Connor couldn't figure out how to approach the subject yet again.

He wasn't at all happy with the process he'd made getting Jaidyn to agree to be his mistress. The sad truth was that although he felt that connection with Jaidyn growing deeper with every passing moment, there was this core inside her he couldn't reach. Something serious was holding her back and for the life of him, he couldn't figure out what it was. With only three days left, it drove him to the brink of desperation.

One thing was for sure. It wasn't anything they did in the privacy of the captain's quarters. Jaidyn responded to him. So much so that she had him completely tied in knots. She was an apt and attentive pupil. There wasn't any delight he'd introduced her to thus far that she hadn't reveled in.

They were not just a perfect match in bed. She was fascinating beyond that. Every time he knew she didn't see, he greedily soaked up all of her: her scent; her delicate, freckled porcelain skin; her stubborn chin; her graceful neck; the elegant slope of her body. Everything about her was perfection come alive.

There was something about her that hit him squarely in the chest when she just looked at him, or had him completely hard when he just heard her voice, that smoky, low hum that seemed to come naturally to her. And when she smiled, Connor felt ready—eager, even, to hand her his heart on a silver platter.

But what was she hiding? How could Connor get that last door she'd barred deep in her soul to open for him? What did he do wrong that she didn't trust him with the most guarded of her secrets?

Getting up, Connor put the pair of compasses away, rolled the map, and stored it away also. Then he started to restlessly pace the cabin.

Perhaps she still couldn't see how serious he was about committing. Maybe she held back because she feared that someday he'd leave her and then she'd have nothing. She'd be stranded like she'd been in Grenada.

Would it last a year? Or more? Would he grow tired of hearing her voice? Would he still want to make her laugh? Would he still hunger for her touch? Would every slash of her angered words, every biting pain of her dry sarcasm not leave him hard and aching to make love to her any longer?

He didn't think so. Somehow, somewhere deep in his gut he knew she was different.

Connor stopped in his tracks, staring out the windows. The sun illuminated him, and it was as if that foggy haze in his brain was lifted with the hot rays of light.

The truth was he couldn't picture himself tiring of her any time soon. As a matter of fact, he wanted her with him indefinitely.

Oh my God. He was in love with her. Truly in love with her. He loved Jaidyn from deep in his soul and with all his heart.

The explanation was so simple and, Connor realized, had been there all the time.

Still, the revelation was shocking. A month ago he'd have laughed about it, called it hopelessly pathetic. He'd have set out to prove to everyone, especially to himself, there was no woman he couldn't walk away from. But now Connor didn't feel like laughing at all. Having prided himself on being a lone wolf that no woman could tame, he was finally brought to his knees.

Strolling closer to the windows, he braced himself against the wooden frame of one, staring into nothing.

What the hell would it take to make her understand the depth of his feelings for her?

And what on earth could he possibly do to avoid the authorities in Georgetown?

He wouldn't trust anybody else, not even a few men from

his ship, with her safety simply because there was no way he could protect her then. And he sure as hell was going to protect his woman. She might not see it that way, but Connor surely did.

An idea snuck into his head and made him suck in a deep breath and hold it.

So, disguising himself as his brother was out of the question, but why couldn't he disguise a Dutch-flagged ship called the *Coraal* as . . . say . . . an English merchant's ship called . . . what?

Yes, the *Viola*! Oh that was good. Very risky, but good.

Under the flag of the *Viola* he could sail right into George-town this time, instead of just sailing close to where he'd grown up.

Connor felt like rubbing his hands and shouting "Eureka!" but he was jolted out of his thoughts as the door behind him burst open.

10

Jaidyn entered the captain's cabin, still thinking too much about too many problems she couldn't solve at the moment or any time soon. She kicked the door behind her shut with her heel, like one of her cousins would and not like the lady she was supposed to be.

She was rather peeved—a very ladylike phrasing for how she felt. Jaidyn was irritated about everything, starting with the fact that her mother's death had forced her into this situation. She was furious that the man she'd believed to be her father had died and left her to struggle on her own. She was fuming that her maid had betrayed her, and Jaidyn couldn't quite find the words for how angry she was that it had all come to this.

Truth be told, though, she was just disappointed in herself. Disillusioned and frustrated. Being royally annoyed at the world was much easier than facing one's own failure, though.

A slight commotion near the windows made her jump. Jaidyn squeaked, her hand to her throat. "Connor! I hadn't expected you here."

Half of him was cast in shadows, the other half of him caressed by the sun. When he turned to her, it was as if he was surrounded by an aura.

Squinting until her eyes adjusted, Jaidyn took a shaky breath. "I've just looked after May Hem. She's getting fat, but nothing that a little exercise couldn't remedy. What have you been up to—here? Alone?" Goodness, she was babbling like a wayward child caught red-handed.

"Charting." He shrugged. "Thinking."

His black hair was loosely tied at the back of his head with one stray strand of hair tickling his chin. The black shirt he wore gaped open until half of his perfectly defined chest was visible. Those black breeches that hid under those knee-high boots . . . He looked very much like the devil incarnate. Dark, forbidden, tempting her to hand over her soul. And Connor tempted her very much. In every possible way.

"Thinking about what?"

"You." He was looking at her with that disconcertingly comforting smile that caused excited butterflies to reel in her stomach.

"Oh?" Jaidyn swallowed the sudden onslaught of lust.

Good Lord! It was time she started thinking with the brain God had given her, not with her lust-driven body or her utterly unreliable heart. No matter how much she wished it could go on, the end of their affair was tangible, looming right there on the horizon. She had to rely on her reason alone and not lose sight of her goal.

But she couldn't deny she always felt a kind of dizzying freedom with him when he reached into her soul and plucked the deepest desires from her. As if he could read her thoughts.

Sudden greed overpowered her to experience that freedom now more than ever. She needed him to take her, to obliterate every thought plaguing her soul. She needed him to push her to the beyond, to where there was only pleasure, release, completion. Where all that filled her was her love for him, and the rest of the world fell away.

Coyly fluttering her lashes, she stepped closer. "Perhaps I should tell you that I had impure thoughts again about Mr. Parrish."

She let her gaze sweep over him, lingering on the bulge growing in his breeches. He was still leaning with one arm braced against the window. But Jaidyn could see his body give a subtle jolt of realization.

Goodness, he was making her quiver and itch on the inside, even more so when she thought about him ripping her clothes off, pushing her onto her back, and having his wicked way with her. But he was too much in control for that.

"Impure, you say?" He'd make her beg for fulfillment, Jaidyn could see it in his eyes. Release wasn't going to find her any time soon—and she was going to enjoy every moment of it.

With an exaggerated sigh, she nodded gravely. "Yes, I'm afraid so."

A smile flitted across Connor's face just before he started to rub the corners of his mouth down to his chin. "Well," he hummed, acting as if deep in thought. "In that case I should probably get you acquainted with my birch rod."

"Uh . . ." Jaidyn was taken aback. "Is *that* what you call it?" She had heard that some men gave their members colorful names, but she'd never believed Connor to be one of them.

Snorting a laugh, Connor shook his head. He opened the chest next to him. Jaidyn knew it contained all sorts of pleasurable toys. Just seeing him reach for the lid had tingling anticipation reel in her belly.

Her eyes fell on the box that held the breast clamps. A shiver skittered down her spine and her nipples instantly hardened as she remembered the excruciating pain they caused. But she also recalled how they thrust her to the precipice where pain and pleasure were completely muddled. Her core clenched and Jaidyn tensed. She looked away, but it was too late. Connor had seen her stare at the case for a heartbeat too long.

"Impure thoughts, indeed." Amusement frothed beneath the surface of his words. He reached for the case and put it next to the tray of glasses and beverages.

"This," he explained as he produced a bundle of leafless twigs bound together, "is a birch rod. *My* birch rod."

Her lips formed an "oh" she didn't utter. Jaidyn couldn't help but wonder what it would feel like. Her body heated up so fast, she had to bite back a moan.

"So . . ." All expression dissolved from his face. Jaidyn felt stirred by his glance, by that air of intimidating authority that surrounded him all of a sudden. "You admit to having been naughty again?"

"Yes, sir."

"You know what that means."

She inclined her head, trying to not appear too eager. "Definitely, sir. But—"

"I don't like that word at all. You know that."

Jaidyn thought she could hear that low growl vibrating in his chest. Her mind melted like butter left in the sun, leaving her body a buzzing puddle of ache. "I do, but please let me request most humbly to not be tied down this time."

"Unless my memory fails me, you've always liked being tied down. Last night when I woke you up, for example, you—"

Quivering inside, Jaidyn tried not to think of how completely helpless she'd been to his wicked seduction then. "I would have screamed, but—"

He smirked. "You had your mouth full."

"True, but afterward—"

"Then you did scream. They must have heard you all the way back to Grenada."

Jaidyn grimaced.

He narrowed his eyes, and his perusal felt as if he stared right into her spirit. "Very well. I'll consider it."

The air in her lungs left her in a rush. "Thank you, sir."

"Now kindly get rid of your clothes and step up to the table."

"Yes, sir."

In three quick strides he was at the door and locked it. Then, Jaidyn assumed, he went back to get his birch rod. She didn't know for sure because she was busy opening the laces of her dress.

The lid of his pleasure chest fell shut with a dull thump just as Jaidyn stepped out of her garments. Without looking over her shoulder at him or what he was doing, she left her clothes in a bundle on the floor and padded to the table, leaning over it.

Her blood was rushing through her veins so fast it resembled the sound of the disgruntled sea in her ears. She felt him at her back. Relentless arousal thrummed through her. Anticipation sent a fresh gush of moisture to her throbbing folds.

"Face me." Connor's husky voice was filled with the steely tone clad in silk and jewels that he used with her.

When she turned, their eyes met and she forgot to breathe. His mesmerizing gaze was absorbed, intent, his whole body exuding that sensuous and all-devouring hunger, entirely predatory, entirely sexual, as though he knew all the secrets of her desire. Jaidyn couldn't move. She felt paralyzed by the raw need staring at her. That dark heat he seemed to radiate seeped into her and was like a spark to dry tinder. Longing flared in her body.

Connor lowered his head to nuzzle the underside of her jaw. Her heart quickened when his tongue traced a pattern on her skin right down to her breasts. Then his tongue flicked over one nipple and Jaidyn gasped, her lids suddenly too heavy to keep her eyes open.

His wet mouth claimed her breast, softly sucking it. His

teeth played clever tricks on it. A gentle nip. A balmy lave of his tongue. The warmth of his breath cooling the wet trail. Then the cruel bite of the clamp.

Jaidyn groaned and tensed, biting her lower lip to fight the horrendous pain.

His lips brushed her other nipple. A kiss as light as a feather. A quick flick of his tongue. A gentle suck. His teeth nipping. One last lave.

Groaning louder this time as the clamp latched onto her, Jaidyn wheezed in a deep breath. "Please! I can't take it."

She heard Connor's low, knowing chuckle. "Oh yes you can."

"No . . ." Jaidyn's wail ended in a long moan. Stifling pain gradually turned to searing pleasure. Sweat broke out along her spine as she fought the strange allure, those talons of unadulterated lust that slashed into her belly. More cream surged from her core and wet her already slick folds. Like last time, the lines between pain and pleasure blurred and sent her soaring. Her core clenched, tightened, and sobbed for him to fill her.

"That's it. I knew you'd learn to appreciate the bite of the clamps. Turn around now."

"Y-yes, sir," Jaidyn stammered, blinking her eyes open. Her knees were too weak to support her any longer. As she quickly turned, her hands sought the edge of the table, clasping it to the right and left of her until her knuckles turned white.

Connor wrapped his fingers around the back of her neck and squeezed it hard as he pushed her down. "Lie down. I want your ass high up in the air."

Her maltreated nipples brushed the surface of the table and a fresh bolt of pleasure-pain shot right to her core.

"Ohmygod," Jaidyn panted. She was throbbing, she was aching, and she knew she was going to crest right now just because of the intensity of the sensation. Rolling her hips against the table as she instinctually sought the pressure she needed, she gasped, "I'm going to—"

"Hold. It. Back."

She shuddered as she fought off the climax, whimpering with the lust threatening to drown her. "Yes, sir," she hissed. "I'm sorry, sir."

"You're very talkative. And you're wiggling your extremely tempting backside a little too much." His fingers dug into the soft flesh of her buttocks shortly before she felt his right hand traveling down her cleft to bathe in the cream coating her folds there.

Jaidyn cried out. The last thing she needed as she hovered on the brink of a gigantic orgasm was for him to touch her. Wound so tightly, she clenched her passage, moaning even louder as she felt one finger thrust into her. A cascade of desire washed over her, causing her body to quiver with the fresh assault to her already sensitized core.

"Let's see how you like this." She heard Connor press the words out, and suddenly his finger left her sheath and entered her farther back. Jaidyn moaned helplessly as he wiggled the digit a little just before he thrust deeper. Sucking in a deep breath, Jaidyn gasped as he retreated just to enter her once more, a little deeper this time.

Gooseflesh broke out all over her like the ripples of water. Even her scalp tickled with the force of this new pleasure that quickly turned into an earthquake, his finger being the epicenter.

"Oh God, Connor," she moaned as she felt him enter her with a second finger, spreading and filling her to the brim. She felt herself open to this prickling tingle. Her juices overflowed, dripping down the inside of her thighs.

When he began to slowly pump in and out of her, Jaidyn couldn't help but thrust back, craving the white-hot, blistering intensity his stimulation brought. She was vaguely aware of him pushing something else into her weeping sheath, something inanimate, but smooth and warm nevertheless.

Jaidyn whimpered pitifully as his fingers left her, but that other thing soon replaced them. It was a little bigger than his fingers had been.

Throwing her head back, Jaidyn gave another loud moan as whatever it was, was pushed deeper into her. She felt herself widen to accommodate it, marveling at it fitting so snugly into her tight passage. She hadn't thought she could take it, but it was seated in her now, and with every roll of her hips, she felt its sweet prickle. It moved with her while part of it was still outside, spreading her cheeks.

The ecstasy was back, this time even more forceful than ever. It roiled in her body and tore from her throat in a scream. "This . . . this is . . . too much!"

"You know what to say if you feel you can't take it."

Chronometer, yes, Jaidyn knew *chronometer* was the only word that would stop him, but she wouldn't say it. Couldn't say it.

"Nonono-oh," she wailed, shaking her head. It wasn't beyond her bearing. She loved this abandon too much, craved all the sensations crashing in on her from all sides.

Connor chuckled low, the sound wickedly seductive. "Still refusing to keep silent? Maybe I should gag you, then."

Jaidyn heard his footsteps as he was walking around the table until he stood in front of her. Staring down at her, his face closed and blank, he opened his breeches slowly.

Licking her lips in anticipation, she felt another fierce gush of cream surging from her passage. He held his member tightly in his fist, pumping it slowly, and Jaidyn scrambled up on her elbows, opening her mouth. She was eager to taste him on her tongue, to feel him in her mouth.

When he was close enough, her greedy mouth engulfed him

and immediately sucked him deep into her throat. Jaidyn gave a relieved moan she felt vibrating in his member.

"There now. That's much better," he croaked, his hands fisting in her hair to hold it up. She didn't mind the little pinpricks on her scalp as he held her head tightly to keep her still. Connor moved into her mouth and she opened even wider, letting him take charge of the rhythm—of her.

Desire flooded her as he pumped in and out of her while the tickle of the plug still seated deep in her rear turned into a steady itching hum. Over and over, he thrust his member into her mouth, sometimes so far back she almost gagged.

Sweat beaded on his forehead and she tasted a spurt of that salty aphrodisiac at the back of her throat. Keenly she swallowed it, yearning for more.

A sudden shiver raked his body.

What had that been? Jaidyn's own desire was completely forgotten for the moment. He'd always been very enthusiastic about her sucking him, but that reaction was entirely new.

Next time he was deep in, she swallowed again. Connor moaned, his eyes going half-mast. His hips responded with another frantic thrust.

So this was his Achilles' heel, Jaidyn thought, concentrating on taking him deep and working him like that every time he was in her throat.

Suddenly he pulled out of her, groaning low.

With a whimper, Jaidyn sounded her protest, stretching in a vain attempt to get close to him again. But Connor only rolled his hips even farther back and out of her reach. With a frustrated moan, she gave up struggling.

Lifting her chin, she saw he'd bent his head, shaking it. He was gulping in air. Once he had his breathing under control again, he slowly raised his head and met her gaze. The same hunger she felt churning in her darkened his eyes to a midnight blue.

"Please, sir," Jaidyn begged, knowing what he wanted to hear. "Come down my throat."

Straightening, Connor pulled the black shirt he still wore over his head. His dark hair came undone, skimming over his chin and neck. His shoulders rippled as he rolled them. Then he blew out a long breath and took one step closer to her, gritting his teeth.

Gathering her hair up again in his hands, he moved his hips forward, thrusting into her waiting, open mouth.

Jaidyn shuddered. The feel, the taste of him, back in her mouth, deep in her throat was so heady, so unbelievably ecstatic, the spiral of lust in her belly had her core clench once more with the impending tempest.

Trying to tear his control into pieces, she bathed his cock, bombarded him by swallowing even harder, even faster the deeper he thrust into her mouth. Every muscle in his body was tense and trembling. His response to her laving and sucking him was urgent, his hips' movements frantic, almost out of control. She heard him moan and let him take whatever he wanted, whatever he needed from her.

A tremor washed over his body, right down to his member. Jaidyn felt the vibration on her tongue, the quaver right before the storm would break.

He let out a choked cry and, as his seed spurted down her throat, Jaidyn swallowed voraciously.

When he slipped out from between her lips, she couldn't help the broad smile on her face. She'd just broken him down, robbed him of his iron defenses.

But with that rush of excitement, her own neglected desire rebounded with full force. It wasn't just heat that slung itself like ribbons through her body; her blood was boiling lava. It wasn't just her fast pulse that beat between her legs; it was a ruthless, pounding ache that demanded relief.

"Connor. Take me. Please take me now. Please," she pleaded

breathlessly. Jaidyn was sure she'd go insane if he didn't take her now, but somewhere deep down she feared he wouldn't.

All she got in return was a condescending chuckle. "You plead so beautifully," he whispered right into her ear. "However, I must refuse."

Squeezing her eyes shut, she felt tears of frustration dot her lashes.

"Not so smug anymore now, are you?"

She heard him walk around her. "I love your ass, but I like it even more when it's a deep, angry red."

After a swish, the pitiless sting of the branches of the birch rod pricked her skin. Jaidyn jumped at the biting pain, groaned as the flaring heat on her backside turned into a fierce tingle, adding to her misery. She didn't have time to decide whether she liked the sharp bite of the birch rod or not. She heard another swish, and it landed farther down, where her thighs met her buttocks.

Jaidyn pressed her lids together even more tightly, trying to focus on not stumbling just yet over the precipice into the abyss of the raging orgasm that was looming. It was going to come as fast as lightning if she wasn't careful. Collapsing on the table, Jaidyn gave herself up to the vicious pleasure and held on to her sanity with what little strength she had left. Another sharp pain had her body seesawing between ecstasy and distress, and another bite of the birch rod had her core pulse severely.

"I think that's enough," she heard Connor say as if from far away, and the sweet torture stopped suddenly. The skin on her backside down to her thighs felt as if it wasn't sure where to pucker. Her arms twitched erratically, the muscles sore from gripping the table too hard for too long.

His hands lifted her upper body just far enough so he could reach her nipples and free her of those terrible clamps. The blood rushing back to her breasts speared her core like a hot poker. Then she felt him moving that plug in her, turning it a few times before he imitated slightly pumping movements.

Those small thrusts in her backside had her pleasure spike once more, build even higher and was about to turn into an inferno—

Too soon Connor pulled the plug out and was gone. She was left alone with her pent-up desire, passion thrumming so hard and fast and unrelenting through her body that she was ready to cry and moan and whimper in despair.

"You've earned your reward." His voice was silken whispers that sent multiple shudders down her spine. "I'll put these away, and when I come back I expect to see you spread yourself for me. Either your creamy lips if you want me to fuck your pussy, or your cheeks . . ."

Jaidyn hadn't thought it possible she could react any more, but at his words desire shot through her yet again, increasing the fierce, steadily pulsating ache in her core. She couldn't stand the wait until he'd be deep inside of her, and what he'd shown her so far tempted her with the promise of ecstasy.

She also remembered how hard it had been to accommodate just two of his fingers. His member certainly wouldn't fit, but the erotic memory of how he'd felt, how that plug had felt when he'd wiggled it . . .

Her body made up her mind for her because when she heard him approaching, she reached back—and spread her cheeks for him.

Smooth, thick liquid trickled down the cleft of her cheeks. Jaidyn gasped in surprise, quickly braced herself on her elbows and bent her head to look over her shoulder.

Totally absorbed in his task, Connor was putting the lid back on the tiny flask before he put it aside. His fingers, shiny with the oil he'd used to lubricate her tight entrance, dug into her cheeks. When he leaned forward, he rubbed his very impressive erection into the cleft of her buttocks until it, too, came away shiny, oily, lubricated.

Without lifting his head, his eyes wandered up and locked onto her gaze. A corner of that arrogant mouth kicked up and his hands gripped her waist. The corded muscles in his shoulders flexed. Veins bulged in his forearms as he held her down tight, keeping her in place with his vise-like grip.

The thick column of his member nudged between her cheeks and Jaidyn mewled, but whether it was because of trepidation or anticipation, she didn't know.

The lubricated, broad tip pressed against her, stretched her. There was a slight burning sensation as her tender flesh was opened so wide she thought she couldn't take it. She wanted to tell him it didn't work, she was too tight, he'd never fit. But suddenly, as he glided past the barrier of the ring of muscles, mind-numbing pleasure like she'd never known before swamped her.

Jaidyn crumpled on the table, her body as weak as jelly. Connor dug his way inside agonizingly slowly, and every inch he burrowed deeper, she welcomed.

The erotic edge had never been more tempting, more overpowering. She moaned with bliss when she was stretched so completely. But the pleasure didn't stop there. He pressed into her even more until she felt him up to the hilt in her.

There he stayed, completely unmoving. Panting hard, she felt her muscles flutter to accommodate him. Every other breath left her lungs in a low moan.

Then that zing of lust shot up and down her body as she opened entirely for him.

Connor started moving a little and then gradually more. Bittersweet, slow and long thrusts shook her very being with their intensity.

Ecstasy was coursing through her and Jaidyn didn't think she could stand one more second of it, couldn't hold back any more from what Connor had denied her for so long. As though he could read her thoughts, he croaked, his voice no more than a sensual rasp, "Don't hold back any longer, Jaidyn. Come. Come for me as much as you can."

More heat was thrown onto the fire raging in her body and between her legs as his strokes quickened. Screaming, she clamped down on him. The orgasm she'd been holding back for too long slammed into her, as sharp as a knife, shredding her mind to pieces. Release so sublime found her and robbed her of the ability to breathe. Her vision blurred as he slid in ruthlessly, disemboweling her every time he retreated.

Her orgasm didn't end. Instead it went on and on, her core fluttering so hard Connor could hardly move in her tight sheath. Despite that he began to ride her faster and harder.

One last brutal thrust, a savage bark, and he came also, long and hard and powerful. And once again Jaidyn burst into so many scorching little pieces her consciousness dissolved.

11

Jaidyn paced Connor's cabin like a caged lioness. She had no idea what to do with herself. Their destination was only days away and she was getting very anxious.

She'd never allowed herself to need anything as much as she needed Connor. The thought alone should scare her, but it didn't. Seeing him, looking at him, feeling him, and touching him in return, when his musky rose scent tickled her nose, when his deep voice resonated in her body and mind, a sense of tranquility settled over her. When Connor was near, everything eased.

His lovemaking in the night had acquired something like a desperate tinge. She rarely saw him during the day now. He'd asked her to stay put while the crew was busy with something—he hadn't said what exactly.

Of course, she hadn't been happy about it, but at least he'd *asked* and not demanded.

Up until now she'd been able to go wherever she wished. She didn't understand when suddenly she was stuck here. Jaidyn didn't like it all. There just wasn't enough space or enough to do in the cabin for her to be able to work off all her nervous energy. She hated the tightness in her chest and rolling in her stomach; it made doing nothing agonizing.

After a few more laps around the room she threw up her hands in disgust as she stomped across the wooden floor.

This was ludicrous!

Jaidyn was torn between wanting to memorize every nuance of every experience with Connor and wanting to forget it all so it would be easier to walk away. She couldn't even look at anything in the cabin without it reminding her of Connor and the way he made her feel. She couldn't look at the table without remembering how the warm wood dug into her hips as she bent over it, or the bed without thinking of how good it felt to lie in his arms in the aftermath. And she refused to let her gaze go anywhere near that damned trunk filled with all his "treasures."

Moving away from the table and trunk, she was left with no choice but to confine her pacing to a small path back and forth in front of the large stern windows. So she was left with staring out at the empty sea.

Out of the blue, there was more to see than just a vast, nondescript ocean. Jaidyn stopped short, jumping back in surprise. A pair of bare feet in need of a bath dangled into her view. Then, with a slow, jerky motion, legs in dingy canvas pants followed.

Cautious, Jaidyn moved closer to the window. Soon it was easy to see the wooden plank, where the sailor sat, was attached to two ropes, and he was obviously being lowered from above.

What in the world was he doing? Jaidyn wondered as the rest of the young and slightly diminutive member of the crew came fully into view.

Seeing her staring though the panes, he tipped his imaginary hat with a smile. Not sure what else to do, Jaidyn waved back. She continued to watch him, trying to understand what was happening as he started to work on something.

She shook herself back to her senses. Eager to investigate,

her mind jumped into action at the opportunity for something besides her feelings for Connor to think about.

Jaidyn moved around the windows, trying to see exactly what he was doing, but she couldn't get a good look with the windows closed. Whatever he was doing, he was too flat against the hull for her to see.

She really should just let it alone and go back to her pacing. It was ship's business and no business of hers. Jaidyn was just a passenger. Why should she stick her nose into the crew's business?

But she was a passenger paying dearly enough that she should be able to make simple inquiries if she chose to.

Moving away from the window, she took another full turn around the room while continuing her inner debate.

Who was she kidding? She couldn't take the curiosity and she knew it. Plus, something strange was going on, and finding out what would at the very least give her something else to do for the moment.

If she couldn't find out or if she objected to what it was, she'd also have an excuse to get out of the stifling cabin and confront Connor. And she'd rather confront him than sit alone and face her worries about him.

Jaidyn moved back to the bay of rear windows. She couldn't see the sailor anymore. The ropes were still there, so she guessed he'd been lowered to the next deck. Careful to avoid the windows that the ropes passed in front of, she opened one to the right of where she thought he should be.

Swinging it wide, she leaned out the window as far as she dared, thankful her pale blue flowered day dress had a demure neckline. Jaidyn looked down to find him painting.

She was disappointed. With the salty air and crashing waves, ships often needed to be painted. It wasn't really anything mysterious or interesting all at.

With a maudlin sigh, she started to close the window—

But it would make much more sense to do something like that in port and not while at a full sail.

She looked out once more to see that the young sailor was in fact painting right over the word "Coraal."

Why in the world would he paint over the name of the ship? That didn't make any sense.

She tried to contain her growing excitement as much as she could as she bowed out again. Bracing both hands on the sill and leaning her whole upper body out, Jaidyn watched him for a while, debating the best way to get his attention and not startle him off his precarious perch. Having not come up with a better plan, she cleared her throat with unladylike volume.

Gripping one of the ropes for stability, the sailor looked up toward the noise. "Afternoon, miss."

"Afternoon to you too. Say, what are you doing there?"

After a pause, he replied, "Painting, miss."

Well, he had no problem with stating the obvious. She'd have to try again. "Yes, I can see that. But what are you painting, exactly?"

His sun-darkened face looked thoughtful for a moment. "Painting this part of the ship, miss."

Stating the obvious seemed to be his only talent, outside of painting, of course. "I must say that is fairly apparent, but why are you doing it?"

Once again he thought before he spoke. "Orders, miss."

Now Jaidyn was beginning to realize he thought a little too much about his answers, like they were designed to be obtuse on purpose.

She took a deep breath and, tamping down her anger, tried once more. "And what exactly were those orders?"

"To paint this part of the ship, miss."

Jaidyn held back her frustrated growl and plastered on what she hoped was a pleasant smile. "Very well. Enjoy your work, then."

"Thank you, miss. Good day to you, miss."

"Good day to you too." Jaidyn pushed off the sill and straightened, shutting the window with more force than she'd intended. She didn't think she'd ever had a more useless conversation in her whole life.

Painting over "Coraal." What an odd thing to do. Why would Connor want to paint over the moniker of his beloved ship and do it in the middle of the open ocean?

One thing was for sure; she wasn't going to stay cooped up in the cabin any longer. No, not one moment longer. She was going to find the captain and get to the bottom of this.

Jaidyn stormed up the stairs with dogged determination to get to the truth of the matter. On deck, though, she was immediately stunned by the frenzy of activity. She'd thought the drills had been hectic, but they were a stroll in the park compared to what was happening now. Every able body on the ship—with the exception of herself, she noted with annoyance—was fast at work. Connor, Mr. Parrish, the two second mates, and Mr. Matthews shouted orders nonstop, left and right.

The rigging was alive with action. Sailors at dizzying heights with little regard to safety were hauling, treading, and knotting ropes. It looked as if they were changing all the sails. There was crew on the deck as well, running in every direction, except for a small group sitting in what could only be described as a sewing circle, working on large pieces of sail.

Mr. Stiles sat close by the group working on something that looked like a flag—a British flag, in fact. She looked up the main sail to see the Dutch flag had been taken down. Even though Connor was Irish by way of the Colonies, he'd told her both his ship and that of his partner flew a Dutch flag, Reinier being Dutch and the Dutch having a strong reputation in merchant shipping.

There was no doubt now. Something serious was happening,

and she had to know what. Steeling her spine to the task, Jaidyn approached Connor, determined to have the truth, no matter how hypocritical it was for her to expect it.

"Connor. What's going on?"

He didn't hear her over the din of orders. In fact, he hadn't even noticed her standing there.

"Connor, a word please."

Still no response. She wasn't sure if he wasn't hearing her or ignoring her on purpose. She tried again with as much volume as she could muster. "Captain O'Driscoll, what is going on here!"

Unfortunately she'd hit a rare lull in the noise level. Not only Connor but the whole ship turned in her direction.

Connor's gaze was level and his face void of emotions. "I thought I asked you to stay in my cabin."

For a split second she wanted to slink away, but with everyone watching she stood her ground. "You did, but I chose to venture above anyway. I saw activity out the stern windows and want to know what he was doing."

"Did you ask him?" Connor's calm demeanor was unnerving. She guessed that was the point of it.

"Yes. He said he was painting on your orders. But what he wouldn't say was why."

"Maybe he was just too busy for a long conversation. We are all very busy today." At that, Connor turned as if to go back to work, dismissing her.

She'd had enough of people ignoring her and avoiding the issue. "Yes, that is quite obvious. But I'd like to know why he is painting over the name of this ship."

"Because I asked him to."

Apparently everyone was meant to be obtuse today. Jaidyn crossed her arms over her chest. She could feel her face beginning to turn red. She wasn't going to accept that as an answer. "Yes, but why, pray tell, would you ask him to do that, hmm?

And why are you changing the sails? Why have you taken the flags down, and what in the world is Mr. Stiles doing with that British one?"

The whole crew seemed to turn away then, unhurriedly going back to their business. She didn't blame them for not wanting to be a part of what she was sure wouldn't be pleasant. She didn't care; she welcomed it.

"Jaidyn," Connor began through clenched teeth, but stopped to take a breath, and, with more cool but with just as much steel, he started again. "As you can see, there is a lot to do here, so if you'll kindly just go back to the cabin, I'll explain it all to you later."

Stomping her foot, Jaidyn had reached the limit of her temper. "But I demand to know now!"

Connor whirled around. "You what?"

He seemed to go completely cold, so much so that it made Jaidyn shiver. The look in his eyes was more dangerous than she'd ever seen it.

She realized then she'd gone too far. She should probably back down, but she refused to go all the way. When she spoke, her head was down and the voice so soft only Connor could hear. "I've paid every price you've asked for this trip. The least you can do is keep me abreast if something is wrong or our plans have changed."

She dared to look up at him through her lashes. After several deep, calming breaths some of the fierceness in his look was gone.

"Come with me." Connor reached out to take her arm.

Jaidyn let him lead her back to the cabin without a word to break the tension. Once inside, he let go of her arm and walked away, taking up her earlier hobby of stalking the floor.

She could see his mind working. It looked to her that whatever he meant to say, he was choosing his words carefully. She almost regretted forcing the issue.

Waiting, Jaidyn tried to compose herself by smoothing her fingers down the front of her dress, resisting the urge to ball her dress in her hands. At that instant Jaidyn did lament her foolishness. The sense of something unpleasant brewing was palpable. This was much more than she'd bargained for.

Finally, Connor walked over to stand right in front of her. He started to speak but then hesitated as though his mind was still engaged in some internal debate. He seemed deeply troubled.

Jaidyn felt the desire to ease his pain. "Connor, I . . ."

"Don't—" He quickly raised his hand to stop her. "You will listen and not speak until I have finished. Is that clear?"

"Yes, sir," she said, regretting using the words from their love play as soon as they were out of her mouth.

Connor growled at her and moved toward the window, looking out at the ocean for longer than Jaidyn was comfortable with. When he finally turned back to her, the look on his face was one of resigned determination.

"You want to know what's happening, do you? Well, I suppose it's high time to tell you. I've been to Georgetown before. You see . . ."

They both suddenly turned to the window as a jauntily whistled tune came from that direction. The painting sailor, whose presence had started it all, was happily whistling as he was being hauled back up. He waved to her again with a broad smile, then saluted Connor before he was lifted out of sight.

Jaidyn brought her hand to her mouth to stifle a laugh. The incident served to cut much of the tension. Connor just shook his head; nevertheless, some of the worry eased from his shoulders.

Sitting on the edge of the bed, he motioned for her to join him. Much of her anger had dissipated. She was ready to listen openly to what he needed to say and sat down.

"Some years ago I was accused of and tried for smuggling contraband. I was—*am* innocent. But I couldn't prove it. I thought it was for the best for everyone if I—"

"What? Tucked tail and ran?" Jaidyn sputtered, despite her vow to listen attentively and not interrupt him.

Connor grimaced. "It's not that simple. Although I was innocent, not even my own brother believed me in the end."

"It is. It's slander, and you've got to do something about it!" And his brother—

He had a brother?

Oh yes, he'd mentioned a brother already. But in what context?

"I cannot. There's only one person who can set things right and, God knows why, but she won't say a thing to put an end to the vicious lies."

Jaidyn almost jumped up at the mention of another woman in Connor's past. She worked hard to tamp down her sudden jealousy.

"And when I left, there was trouble. Someone was hurt. I later heard he didn't survive his wounds."

"So you'd rather live in exile for God knows how long."

Connor shrugged resigned shoulders like nothing else could be done.

As Jaidyn began to understand, her chest grew tight and her stomach tied in knots. "So if they catch you in Georgetown, you'll be arrested and hanged."

She could sense his hesitance before he gave a terse nod. "I hope to minimize the danger by disguising the *Coraal*, though."

Jaidyn was addled. All the chaotic thoughts rattling her brain made her feel as if she were wading through water. "Why did you agree to do this?"

"Well, technically, if you'll recall, I agreed to take you to the Colonies before I knew exactly which port." Connor attempted an awkward smile. It was probably meant to reassure her, but it failed to ease her confusion or help her sort through the welter of puzzling thoughts.

"But why didn't you tell me as soon as you knew where we were going? I wouldn't have held you to the bargain. I would have never agreed—"

Connor cut her off before she could continue. "Exactly. I wasn't going to let you change your mind or worry for the entire journey either. You need to get to Georgetown, and I'm going to be the one to take you. I would not change what's happened for all the world."

All her thoughts suddenly combusted, leaving only stillness in their wake. She was stunned.

No one in her life had ever gone so far for her. He was being completely unselfish, putting his life on the line for her needs. He was risking his life for her!

In that second she knew the truth. She loved him. She loved him with all that she was, and the thought of what might happen to him because of her was too heavy to bear.

"Connor, I don't know what to say." Her mind couldn't wrap itself around everything she knew now.

"You don't have to say anything. Besides, there is nothing to worry about. It's a good plan. There is nothing to be done but enjoy the rest of the trip." Connor gently gripped her chin so that their eyes met. "Promise me. No worries."

Jaidyn couldn't respond or she'd choke on the tears she could barely contain.

He risked everything for her, and she was going to leave him.

She couldn't find the words to come close to expressing what she felt. So she did the only thing that she could think of, reaching for Connor. And he welcomed her into his arms, hugging her while her fingers dug deep into the muscles in his back, pressing him to her with everything she had.

Connor was everything Jaidyn wanted, and she couldn't have him. Ever.

She'd always pictured herself married to a man who adored her and who she loved in return. With her financial and social status, she could have afforded a man of her own choosing to build a family together.

Instead, it all had come down to this.

Jaidyn felt cheated. Nothing was as it was supposed to be, least of all Connor.

He touched her soul in a way Jaidyn knew no other man ever could. She didn't need hundreds of past lovers to be sure. Connor was the one; the one man who called to her heart. The one Jaidyn knew a woman rarely—if ever—found.

But instead she'd consigned herself to a life of loveless matrimony. All there'd be to sustain her for the rest of her life were the precious memories of a glorious time with him.

Connor was a good man. Any woman would be proud to call him hers. But it would never be Jaidyn.

12

Grenada was so far away now Jaidyn couldn't imagine it even existed. Georgetown, on the other hand, was right there, behind the horizon. She thought she caught a whiff of civilization tainting the air. The breeze wasn't the friendly, comforting whisper along her arms any longer. It didn't play with her hair or her skirts anymore.

Jaidyn swallowed the well of tears. She had made her choices. Now she had to live with them. How she wished circumstances were different. But wishes didn't change a thing nor lessen the pain of the harsh reality.

"Still feels like the first time, doesn't it?" The wind carried a hint of roses and sandalwood.

Jaidyn turned her head in Connor's direction. "Being aboard a ship?"

"No." She felt him stepping up behind her. His body warmed her back and his arms came to lie on her waist. "Watching the sun go down. I always feel that way. Don't you?"

Perhaps she did; Jaidyn hadn't really paid attention to the fat sun squatting in the sky and scowling at her.

Turning in his arms, her hands came to rest on Connor's chest. She buried her nose in the niche where his neck met his sternum. He wrapped his arms around her, his cheek resting on the top of her head. Jaidyn felt secure and protected with the strength of his hard chest against her cheek as he held her. The world could fall apart now and she wouldn't even mind. She closed her eyes and breathed in his scent.

Take me far, far away. Jaidyn wanted to say the words, but couldn't.

"In little more than an hour night will fall. I'd like to land in Georgetown in the night. I thought we could anchor in a port a little outside, still far back, but among the other ships. It's far less suspicious than being the only ship in an empty port."

She smiled into the shirt he wore when she felt his arms wander down her back, cupping her buttocks and pressing her closer to him. His engorged member pressed against her belly.

"So we still have some time on our hands."

Connor kissed the crown of her head and her pulse lurched. She couldn't help the pleasant shiver down her back. In his arms she felt free . . . liberated. Cherished. Connor gave her everything her body, her mind, and even her soul craved.

"Do we?" Her words were muffled against his shirt.

"You seem a little distracted." Grasping her elbows, he held her back to search her face.

"It's nothing. Really." Try as she might, she couldn't look him in the eyes. She snuggled close again, playing with the lapels of his black shirt. All that counted now was each moment that she could spend with him still. She wouldn't allow anything to stain that.

"I have a gift for you."

Leaning her head back, she stared up at him in surprise. "A gift? For me?"

He nodded, grinning. "I'll show you."

Grasping one of her hands, he tugged her along. Jaidyn followed, unreasonably giddy with the idea Connor had a present for her. Down the stairs, to the right, and the door of the captain's cabin fell shut behind her.

In the middle of the table stood a wooden chest, richly embroidered with butterflies . . . no, they were . . . Jaidyn stepped closer. They were dragonflies . . . No! They were pixies! Jaidyn laughed at the sight. Her father had always called her a little pixie when she'd been bad.

Where had Connor kept that chest all this time? She looked at him with the question in her eyes.

Connor chuckled. "I'm afraid I have a penchant for decorated chests. I found this one in a small shop in Boston and had it stored aboard the *Coraal* ever since. Do you like it?"

Jaidyn jumped, clapping her hands. "I love it!"

"There's something in it too."

Inside, the box was padded and lined with purple velvet held down by tiny brass nails. Opening the lid some more, Jaidyn saw something she thought she recognized. "That's what you've been working on when you thought I didn't see."

Connor hummed. "Take it out."

Tilting her head, Jaidyn contemplated the item. She decided that the thick, plaited end must be some sort of handle, so she grabbed it in the middle between the big and the small knot, her thumb and forefinger closing beneath the smaller knot. When she lifted it, the numerous slim leather thongs spread from the small knot and swung softly. The leather was warm in her hand. It shone, new and well-oiled. Jaidyn was completely fascinated by—

"What is it?"

"It's called a Captain's Daughter."

Looking up at him, she felt her eyebrows sneak up on her forehead. "A what?"

"It's a cat." Connor took it from her and with a flick of his wrist, the leather thongs curled into a perfect spiral. "A cat-o'-nine-tails."

Jaidyn was still perplexed. "And what's it for?"

At that, Connor's lips parted and he gave her a toothy grin. "You."

"Me?"

With a curt nod, he almost growled, "I'll show you."

With one stride, he was at his treasure chest. He took something out that he stuffed into his belt, then he pivoted and strode to the door, locking it.

When he turned, his face had changed into an austere mask. His calculating gaze blazed with that dark, sparkling allure. "Off with your garments. Now."

Jaidyn had difficulty breathing. She felt a whimper in her throat. Connor's sharp, serious tone made her feel like a triangle had been hit, only instead of a high-pitched ring, sudden need vibrated through her.

"Yes, s-sir." Arousal made her voice degenerate to a palsied whisper.

Her gaze was riveted on those leather thongs dangling by his calf. Without thought, she reached for the laces of her dress, her hands too shaky to work efficiently. Impatient to get out of her suddenly confining garments, she tore at them, desperate to get rid of the suffocating wrappings.

"Brace yourself against the table," she heard him order just as she peeled the sleeves off. "Legs spread wide."

Her hands found the edge of the table and held on to it.

"Bend your head. Watch."

A fierce shiver raked her body as she obeyed. His hands cupped one breast from behind, thumb and forefinger playing with the erect nipple, twisting it gently one moment, pinching it hard the next. His other hand joined the wicked game, the leather thongs wrapped around his palm. The thick knob at the end of the handle and then the handle itself rasped the peak lightly. The difference in sensations, sharp pinpricks versus smooth leather that smelled of him, had her breath leave her in a sharp gasp. Every pore was flooded with hunger until she thought she was drowning in eagerness. Waves of desire washed over her, lapped at her body, pooled in her core.

"Are you slick with want already?"

At his words, desire slammed into her. Her heartbeat turned frenetic, as did the anticipating pulse between her legs. She thought she had been moist already, but she felt a hungry gush of cream surge out of her at his question, wetting her already slick folds even more.

His free hand roamed down her body and cupped her mons, his fingers probing and spreading her dewy nether lips while his other hand kept to the primal rhythm sawing away at her nipple. Panting, she gave a low moan when she felt her secret muscles ravaged with tiny contractions as his thumb played over her sensitive knob and he rubbed her entrance with the pad of one finger.

But he left her too soon, drawing her moistness over the apex of her thighs with his fingers. A moment later she caught a glimpse of his hand between her legs, holding a small, knobby thing that vaguely resembled a miniature member.

Entranced, Jaidyn watched Connor spreading her lips with the knobby plug, bathing it in her juices just before he gripped it harder and pushed it into her slick sex. Her muscles sucked it in immediately and Jaidyn cried out, feverish with lust. She arched her body, thrust her hips down. But it seemed the harder her breaths came, the slower he moved the plug in and out of her. Jaidyn groaned, seeing her juices trickle down his hand. She wanted more, relished in the wicked pleasure the plug brought.

"Move closer to the table," she heard him say, his voice degenerated to a feral rasp.

Jaidyn tottered a step forward until the hard wood of the edge of the table bit into her thighs and she felt a dull throb against her mons. The hand he held the cat in now came to lie on the small of her back.

Her core pulsated around the plug seated inside her in the same rhythm of the deafening beats of her heart. She threw her head back and let out a high-pitched cry when Connor slid the plug out of her quivering core and positioned it at her tight entrance. Without effort, it slid past the barrier. Groaning, Jaidyn welcomed it and the dark pleasure it brought.

Both his hands left her. Jaidyn mewled in anticipation. She knew he was going to use the cat on her. Would she feel the impact deep in her muscles like she'd done with the rope? Or would it deliver fitful, fiery stings like the birch rod had? She fought against her instincts and tried not to tense her muscles.

At first, she only registered the crack of the cat. Then she felt its bite on her backside. It had landed with tiny, successive smacks. Jaidyn bent and squirmed, her body instinctively trying to evade the pain.

Her skin started to tingle and the ache altered, turned into honey-sweet pleasure. Jaidyn delighted in the cat's pitiless caress. Its kiss wasn't as sharp and pricking as that of the birch rod nor as deep as the ropes. It was as smooth as the instrument itself looked.

Again the leather thongs landed on her skin, creating that tickle that rushed headlong into her core, spearing it with desire and leaving it sobbing for more. Jaidyn thrust her hips up toward Connor, silently begging him to continue the precious torment with his loving, ruthless caress.

Titillation, want, and desire tangled up in her belly, sizzling down to her core. Jaidyn knew a climax was bubbling in her stomach, throbbing between her legs, tickling in her anus. The pleasure kept right on building, rising inside her with such force it made her feel faint. The effort to hold back was almost too much.

The next few strokes with the cat came fast and her eyes shuttered. Moaning, she felt herself climbing toward an ecstasy that threatened to overtake her.

Her core was on fire, relief so close she teetered on the edge. She whimpered for it, but held back. She knew it pleased Connor if she denied herself until he allowed her to crest.

But divine pleasure assailed her senses, a multitude of sensations that almost shut her brain down and immersed her in pleasure so raw, so heady she swore she was going out of her mind.

Her skin rippled, her nipples ached in abandonment. Her pulsing, weeping core and that tingle in her rear, it all cumulated to a fiery conflagration. She needed so hard to crest, but her body coiled and waited. Only Connor could grant her relief from this.

Jaidyn licked her lips dreamily, her body swaying gently. Connor was pleasure; she was a slave to pleasure. The words rumbled in her brain over and over again.

Throwing her head back as the cat landed where her buttocks ended and her thighs began, Jaidyn let out another gasp. The vibration so close to her drenched core had her cry out with the tiny scrap of relief that was just out of her grasp. Passion boiled beneath her skin, streaked through her veins, and sizzled like a bolt of lightning down to her throbbing sex, scattering any rational thought. Behind her closed lids she could see sparks flying, pulsating with every stroke he delivered.

Then she realized that behind all those numerous buzzing fireflies there was . . . a strangely peaceful place. Each stroke of the cat felt like it gradually scratched away the wax on a honeycomb. Her sanity liquefied and trickled like treasured honey from her. Jaidyn let herself drift to that place and found herself swallowed up by the scorching bliss that welcomed her and annihilated any rational thought.

Twirling the cat in his wrist, Connor let it land on her backside, this time with a little more vigor than before. Her moans and gasps blurred into each other and he saw she rested her forehead against the surface of the table.

Next time he brought the cat down, he used as much force as he believed she could take in her current state of arousal without hating him for the marks in the days to come.

Jaidyn squirmed and let out another breathy moan. Thin welts started to show, a crisscross of horizontal lines that rose from the pale skin of her backside and upper thighs.

Excitement sluiced his control until his toes tingled.

Once more he spanked her hard and then, without giving her time to process the pain, he turned his hand, twirled his wrist, and let the cat snap forward fast only to pull it back immediately. The cat's thongs landed right between her spread legs, each tip nestling against her sex, biting her vulva before they fell away.

At that she let out a deep, long groan that sizzled through his body and licked at his skin, called to him. Need slammed into his gut and Connor tightened the grip on his slipping control.

Again he flogged her left cheek hard, quickly followed by a harsh swing to her right buttock. When she yelped, he let the cat snake between her legs. A visible shudder skittered through her body and she let out a long moan.

Now Connor concentrated on the sensitive skin on the inside of her thighs, which were glistening with her juices. The ethereal skin on her backside was flushed with too many crimson welts, some of them already fading. Others would still be visible tomorrow.

With careful strokes the cat landed from below, the thongs

wrapping around her thighs, a few of them always kissing her core. Perspiration covered her body that swayed to those strokes in a primordial rhythm. Sometimes Jaidyn let him hear a breathless moan of pleasure, at other times she gasped or grunted in pain. But always her passionate sounds ended in blissful sighs. Too soon her thighs turned an angry red as well.

Jaidyn had become eerily silent. Connor's hand fisted in her hair and he forced her pliant body upright. Her eyes were closed, tears dotted her lashes. Taking only shallow breaths through her slightly open mouth, she was smiling as though she was dreaming.

She'd floated away to that place where he couldn't follow.

With Jaidyn, Connor thought as he tamped down the over-whelming pride expanding in his chest, using the cat-o'-nine-tails was perfect.

Placing the cat on the table next to her, Connor cupped her chin.

"Jaidyn." He spoke softly, trying to gently pull her mind back into her body. "Darling. Come back to me."

Connor rained tiny kisses on the tip of her nose, her cheek-bones, and her chin. Then his mouth settled on hers. He felt her lips quiver shortly before she responded to the kiss, moaning into his mouth as he flicked the tip of his tongue over hers.

Nipping and sucking her lips before he kissed her deeply, he felt the strength coming back to her body. She held herself up-right now, thrusting her tongue back into his mouth, letting it tangle with his. He suppressed the pleasant shudder as she thrust her bottom out and it bumped against his engorged cock.

"Connor," she whispered as they ended the leisurely explor-ing kiss and her eyes fluttered open. She smiled at him and his heart missed a beat.

"There you are again."

"Please . . ."

"What, Jaidyn?"

She was the most beautiful woman he'd ever seen, especially now as her cheeks were flushed, her eyes dilated and misty, her lips wet with his kisses. And her scent . . . marvelous. So spicy, so sweet. It was wrapping him in Oriental silks more exclusive and precious than he'd ever seen.

"Take me, Connor." She didn't demand; she pleaded softly.

Turning her in his arms, he slowly, almost gingerly lowered her upper body to rest on the table before he reached down and opened his breeches. His cock fisted in his hand, he guided it toward her pussy.

Her moist nether lips happily parted for him and inch by agonizingly slow inch he stuffed her, relishing every moment. She was beyond tight with the plug in her ass. Her muscles constricted around him, struggling to accommodate him. Inexorably, he sank deeper into her slickness until at last he was seated up to the hilt in her.

Allowing himself to revel in her long, low moan for a little longer than he should have, he eased his cock out equally slowly until he almost left her completely. Once more he slid into her and retreated just as slowly, but with her ragged loud pants he couldn't hold back any longer.

Connor settled into a rhythm of lazy strokes that created a delicious friction. Tiny explosions sizzled from the base of his spine down to his anus and up his cock. Trembling all over as her cunny constricted around him like a tight, wet fist and began to milk him without mercy, he groaned and started to shove into her harder.

Jaidyn scrambled up, her hands anchoring at the back of his neck. Connor lifted her legs and splayed them over his elbows, his hands finding her waist again to keep her in place. Her breasts swayed in the rhythm of his thrusts.

Pulling his upper body closer to her, she found his lips. Connor responded to her greedy kiss. Entwined like this, his hungry mouth locked on hers, his cock seated so deep in her, he felt the climb to the peak coming fast, much faster than he'd thought. Need threatened to steal his control, his sanity, his very essence. Connor was burning alive. He was going to perish in the fever that laved his skin and turned that growing pressure into roaring lust.

Their lips parted but they still were close, so close that they could drink each other's pants and moans. Connor tried to push the sharp ache about to crest back for just a little longer. His every breath was filled with her scent, his every thrust was accentuated with her mewls and whimpers.

Jaidyn let go of his neck and braced herself for his hard and fast thrusts by gripping the edges of the table. When her moans turned guttural, he could almost taste her impending orgasm in the air.

"Come, Jaidyn," he croaked, his command suffused with passion.

She froze. She shuddered. She let out a raw scream as her climax washed over her, broke like surf on the beach. Her cunny gripped him hard, but Connor drove into her, over and over, frantically, close to desperation. She was made for his cock. He wanted to stuff her and make her scream some more.

Her pleasure blasted through him, spiraled down his spine with head-spinning strength. It hurtled him toward the cliff that stood over an ocean of passion so intense he lost control of the orgasm he'd been trying to deny for just a thrust longer.

She wasn't just the embodiment of temptation for him. He wanted more, so much more. He wanted the right to give her her heart's desire and be everything she wanted—needed.

Dizziness crashed over him and Connor felt himself hit the surface, then drown in the sea of pure bliss. Pleasure ripped her name from his lips in a hoarse cry as he filled her with his semen.

When he was as deep inside her welcoming warmth as he was now, he knew. Simply knew the connection was there. It was magical. Awe-inspiring. She was in him, forever in his heart, and he wanted nothing more but for her to stay there forever. To keep her safe. To give her pleasure. To be rewarded with her happiness.

Boneless with the devastating ecstasy he'd just experienced, he sank down on top of her, struggling to get his erratic heartbeat under control.

"Thank you," she slurred after a couple of deep breaths. He could hear the smile in her voice.

"It was my pleasure." Light-headed, Connor broke into a low chuckle that ended in a groan as he felt himself slip out of her. Reaching down, he slid the plug out of her before he wrapped her in his arms and kissed her neck down to her shoulders and up again.

A weird and wonderful peacefulness spread in him. True, his body craved hers, but it was more than that. He reveled in the closeness afterward that he'd experienced only with her. And when he didn't have her naked and panting and wet beneath him, he wanted to hold her, just hold her.

Fulfillment and craving, hope and desire constantly warred in his soul. But above all that, yearning to protect her and make her happy beat in his chest. Connor wanted to seize and devour her, cherish her, dominate and at the same time serve her.

He couldn't let her go—ever. It would be like ripping a piece of his own heart out of his chest and bleeding to death slowly.

He couldn't let her go. He simply couldn't.

But he didn't want her as his mistress any longer.

"Jaidyn, marry me." For a moment he was shocked that he'd asked her, but relief and jubilation rushed over him the next. Yes, he wanted her to be his wife. She had turned out to be everything he'd dreamed of.

She'd completely stilled in his arms.

"Marry me," he repeated and, swallowing the lump in his throat, added, "Please."

Her whole body quavered. He lifted his head to look at her. Jaidyn turned her face away but not before he caught the moist sheen on her cheeks. She was shedding silent tears.

"What's wrong?" Connor fought the confusion at her reaction. Were they tears of joy? Certainly not; elation looked entirely different. "Tell me."

She let out a sob that slashed his gut to pieces. Connor gave her the room she needed and reaching down, he closed his breeches.

"I can't!"

Uttering soothing noises, he leaned over her again. Connor petted her, trying to comfort her as she broke down completely. "Shh, Jaidyn. It's all right. Of course you can tell me. You can tell me everything."

"No," she wailed, shaking her head quickly a few times. "I can't *marry you*."

Straightening as if she'd burnt him, Connor tottered back a few steps. "What?" Sudden rage stirred in his gut. "Why not?"

Sitting on the edge of the table, Jaidyn hid her face in her hands, weeping harder and louder. "Because . . . because I am already married."

"You're . . ." Dark violence churned in his belly, like the lava of a volcano ready to erupt at any moment.

"To whom?" He had to grit his teeth to keep the snarl out of his voice.

"What does it matter—"

"To. Whom." He wanted to put a fist through the wall; he wanted to curl up and nurture those lacerations her words had delivered to his heart. But above all he wanted to hurt her as much as she'd just hurt him. "I want to know whose wife I've fucked these past weeks."

13

That served to let Jaidyn find solace in her own anger. She stood, letting him see the bright fire of her temper burning in her eyes that matched the fury in his voice. With her chin thrust up, she walked toward where she'd left her garments and managed to don them hastily, yet with as much dignity as she could muster.

"I don't know him," she finally replied, avoiding his glare.

In two quick strides he was at her side. His hand gripped her elbow tightly and he shoved her around to face him.

"What do you mean you don't know him?" Connor looked like he was hanging on to his control by a thread. "How can you be married—" He left the question unfinished as sudden realization lit his eyes.

"We were married by proxy," Jaidyn confirmed, fighting not to squirm under his hard stare.

His hand fell away and he took a step back. Jaidyn could see his eyes dull as if this was more than he could bear. One hand flew protectively over her heart, the other covered her mouth to hold in the sob she felt. A fresh well of tears flooded her eyes.

Connor, strong, powerful Connor was defeated. By her hand.

Frowning, he turned his back on her and paced to the other side of the cabin. His hands dove into his hair, fingers curling. The braid came undone.

"Jesus," he gasped. His shoulders slumped. "*He* is in Georgetown," Connor stated over his shoulder.

She couldn't believe it had come to this. He detested her. She loved him and hated herself and the husband she never met.

There was nothing more that could be said.

Jaidyn stormed out.

The knock on the door was a little hesitant. Connor knew only one of his crew would dare to bother him. He let the lid of the chest holding his weapons drop and squared his shoulders, facing the door.

"Come," he barked, wondering what business it was now. They'd anchored in Georgetown and he'd given the men leave. Only none of them had gone.

"Captain . . . sir?" Maxfield seemed to search the room and when he found Connor, something flickered in his eyes. Caution or worry.

Whatever it was, it was something Connor didn't want to deal with at the moment. "Mr. Parrish?"

"I thought . . . maybe . . . I might have a word with you."

If he kept on stammering like that, Connor's patience would snap. "About what?"

Maxfield shut the door behind him. His gaze roamed the cabin, restless, on edge. "I—"

The next instant Maxfield jumped into action and came close, so close. Too close. "I see how you suffer," he whispered. "You shouldn't suffer like that."

"Is that all?" Connor didn't want to talk about it. Especially not with Maxfield. "Very well, you may leave now," he sneered, turning his back.

Maxfield's hand wrapped around the other man's elbow, tugging. Connor whirled around, gripped Maxfield's neck and shoved him into the wall behind him, gritting his teeth. "Insolent, are we?"

He didn't fight back, just stood on tiptoes. As Connor's choking grip increased, Maxfield's eyes dilated. "She's not worth it," Maxfield pressed out. "She's not worth any of this."

Connor felt him growing hard against his thigh. He released him as if the touch burnt him. Taking a step back, Connor tried to calm himself.

This wasn't a good idea. Not in the mood he was in.

Maxfield stepped up to Connor. "I knew it would come to this, but I've waited. I've tried to be patient." He cupped his captain's face in his hands. "Let me make it better. Just like old times."

Tilting his head, Maxfield brought his lips close to Connor's. His hands wandered down to Connor's shoulders and farther down, caressing Connor's chest like only a man would, with none of the hesitancy a woman had. When Maxfield's hands reached his belt, Connor stopped their advance, shaking his head.

"I can give you what you need," Maxfield whispered into his ear, his lips brushing Connor's earlobe.

A pale shiver of arousal tickled down Connor's spine. "And that would be?"

Maxfield's eyes sparkled as he heard Connor's croak. He lowered himself to his knees in front of Connor, his hands opening his shirt. He pulled it over his head slowly, then shook it off, looking up at Connor with eyes that were dark and sweet and full of hope.

Maxfield caressed himself. Connor couldn't look away. His eyes followed as Maxfield's fingers dug into the blond hair that dusted his pectorals, down to where the patch narrowed to a fine line as it reached the rim of his breeches.

For a heartbeat, Connor couldn't move. Even if he could, he didn't know where he wanted to go. Did he want to take a step forward and encourage Maxfield? Or did he want to take a step back? Or did he want to go to his treasure chest and get the riding crop?

This was not a good idea—not in the mood he was in, Connor repeated in his mind.

But, oh, it was tempting.

Maxfield rubbed the bulge in his own breeches, tilting his head, his eyes never leaving Connor. His gaze was alluring. It felt like a good tug on his balls. Maxfield liked to do that when he sucked Connor off.

Suddenly breathless, Connor shook his head again. "No."

"Let it out on me. You know I can take it. I know you want to. As much as I want you to." Maxfield's incessant whispers increased the pounding in his cock. The younger man's gaze zeroed in on Connor's growing rod and he licked his lips suggestively.

Jaidyn was ready to run, ready to get as far away from Connor as fast as she could. Yet somehow she found herself dragging her feet to disembark.

The only place to go was to her father. Now that the time had come, she didn't know if she could do it. Not when things with Connor were like this.

What if things with her father turned out to be just as bad? What if after all this he didn't want her, either?

She couldn't stand the thought of facing him then having no one. She did have someone, though. She had May Hem. At least May Hem would be with her.

In the hold Jaidyn began preparing the horse to leave. She

got the bridle and bit down off its hook, then threw the blanket over the mare's back.

Her heavy sigh turned to a sob. Instead of reaching for the saddle, Jaidyn leaned her cheek against May Hem's warm hide.

"What am I doing, girl? I've never been one to run from a problem. But I'm not running. I came here to see my father, and that's exactly what I'm doing. It's time to finally have this done with, just like Connor is done with me." Jaidyn patted the horse's smooth flank as she whinnied in sympathy.

"I've hurt him so badly, May Hem. If you could have seen the look on his face. It was horrible. I had no idea he would be hurt like that. I never thought—I never hoped that he could feel so deeply for me. I thought it was all just a game to him."

The idea came so unexpectedly, Jaidyn jolted. She stood back up, wiping her eyes and nose with the edge of her sleeve. Could it be?

What if he really . . . ?

She wanted to believe it so badly. Her heart wanted to grab at that thread of possibility and hold on for dear life.

Well, if he did feel so much for her, then maybe instead of going to a husband she'd never met and who never wanted much contact, much less expect her to fulfill her wifely duties, she could stay with Connor. Maybe they could find a way to be together. There was still a chance she could love him and be with him.

May Hem stomped her hooves impatiently. Jaidyn gave her a sad smile. "Oh, my sweet girl, I know you're ready to get off this ship, but I can't go just yet. I've got to go back and make him talk to me. I've got to know. I couldn't live with myself if I left without ever knowing if he feels for me like I do for him. Surely you understand that."

The mare raised, then lowered her head before shaking it from side to side, neighing. Jaidyn wrapped her arms around the horse's neck, kissing her cheek. "Hold on, girl, for just a little bit longer."

Love made her fly up the stairs. Jaidyn was hoping against hope it was true.

For Connor, Maxfield's offer was . . . unsettling. Seductive, true, but that he didn't react with his usual enthusiasm was unnerving.

But why should he hold back? There was nothing—nobody that kept him from doing what he wanted. Maybe a good hard ride was just what he needed to find his usual detachment again. And Maxfield liked it rough, especially after a long and thorough treatment with the riding crop.

Connor didn't think when he went to the treasure chest; he didn't think when his hand wrapped around the crop, nor when he positioned himself behind Maxfield. He gripped the riding crop in his hand tightly.

But he couldn't make himself take that first sweet, zinging swing.

Connor was repulsed by himself. He opened his death grip on the instrument and the crop fell to the floor. His fingers dove into his hair and he rolled his eyes skyward in despair.

This was not what he wanted. Not even remotely. He wanted *her*—and it was tearing him to shreds.

Jaidyn had ruined him for anybody else.

Maxfield turned, his hands quickly working the fly of Connor's breeches. Before he could get anywhere near his cock, Connor roared, "No!" and shoved him away.

A sharp gasp had him look up. Jaidyn was standing in the door, taking in the situation before her, her eyes round and unblinking like an owl's. Connor refused to look embarrassed.

Maxfield reached for his shirt. He got up and his gaze darted between her and Connor. The pain of being cast aside shone clearly in his hazel eyes, but Connor thought there was also something else. Carefully subdued anger.

The younger man averted his gaze and nodded toward Jaidyn. "Miss Donnelly."

"Mr. Parrish."

Without another word, Maxfield stormed out.

Connor couldn't look at her for fear that the hurt roiling in his stomach and ripping his heart to pieces would show. So he went back to the chest he'd shut before Maxfield's intrusion and resumed preparing his pistols and daggers.

"Connor. I—"

"What?" His eyes narrowed at her. The underlying growl in his voice served to stop her in her tracks.

"Can we talk about it?"

Loading the smaller pistol, he ground his teeth. "There's nothing to talk about."

She rolled her lips under and took another step toward him. "You may have nothing to say, but I do."

"Fine," Connor snapped, securing the pistol in his belt at the small of his back. He started loading the larger pistol. "I don't want to hear it."

"Please, Connor. At least let me—*What* are you doing?"

"What does it look like?" He squeezed the larger pistol into his belt at his front. Reaching for two daggers, he secured them in his boots. One last dagger was slid into its sheath and attached to his left forearm with leather straps.

"Good Lord! You're not thinking of—"

"What I'm thinking," he cut her off, "is none of your business." He went to get his coat, shrugging into it. "Besides, why do you care?" Righting his cuffs, he settled a callous gaze on her. "Or more to the point: since when?"

Jaidyn went in an arc around him until she stood with her back to the tray of decanters and glasses. "Look, there is no need for you to leave the ship. Winston can take me ashore. There is no need for you to risk being seen."

Connor chuckled, but the sound was void of amusement. "Very good. But there's no need to keep this up any longer."

"This isn't an act, Connor. It never has been. I—"

That was it. Connor could no longer hold the red-hot fury in him back. "Mr. Matthews and you can do whatever the hell you like." Moving toward her, he pointed an accusing finger. "But I'm going to take a stroll through town and see if anything has changed since they branded me a criminal. Maybe have a pint or a dozen before saying hello to my loving brother."

Even though they weren't close to each other, Jaidyn took a small step back, bumping into the cabinet. "Connor, you're just being foolish. And you're going to get yourself killed for it."

"No, my dear, what was foolish was ever getting involved with a manipulative harpy like you. I knew you were trouble. I knew it when I left you that first time. I should've never come back." He whirled, giving his back to her.

"Connor! You're being ridiculous. Don't say that."

Agitated beyond bearing, he began to pace the room. "You're right there, Miss Donnelly. It was ridiculous to think you were doing anything but using me to get exactly what you wanted. Happy now, my lady? You've had your fun and now you'll have your husband—and all you had to do was open those pretty legs of yours."

"Stubborn bastard! It wasn't like that and you know it."

Connor turned back to her. "It wasn't? Yet here we are. I'm risking my life and you're going home to your husband in town. How is it not?"

Ginger brows snapped together as her eyes narrowed. She opened and closed her mouth, but nothing came out. Connor knew there was nothing she could say. It was the truth. But it didn't make him feel any better.

"I wonder. Do you think your husband will be able to make

you come so many times you can't breathe, can't think? Do you think he can help you find that place where it all falls away? Be sure to let him know who to thank for breaking you in." Connor had to stop himself from spitting on the floor or screaming his rage at the thought of her with her husband.

"That was cruel, Connor. How can you be such a cur?" Jaidyn looked hollow, empty and forsaken, but he wasn't going to let that fool him.

"It seems to be easy with you around." He needed to get away from her. Fast. "I've brought you here. You've paid for passage." Connor spoke with a casualness he didn't feel. "As far as I'm concerned, we're even."

"Oh really? If that's what you think of me, then maybe I should pack my things and leave as soon as possible."

Already at the door, Connor turned his head. "That might be best."

A glass shattered on the wall dangerously close to his head, but Connor ignored it. He just left.

14

The leather of the large chair rumbled as it stretched when Connor sat down. Its twin sat empty on the other side of the table. He leaned his head back and inhaled deeply. Fading traces of soft soap and furniture polish mingled with the faint scent of cold cigar smoke from the thick carpet under his feet.

It still smelled like home, Connor thought. And it still felt like home.

Being here again after all this time was like all the burdens had suddenly fallen off his shoulders and everything would turn out right in the end.

All but one worry. That nagging pain still remained no matter where he was.

Now that the house was asleep, the ticking of the pendulum clock in the hall was so loud it almost drowned out the excited song of crickets outside. On the other side of what was now Kieran's house, Connor could hear a lone coach rattling by, the horse's hooves beating a tired clip-clop on the cobblestones.

Otherwise the night was quiet, but Connor knew it wouldn't be long until Kieran showed up. He didn't know how his brother did it, but Kieran had some sort of sixth sense when it came to intruders. Inwardly, Connor winced when he realized that he was now an intruder in this house as well.

An almost inaudible squeak of the wooden floor in the hall had him perk up his ears. He grabbed the match next to him and lit the candle. When he looked up, he saw the barrel of a pistol pointed at him.

Behind it stood his brother. The pupils in his pale blue eyes shrank to pinpoints in the sudden light. Other than that he remained as still as a statue.

"Kieran," Connor greeted him, although the temperature in the room seemed to have dropped considerably all of a sudden.

"Brother?" Dropping the arm that had pointed the pistol at Connor, Kieran turned and sauntered to the sideboard. He'd taken the time to dress, Connor noted. He wore a shirt and breeches, but no shoes. His long black hair hung loosely down his back.

He placed the pistol on the cabinet and filled two glasses with brandy. When Kieran came back to where Connor sat, he set one glass right in front of him, raised it in a silent toast, and sipped at it without waiting for Connor.

He swallowed the amber liquid with a gasp. "To what do I owe this honor?"

Connor reached for his glass. "I wanted to see you."

"And risk your head by doing so?" The tone in his voice made it quite clear that Kieran didn't believe him. Even that wasn't new.

"Nobody knows I'm here."

"Let's hope it stays that way," Kier mumbled into his glass before he downed the rest of the brandy.

"I trust my crew."

Kieran snorted. "Still idealistic."

Connor set his glass down with a loud clunk. "No, I just refused to completely lose faith in people. Well, most people."

"You never had to." Kier's cold stare settled on Connor.

"I'm reminded of never trusting anybody again every day." He pointed at the thin scar on the left side of his face that started at his brow and ran down his temple, ending just above his cheekbone. With a growl, Kier got up, taking his glass with him to the sideboard to refill it.

Seeing how coldhearted and bitter his brother had become hurt Connor like a jab in the stomach.

The tension left Kieran's shoulders a bit. "But it's good that you're here."

Connor's heartbeat pitched and he fought to not let the hopeful smile he felt tugging at his lips show. Maybe they could finally make peace.

"Yes," Kieran nodded, crossing the room to the desk. "Do you mind signing this while you're here?" He retrieved the paper in question and laid it out for him.

Connor strolled to the desk and reached for the quill. Dipping it into the ink, he signed the document as quickly as usual. When he turned back, he saw Kieran watching him with an unfathomable grin.

"You never read any of them, do you?"

"No. I trust you." Straightening, Connor looked out of the windows, absentmindedly touching the pistol at his front hidden underneath the coat.

"Is someone waiting for you? Don't let me keep you."

"No." Connor shook his head and leaned against the frame of the window. "Nobody's waiting for me." He wished Kieran didn't catch on to the sadness in his words, but they were brothers and Kieran knew him too well.

Good Lord. Connor exhaled and turned until his back was supported by the wall between the two windows. The ache didn't lessen. If anything, it increased with every desperate beat of his heart.

"What bothers you?"

Should he tell him? He'd come here to talk with Kier about

it, hoping he'd feel better afterward. But those nagging doubts right now . . .

"I know. Now."

Leaning forward, Kier glowered across the table at him. "What do you think you know?"

"How you felt. Then."

Lips grim, Kieran averted his gaze. "I don't know what you're talking about."

"This woman . . ." Connor snorted as he reminded himself that she wasn't just that. She was a liar, a . . . "That fork-tongued viper played me for a fool."

"I see." Kieran leaned back with a self-satisfied smirk. "One of your lovers is giving you a headache."

A heartache was more like it. "She's not just a lover. I . . ." Connor swallowed the lump in his throat and closed his eyes, whispering, "I love her."

He heard Kieran sucking in a deep breath. "So? Run. That's the best thing you can do. And we both know it's the one thing you're good at."

Connor was sick and tired of Kier's accusations. Did the man have no heart?

No, not anymore. It had shriveled to an icy clump.

Would Connor end the same way?

Pushing himself off the wall, Connor stomped to the table. Reaching for the glass, he threw his head back as he gulped the contents down, then set it on the table. "Coming here was a mistake."

Kieran only shrugged. "You'd better leave, then."

Connor just shook his head and left, vowing to never look back. His twin was beyond redemption. Not even Connor could help him anymore.

The water gave another low, content gurgle. Jaidyn's eyes began to burn and only then she realized they were so dry because she'd forgotten to blink as she'd stared at the small bubbles of air surfacing every once in a while next to the *Coraal*'s hull.

I want to be with you. Why hadn't she said it?

The steady glow of the stars above gradually paled as the sky changed from inky blackness to anthracite. It was close to dawn now, and Connor was still nowhere in sight.

Prying her hands off the railing, Jaidyn turned. She couldn't just keep on standing there.

It was as though the ship's planks themselves exuded a peculiar kind of alertness everywhere she roamed, careful not to make a sound. Knowing what she did now, it didn't come as a surprise to her that the crew didn't dare leave the ship because of the danger looming over their captain's head. Some men slept restlessly on deck with one eye open, close to where they worked during the day.

Below deck, the eerie silence felt oppressive. Jaidyn wanted to scream her frustration. This was all her fault, and all she could do now was sit here with her hands crossed in her lap? No, something had to be done.

But what?

May Hem snorted a whinny, not in the least happy to have been roused from her nap. Georgie immediately scrambled up, blinking hastily, his hand moving to his boot. In what little light there was, Jaidyn could see him unsheathing a dagger.

"Georgie, it's me," she whispered and instantly his head snapped in her direction. His scowl softened as soon as he recognized her, and he let go of the weapon. Obviously relaxed, or as unperturbed as he could be under the circumstances, he leaned back, drifting back to sleep again.

Jaidyn walked closer to May Hem. The horse nibbled at the laces of Jaidyn's pale blue dress before she poked her in the shoulder with her nose.

"I know," Jaidyn murmured. "I'm worried about him too,

but there isn't anything I can do right now." With another whinny, May Hem presented her neck and Jaidyn patted it.

When she thought she heard a sound, Jaidyn pivoted, squinting into the darkness. It was impossible for her to make anything out, yet she was sure she'd heard something there.

If she placed one foot in front of the other, she'd eventually reach the door to the storage room. With her arms outstretched to avoid bumping into something, she padded forward.

Another gurgle of water had her jump. The sudden crack of the planks was earsplitting. Inside the *Coraal* the friendly babble of the sea lapping at the hull didn't sound as soothing.

There was a dull thumping noise. As if someone had hit the wood with a fist. Then Jaidyn thought she'd heard again that sound. It was closer now and resembled . . . a snivel?

Convinced that something—or rather *someone* was where she was headed, her cautious steps became firmer.

Her fingers brushed the wood that separated the storage room from the rest of the ship. Blindly, she searched for the handle. When she found it, she opened the door and stepped inside.

She almost gasped at the blinding flicker of a lantern, but once her eyes adjusted, she realized Mr. Parrish squatted far back in the corner, his arms wrapped around his body. He was rocking back and forth, biting his lower lip as he tried to swallow another sob. His cheeks glistened with tears; his eyes, red-rimmed and restless, darted around as if he expected a sea monster to charge from the shadows around him.

"Mr. Parrish," Jaidyn took two quick strides. On her knees, she grabbed his shoulders and shook him. "What in God's name is wrong?"

He mewled and, closing his eyes, shook his head. "I'm sorry," he choked out, repeating, "I'm so sorry," over and over again.

"What are you sorry for?" Jaidyn furrowed her brows.

His haunted expression turned on her. "They know."

"Who knows?"

"By now they'll have caught him. Stealthy as he may be, but he's still outnumbered a hundred to one."

Her heart was suddenly beating so hard, Jaidyn thought it might jump out of her chest. She didn't want to comprehend, but she couldn't fight the feeling of impending doom. Briefly closing her eyes, Jaidyn sent a silent prayer skyward, but the bitter lump in her throat remained.

"Mr. Parrish. Pull yourself together. And stop speaking in riddles."

"Oh," he wailed, a despicable sound coming from him. "The shame!"

Jaidyn was tempted to slap the man. Repeatedly. "Mr. Parrish, be more specific."

"I didn't think. I just ran and told the authorities he's here."

Jaidyn forgot to breathe. She couldn't believe what she'd just heard. "What?"

"I-I . . . oh God, I betrayed him."

Hate zinged up her spine, blurring her vision. "Stop whining now, you filthy little worm."

"I can't! I can't . . . He'll never forgive me."

Jaidyn stood, looking down her nose at him. "Connor is a good man. Chances are he will. But you're right. What you did is inexcusable. *I* will never forgive you."

Balled into a bundle of misery, the lout looked up at her, blinking slowly.

"Let me tell you, Mr. Parrish: if they find Connor and hang him, I will personally raise hell to see your head on a pike." With that, Jaidyn turned as regally as she'd been taught.

As soon as she was out the room, however, she clutched her neck as if it would help her breathe. She felt queasy, like a flock of bats were caged in her stomach. Jaidyn was unable to move. Her heart beat a frantic drumming in her ears. Her legs had turned to stone, weighing her down. Icy coldness threatened to immobilize her.

May Hem whickered and stared in her direction. The way back to her blurred and narrowed, but Jaidyn battled against the rising nausea that felt like spiders were crawling up her gullet. She fought against the anxiety that had paralyzed her. After a few steps, moving became easier and Jaidyn began to hastily run toward May Hem. She stumbled, got back up, tottered like a drunk, but forced her way back to the light that shone close to May Hem.

"Georgie," she hissed as soon as she was close enough. "Georgie! Help me get May Hem ready."

Rubbing the grit out of his eyes, he sleepily looked up at her. "But . . . Miss Donnelly—"

"No time for explanations. Hurry!"

"Aye, ma'am."

As soon as May Hem was off the ship and on the dock, Jaidyn mounted her and dashed off. There was only one man she could think of who could help her now. Neil Flaherty knew this town. And she'd learned by heart the directions to his home he'd given in his last letter.

15

Connor hugged the shadows as he walked down King Street back toward Front Street. So much had changed since he'd left. He barely recognized Georgetown anymore. Prosperity was rampant. No doubt Kieran was making sure they profited well from all the indigo and other naval stores going through the warehouses they owned.

Connor knew he was taking a chance heading back to the Sampit River harbor, but all the pubs were off Front Street and he needed to get drunk. The small glass of brandy he'd shared with his brother wasn't nearly enough to dull all the multitude of aches. Right now he wasn't sure Reinier's wife's whole rum distillery would have been enough.

Shite. That summed up his mood. *Shite*.

It really was too bad that after all this time, things were still so tense between him and Keir. It would have been nice to have a brother he could count on right about now.

But at least Connor understood how Kier could have turned so bitter after all that happened with that bitch Gabby. It was so easy for him to see now.

Connor entered the Duck and Dove just off Front Street on Screven and walked directly to the bar. He motioned to the barkeep for a pint of ale and quickly took it with him to a seat at a small table in the farthest corner. He slumped in his chair, hoping the shadowy corner would keep him hidden. Just in case, he pulled his hair out of its binding and let it fall all around his face with his tricorn hat pulled low so his eyes couldn't be seen. The collar of his jacket was pulled up to further shield his face.

It also helped that even at this late hour, the place was crowded almost to bursting. The room had been packed with as many tables as would fit, and they were all filled with reveling patrons drowning out the lone fiddle player. Connor faded well into the background amidst all the drinking men, whoring women, and even a pair of mangy dogs.

He was compounding the risk of being in town by being in public, but he'd run out of options about where to go. Connor wasn't going back home; he wasn't ready to hide out like a hunted rabbit. It hadn't come to that yet.

And he damned well wasn't going back to the ship and have to deal with either Jaidyn or Maxfield.

Poor Maxfield. He should have cut the boy loose a while ago. It was high time he pushed him out of the first mate's nest and let him go find his own way. Maxfield was a fine seaman and more than ready to handle his own small ship. Last time they'd been up farther north he should have made him go home and settle things with Drusilla. It was past time for him to face the music and either break his fiancée's heart or vice versa and get on with his promising career at sea.

For himself, Connor was done with women. Well, no. Not women. He was done with having any emotions for them. He'd been doing just fine before he'd met that wicked red-haired siren.

Finishing off his first pint with a flourish, he slammed it on the table and motioned to the blond-haired buxom serving girl nearby for another.

Connor vowed he'd just go right back to the games he'd played before. Even though he'd be playing those games alone for a time. Reinier was happy with his wife, most likely for quite a while if not from now on.

Why could Reiner find love and not him?

Technically, Connor had found it. He just couldn't have it, and that was so much worse, in his not-so-humble opinion.

He'd said some horrible things to Jaidyn. Maybe he shouldn't leave it like that.

No. Connor shook the asinine thought from his head. Maybe he should. Maybe it would haunt her like everything about her haunted him. Maybe she would remember his words every time she was with her husband, let her feel as horrible as he did.

Where the hell was that wench with his next pint? It was taking way too much time to get very, very drunk.

Finally she was coming his way. "Here you are, sir. I'm Becky, by the way." Connor watched as she took in the high quality of his clothing. "I can get you anything else you be needin'." She sat down the mug and practically dipped her ridiculously ample bosom into it. "Just ask for it."

Damn. Connor should have borrowed something to wear from Stiles so he would look like he couldn't so easily afford what was sadly the best the tavern had to offer.

As much as he'd just expounded on the joys of whoring, he was in too foul a mood and wanted to be left alone. "You can try not to be so slow next time my cup is empty. And do try to keep yourself in your blouse and out of my drink."

"Well, I never!" Becky stuck her hands on her wide hips and stared him down.

"Oh, I am quite sure you have. Many, many times." Connor picked up his mug and drank it half down as she stomped off.

The next pint was served by a skinny woman with black hair. Connor supposed the tavern keeper was hoping it was just personal taste that drove him to say no to Becky and that he could still make a nice profit off Connor with this one. In fact, Connor was sure of it when, as she sat the mug down with one hand, the other tried to snake up his leg.

He quickly caught her thin wrist tightly in his grip.

"Owww, sir. That hurts!"

Ahh. He did like the sound of that, having heard it often through the years.

Unfortunately, Connor didn't think he'd have been interested in her even if he'd been alone on an island for half a year. With a scowl, he let her go. "Then don't go putting your hands where they shouldn't be."

She threw her slightly hookish nose in the air and walked away as regally as possible while rubbing her sore wrist.

Soon Connor saw who he assumed to be the tavern keeper himself coming toward him with yet another pint.

Hell's bells, he just wanted to be left alone! The last thing he wanted was to attract the attention of every whore in the place and the owner, but apparently that's just want he'd done.

"I'd ask you to be more courteous to me staff, sir."

The man was tall and oxlike with brown hair and small eyes. Connor thought he might even be able to give the stalwart Mr. Matthews a run for his money in a fair fight.

"And who might you be?"

"I'm Mr. Kennard, the owner." He sat the mug down hard, spilling a good third of it on the table. Pity.

"Well then, Mr. Kennard. I'd ask your whores ... err ... *staff* to be more respectful to me and leave me be." Connor spoke low, with as much steel in his voice as he could manage.

Both of the tavern keeper's meaty fists came down onto the table. "You'll be wantin' trouble, then, will you?"

Connor sighed with resigned exasperation. For an Irishman he really had no luck whatsoever.

Reaching into his jacket pocket, Connor pulled out enough coin to flood the whole damned place in beer if he'd wanted to. "Not at all, sir. I only wish to drink my ale in peace . . . alone." He stacked the money on the table.

The owner hesitated only long enough to try to make Connor think there was an actual decision to be made. Grabbing the coins, he gave Connor one last warning glace all the same. "See that you keep to yourself, then."

"Gladly." Connor tipped his mug to the man and drained it.

After two more pints, Connor was finally feeling a bit of numbness set in. When the fiddle player stopped in midsong and the whole place went silent, he looked up to see four Colonial soldiers enter. Connor swore under his breath.

Instantly, all his senses went on the alert. Christ, he should have been more prepared! Yes, he was armed for a small insurrection, but by taking a table against the wall opposite the front door, he'd essentially cornered himself.

Hellfire and fuck. Connor wasn't familiar with the place enough to know where the kitchen door led or who would be back there to stop him, so his only way out was the front door diagonally across the main room from him, just down from the bar where the soldiers stood.

They approached the tavern keeper behind the bar. One thing that might be in his favor, Connor noticed, was that the soldiers' uniforms looked the worse for wear. Maybe they were as untrained as they were unkempt. Maybe they hadn't been paid in a little while and wouldn't be as enthusiastic or as vigilant in their jobs as they should be. Plus the idiots only had muskets with bayonets. The long guns were going to be hard to draw in such a crowded place, especially without someone innocent getting in the way.

Just as Connor expected, after a few moments of conversation, Mr. Kennard pointed his way, showing him to the guards.

It was now or never. Connor was going make sure right now that they never caught him. His pulse was racing with excitement as he pulled the pistol in front and aimed above their heads. The iron chandelier crashed onto the bar and onto one of the troops. One was effectively incapacitated, but the other three only came toward him faster.

Connor had one more shot without reloading either gun. He needed anything he could do to slow them down without firing before he could make it to the door. Throwing the one gun down, he reached for the legs of the table. Squatting for as much leverage as he could get, he tossed the table at them with a roar, using it like a giant shield.

The poor soldier closest to it slipped on the spilled ale, slid underneath with arms flailing, and was pinned underneath. Connor darted to the right and toward the door.

Two down; he liked his odds now much better.

That was until he noticed buxom Becky blocking his path to freedom with a triumphant smile.

Thinking on his feet with lightning speed, Connor smiled right back. Turning fast, he sidestepped the officer directly behind him. Connor grabbed him by his neck and shoved his surprised face right into Becky's ample bosom. There was no way the man could breathe as they both fell to the floor with his face buried in her chest.

Connor barely heard the whole tavern erupt in a roar of laughter as he sprinted for the front door.

But he'd failed to notice that the last guard had skirted the commotion and was waiting for him at the entrance.

Reaching for the pistol at his back, Connor rushed headlong

into the last soldier. Pressed against each other, they were too close for the guard's musket to be of any use to him.

Without hesitation Connor shoved his pistol into the other man's ribs hard enough to crack one. "Is it worth it, huh? Old Georgie Boy pay you enough to die like this?"

Both men stared at each other, both breathing hard and both sizing up the will of the other.

After what seemed like minutes but Connor was sure was only a second or two, the last soldier dropped his musket. Connor ran out to disappear into the breaking dawn, happy to be free, but not sure what the hell to do next.

Jaidyn had always had a natural good sense of direction, but having the directions in one's head and seeing the actual landmarks were two very different things. Even so, she was confident she and May Hem were on the right road to her father's estate.

The right road was the only thing she was confident about. Otherwise she was heartsick. Connor was going to get himself killed and she would never forgive herself. All of this was her fault. Well, she thought, some of it was Annie's fault. Annie, who'd betrayed her and left her deserted.

But if she hadn't, Jaidyn would have never met Connor. Did she really want not to have met him, not to have experienced all the things she had with him?

If she were honest with herself, those were precious memories she would cherish no matter what the future held.

Maybe if she ever saw Annie, she should at least thank her for that. Not that she ever expected to see her. Jaidyn had always imagined her long gone, somewhere in Europe with her French pirate going from party to party using her name and sponging off other unsuspecting people like the leeches they were.

May Hem stopped and Jaidyn pulled herself out of her thoughts to see they were at another crossroads. Going over the directions in her head once again, she pulled the mare to the right and continued on.

She wouldn't think of Annie anymore; she wasn't worth even a spare notion.

Her mind drifted back over the last few hours and Maxfield Parrish. Now she knew just how close Connor and he'd been and how much Mr. Parrish cared for his captain. But she hadn't had a chance to process it all. She had so many questions for herself.

She'd seen—and, *oh my*, experienced—the way Connor had been with Reinier when they'd met. Now the image of Maxfield at Connor's feet was burned into her memory. Did it bother her they were men? She should be appalled, but somehow she wasn't. It was just who Connor was, and she loved him for who he was. Connor had been with many women too. But he wanted to marry *her*.

What about the things he'd said in anger? Had he really meant them?

One thing she knew for sure, she would have never betrayed him like Maxfield had, no matter what.

Jaidyn laughed sadly to herself. Wasn't that exactly what she had done? Lied to the man she loved and betrayed his trust?

There had to be a way to make it right. She had to find a way to at least get him out of this current trouble and go back to the life he had before her. For her own sake, she had to make sure he was okay. At least make him see she never intended to hurt him.

Could she handle that? Could she stand knowing he was with Maxfield if he forgave him, or knowing he went back to Madame Poivre's? Or further down the road there'd be a woman who—

Just thinking about it broke her heart into more and more tiny pieces.

But she would endure it.

The road turned by a stream and Jaidyn veered off to let the horse have a drink. They were getting close. It wasn't much farther.

She'd never approve of the way her mother had hidden the truth from her, but she was thankful Neil Flaherty existed. He'd been so nice in his letters, so welcoming. After she lost her family, it was such a gift to still have someone. That he was a commoner didn't matter to her. He'd helped her with no questions asked when she'd got into trouble.

Neil had lost his love and had been forced to spend his whole life without her and his child. It must have been hard to know another man had taken his place, but he'd taken his exile and had made something of himself. Jaidyn was proud of him and happy that he wasn't bitter—at least not toward her. Her father was going to help straighten it all out, and maybe he could even teach her how to live without Connor.

She turned onto the lane that led to the manor, and her stomach was flipping and fluttering like mad wasps.

There was a woman coming toward her, too well dressed to be a servant. Jaidyn wondered if maybe she was a neighbor. As she got closer, Jaidyn could tell the woman's dress was moss green. She'd had a dress in much the same fashion that she used to love.

Jaidyn's hands on the reins faltered and her whole body went cold.

No! *No!* Not her. It couldn't be her, not here.

May Hem sensed Jaidyn's panic. The mare shook her head and stomped her hooves, refusing to move forward.

What the hell was Annie doing here? It never occurred to

Jaidyn that Annie would have ever come here. Where was her partner in crime? What had she told Neil? What if she'd hurt him or killed him?

That thought got her riled up and spurred her into action. She didn't have much time and didn't want the traitor in the way of her helping Connor. Annie was evil, and Jaidyn didn't want her anywhere near her father.

For the moment Jaidyn stood her ground and made Annie come to her. She could tell the instant the rat recognized her. Her spine stiffened and her steps became quick and more purposeful.

"What are you doing here?" Hate dripped from Annie's words.

"What are *you* doing here?" Jaidyn looked down on her from her perch on May Hem. She'd make it clear she wasn't intimidated. "Where is your little French paramour?"

"None of your business," Annie sneered. She tried to step closer but May Hem let out a harsh whinny, making it clear she was having none of that.

Jaidyn snorted at both May Hem's reaction and Annie's pathetic response. "Threw you overboard, did he? Serves you right."

Annie crossed her arms over what had been one of Jaidyn's favorite dresses. "Go away. You aren't welcome here."

"This is my father's house!"

Annie's laugh sounded high pitched and manic. "Don't you mean *my* father's house—since he's completely convinced that I'm you?"

"Impossible." Jaidyn refused to believe it. Neil was her father; he would know her.

Annie smiled as if she was confident she'd won. "Oh really? You'd think he'd be smart enough to know his own daughter, wouldn't he? He welcomed me with open arms. And he loves *me*, not you."

Doubt started to creep into Jaidyn, but she wouldn't let it show. "We'll see about that."

"No, we won't. I will not let you get near the house or *my* father."

"Don't you dare call him that!" Jaidyn yelled, but turned quickly when she heard strong hoofbeats closing in. They had both been so focused on each other, neither had heard the rider approach.

The man on the fine black steed was older and thinner than the young, brawny redheaded man in the small portrait her mother had given her. But there was no doubt it was Neil. Her father. Jaidyn's heart skipped a beat.

"Jaidyn, darling, what's—" As he caught sight of the real Jaidyn, he froze.

Just waiting and staring back, Jaidyn hoped he would see the truth.

Annie was quick to break the spell. "Father, this . . . thing . . . was my maid. You know, that one I told you about that stole all my money and ran off with a lowlife Frenchman. Call the constable, father. Have her thrown in the stocks."

Neil didn't seem to hear her. His eyes never left Jaidyn. "You look so much like her. It's uncanny."

Jaidyn smiled shyly at the compliment. Many times people had commented on how much she looked like her mother, but hearing her real father say it was special. No doubt he believed she was his daughter. "I've been told I have your hair, though, and, sadly, your temperament."

Neil shook his head with a breathy laugh. "That you do. I mean the hair, at least. But I don't understand—"

"Don't believe her, she's evil!" Annie tried to step between them, holding the reins of Neil's horse. "I've been here with you all these weeks. I'm your daughter. I am!" Her voice was shrill with dread and rage.

Neil jerked the reins from her hands and backed away, trying to calm his steed.

"What happened?" He looked directly at Jaidyn, and much of the tension left her. He was her father and he believed her.

"Aboard the *Brightstar* a week out of Southampton, she drugged me right before her lover and his thugs attacked the ship. She told me we had to switch clothes to keep me safe, and in my drugged state I listened. I thought she was a trusted friend as well as my maid. During the raid she stole my identity and left me adrift with a few of the crewmembers from the *Brightstar*."

"That's quite enough!" Neil stopped her and turned to Annie, walking her down with the horse. His eyes spoke of the fury coursing through him, his face a deep, angry red. "Annie, or whoever you are, I want you out. Now."

"But what about my things?" Annie whined.

"Don't you mean *my* things?" Jaidyn interjected.

"You will never go back into my house!" Neil struggled to keep his voice to a low growl, Jaidyn could tell. "If you walk away now, I may not have you arrested."

Annie knew she was beat. Regardless, she stared at them both with loathing in her eyes, threw her nose up at them, and started off proudly down the lane. Jaidyn couldn't resist trying to wipe that look off her face. "Excuse me, Annie, but I believe that is my dress. I would have it. Now."

Annie stopped in her tracks and looked back. "Now?"

"Yes, now," Jaidyn confirmed.

Indignantly, the recreant jerked the dress off her body and handed it to Jaidyn. She started down the road again, this time in nothing but her shift, with her shoulders slumped and her head down.

Neil shook his head. "I'm still amazed what a fool I've been to let her trick me. I did feel something wasn't right, but—"

Having wasted too much time already, Jaidyn turned to him. "Father, something else has happened, and we're running out of time."

"Then let's get you home, so you can tell me all about it."

16

———

A twig smacked Jaidyn's face when she dismounted. Ducking into the shadows next to Neil, she peeped over his shoulder.

They were hiding in what looked like a lovely kind of wilderness bordering on a fastidiously kempt park. At the site of that there was a complex of smaller buildings; one with a smoking chimney that Jaidyn assumed was the kitchen. Voices wafted toward her from there, laughter and singing. A woman hopped down the stairs, a basket in her hand, and made her way to the adjoining garden.

The sun was warming the soil, and the thick, sweet scent of warm grass filled Jaidyn's head. Butterflies were hopping from flower to flower, birds were chirping merrily. It seemed peaceful, but Jaidyn felt anything but calm.

She needed to find Connor, and time was running out. Neil had jumped into motion when she'd told him Connor had been arrested, had run out of the house and straight for his horse. Jaidyn had demanded he explained what he was doing. Neil had told her he knew someone who could help. She trusted Neil, so that was all she needed to hear.

Until now.

Neil squatted down behind a bush and Jaidyn followed suit, pricking her finger on the holly bush next to her.

Bloody brilliant.

Ahead of her, Jaidyn saw a three-story house that reeked of money. Was this where Connor was kept?

Neil seemed to watch the surroundings for any signs other than the merry laughter coming from the kitchen. As far as Jaidyn could see, nothing out of the extraordinary was going on, so why were they still hiding here?

Determined, Jaidyn attempted to scramble up, but her father immediately held her back, dragging her into the shadows until she had to squat down next to him again.

"Where are we?" Jaidyn hissed, trying to wrench her arm out of his grasp.

"Wait here," Neil grumbled, patting her elbow just before he got up.

"No. I'm coming with you."

Her father gave her a patient smile. "I know you want to come with me, but I'd rather you stay here."

"That's very sweet of you, but I will come with you." Jaidyn struggled back up.

"No, you won't!" Neil stomped back into the shade of the poplar tree.

Feeling suddenly crowded, Jaidyn took a step back into the shrubbery.

"I will!" She fought to keep her tone a low snarl.

"You can't!"

"Why not?"

"Why—" Neil was positively puffing with annoyance.

Jaidyn harrumphed. "Well, let's get inside, then."

His face turned a deep red. "You're just like your mother," her father eventually growled, careful to keep his voice low.

Jaidyn didn't know if under the circumstances she should be happy about that compliment.

"Fine," she snapped back, and with her chin an inch higher, she stood up again and stomped toward that house.

"Jaidyn, wait!" Neil pulled her back into the shrubbery again. She didn't grace him with her glare.

"I'd rather you stay here because I'm not sure what's going on in there."

"Why? What is this place?"

"That's O'Connor's house."

Jaidyn blinked. Surely he'd meant *Connor*. Then it suddenly dawned on her that Connor had mentioned a brother. So this was his brother's house?

"For all we know, the authorities might be in there, and if they see you, they'll arrest you, trying to get information out of you by any means necessary." Neil was shaking her as if it would help her hear him better.

Of course. She was an accomplice now, and the authorities catching her would make things even worse than they already were. She hadn't thought about that.

It didn't change that she didn't want to wait helplessly by and let her father and Connor's brother try to help him. "So I'm supposed to sit and wait while you men handle the business like men?"

Neil suddenly seemed to soften as he cupped her cheek. "You're more than apt at taking care of yourself, lass. You've made it here despite everything. But let me just bask in the illusion that this time I can help you and take care of you like a father should." With a sigh, Neil blinked. "I lost you both too early. I loved your mother, love her still, but I'll never see her again. Please stay here and let me handle this. I don't want to lose you—again . . . when I've just found you." He gave a short snivel and wiped his eyes with the sleeve of his coat.

Jaidyn pursed her lips. "Are you crying?"

Looking skyward, Neil blinked a few more times. "Most certainly I am not."

"It looks like it, though."

Shaking his head, her father waved the ridiculous notion aside. "My eyes always turn red around birch trees."

Her forehead wrinkled as she looked up. "This is a poplar tree."

"So? I can't stand poplar trees, either."

"Birches are over there," she said, pointing with her chin over her shoulder.

Neil cleared his throat. "Are you going to wait here now?"

He did sound a little impatient. Jaidyn ripped a leaf off a branch next to her. Crushing it in her fist, she gave in with a sigh. "I'll stay here."

"I'll be back in no time." Neil sounded relieved.

"You'd better," Jaidyn grumbled, dropping the leaf from her fingers. "Or I'll storm the house."

With a sheepish grin, Neil nodded. "I know."

Kieran was beside himself with fury, but he thought it beneath him to let any of it show. His guarded countenance appeared passionless. He stood at the top of the front steps as he watched Gabrielle Talbot, Baroness Wickfield, ascend the coach and back out of his life. Again.

Even though he felt like snarling his implacable hatred, he refrained from it. Why had she come now? Why hadn't she said something earlier? Kier could have saved his brother's reputation and would still have him by his side. Ronan would have never started hating him, and he surely would have never run away because he couldn't stand Kier's presence.

The Baroness Wickfield had just given him all the proof he needed to get his brother back home. If his brother didn't want to stay, fine, but at least his name would be rid of that black stain that branded him a criminal.

Well, provided she had spoken the truth. She'd taken up the habit of lying as soon as she opened her mouth on her wedding day.

No, she'd perfected her skills at deceiving even before that, Kieran recalled bitterly.

He told himself that it didn't matter that she'd remained silent all this time. Nor was it any of his business why she'd suddenly decided to no longer cover her husband's scheme. For the first time in years, Kier held the key to proving his brother's innocence. And surely Talbot wasn't so twisted that he'd get rid of his own wife, like he'd done with all the other witnesses Kier had found, who suddenly disappeared or died in some mysterious way. On the other hand, Talbot was a deceitful, murderous bastard and there was no telling what he'd do once he found out his wife had finally told the truth.

Kieran didn't have time to concern himself with Gabby's fate. His brother came first. Once Ronan was cleared, Kier would have to find a way to undo what he'd done with the incredibly offensive Jaidyn Donnelly. Kier had thought if she was Neil's daughter, she'd be like him in a way. Good God, could he have been more wrong? A pity that woman was the apple of Neil's eye, because this apple had fallen very far from the tree. Granting Neil that favor had probably been the biggest mistake of his life—and he'd made quite a few, he added to his train of thoughts as Talbot's coach jumped and slowly left Kier's driveway.

As soon as the coach was out of sight and Gabrielle with it, Kier whirled around, heading back into the house and to his study. He had to reach his brother. He'd probably docked somewhere out of the way toward the end of the bay. He'd write him a letter first, telling him that it was imperative they meet in Charleston right away.

On the way to his desk, Kier searched his brain for a vague enough wording that would clue his brother in. Something like . . .

There's no need for indigo dye from the East Indies any longer. Indigo dye around here is not as hazardous as it used to be. Meet me at our usual place to discuss further proceedings.
K.

Looking at the letter before him, Kier decided it was perfect for his purpose. He called for Malory, his butler, and folded the note.

Quick footsteps announced Malory was on his way, and Kier looked up to tell him—

Neil Flaherty stood in the door instead of his butler. His eyes darted around the room before settling on him. His shoulders slumped a little with relief, but Neil still looked anxious.

"You're alone?" He said in a clipped tone as he looked around the room once more.

"Yes?"

"Good," Neil mumbled and started pacing the room. "Jaidyn is waiting outside."

"Oh?" What was it that she'd complained about this time?

Nodding, Neil rubbed his face. "I thought it best for her to stay outside in case the authorities were here."

"Why would—" Gasping, Keir realized why Neil would think the authorities might be here. "What do you know? Where is he?"

"Jaidyn told me they'd sailed here together and last night he ventured out and didn't come back. She learned that one of the crew had ratted on him and she immediately came to me for help."

"Neil, you are aware that you don't make any sense at all. Jaidyn has been here for a few weeks already. I know my brother arrived yesterday, and let's hope he's already left."

"So he was here? Then you know already?"

"That he was here?" Keir shook his head. There was something he was missing.

"No. That he brought Jaidyn."

"What are you talking about?" Keir's patience was wearing thin.

"The woman you think is Jaidyn isn't. The real Jaidyn is outside and she's going to storm this house if we don't start searching for your brother right away. And heaven help us then. She's inherited not only her mother's looks, but her temper . . . well, the red hair she's got from me." Neil grinned sheepishly as his chest puffed with pride. "Unfortunately, she also inherited my occasional lack of restraint. That other wench you thought was her was just an impostor. The maid, in fact."

That sounded much more like what Kier had thought Neil's daughter would be like—

Something clicked in Kier's head. His brother had spoken of a woman . . .

Sweet Jesus, and he was going to pay with his life if Kieran didn't find him before the authorities did!

Well, Ronan was smart. He'd find the perfect hiding place unless their stepbrother acting the constable found him sooner.

"Neil, there are several hideouts we must try." Kier dipped his quill and started scribbling on a piece of paper. "If we want to find him fast, we'll have to split up. Here's a list of places. You'll start looking for him from the top of that list. I'll try the others. If we're lucky, we'll meet somewhere in the middle and find him in time."

Taking the piece of paper from him, Neil stalked out through the back of the house the way he'd come in.

Kier bellowed for Malory again and the butler showed up, out of breath and his wig a little crooked on his head. Keir's coat and hat dangled from his arm. "I've taken the liberty to have your horse ready, sir."

Good old Malory had his eyes and ears everywhere. Keir slipped into his coat, donning his tricorn on his way out.

17

The trapdoor stood wide open. Connor attached the fine rope that he'd found above to the trapdoor, then to his wrist, and swung himself down, careful not to tread on the dusty old stairs that hadn't been used for years. He landed with a dull thump, small clouds of dirt puffing around his ankles and covering the tips of his black boots with brownish dust. Turning, he grunted his approval at the still undisturbed stairs.

Reaching for the rope around his wrist, he loosened it, turned around, and tugged on it until the trapdoor fell shut. Slivers of daylight from the crude timbers over his head streaked the darkness surrounding him. Connor didn't need to see anyway; this was a hidden basement of one of Kieran's old warehouses and he knew it by heart.

After one more twirling of his wrist, the rope slid out of the hook on the trapdoor and Connor rolled it up.

The warehouse might have been old, but it was frequently used and it didn't look like the typical hiding place. Maybe this place would keep Connor alive until sundown, when he'd sneak to his ship and leave.

Hiding far back in the darkest recess of that basement, Connor made himself as comfortable as he could get. His eyes got used to the gloom in no time and if he leaned back and peeped around the crate hiding him, he had a very clear view of the stairs and the only entrance. He shucked his coat and waistcoat and sat with his back against the wall. One knee bent, he propped his head in his hand. He had quite a few long hours ahead of him.

Here he was, alone, hiding in the basement . . . and for what? So that he didn't get hanged for a wrong he didn't commit?

But there was someone he had wronged. Connor cringed. After having stewed in his anger for hours, he'd sobered enough to realize that.

Jaidyn. Her scent, her beauty, the taste of her skin, the feel of her body melting into his . . . he'd tried so hard to banish each and every memory of her. But it was in vain. It was probably easier to chop his right hand off than get her out of his system.

Connor's feelings were a massive knot of confusion. He felt possessive about her and it terrified him. His yearning for her burned and had ice-cold shivers run down his back.

He wanted her, but she belonged to another man. Jealousy speared him again at the thought that she could be just as happy if not even more so with that other man.

Connor would have never thought he could feel for a woman that deeply. He wanted to keep her safe and whole. He wanted to be the man she wanted, someone who understood her, who could give her what she needed, what her mind sought, what her body craved.

When Jaidyn had told him she was married, it had been like the red flag to a bull. Desperation had him fling all those scathing words at her.

He'd seen it in her eyes—had seen that he was the reason for her anguish. She'd never forgive him, and knowing that felt like a punch from a battering ram.

Trying to release the tension, he rolled his shoulders, but nothing helped to take the frustration away.

Pride demanded he let her go. Desolation gnawed at him, urging him to hold on to her. He was fighting a losing battle and he knew it. Even if she weren't married and he could be the man she wanted, there was still this bounty on his head. So there was no way in hell they had a future together.

All he could do was pick up the sad scraps of his hurt pride and shattered heart and move on, and come nightfall, he would. He'd said good-bye before. So many times in fact that it shouldn't hurt so much. But this time it was different. This time he was in love and he wasn't sure if his heart could ever recover from the blow.

Dirt rained down on him from the slits in the timbers above. Rubbing the dust out of his eyes, Connor looked up.

He could hear footsteps. The streak of sunlight glinting through a knothole disappeared as someone approached the trapdoor above him.

More footsteps. Connor thought he could distinguish three different sets. He held his breath, his gaze fixated on the moving shadows.

Seconds ticked by. Connor felt his lungs burn, the deafening beats of his heart drowning out every other noise.

The hinges of the trapdoor squeaked in protest as it was lifted. Connor scrambled farther back into the shadows.

No one would find him here, he was sure. Only somebody who knew . . .

Kieran?

Hope had Connor's heart beat even faster and he dared to take a brief glimpse around the crate he hid behind.

Lantern light blinded him. It flickered over the interior, illuminating bits and pieces as if sniffing out the basement, trying to find something or someone.

Connor could hear a low sound that resembled a chuckle but was more like a sniff.

Kieran didn't snort that way.

"You can come out now."

Connor felt his heart plummet. He'd recognize that voice anywhere. There was only one person who could fill it with so much derision that it sounded like it was made of brass.

Hugh Talbot had found him.

How stupid had Connor been, hiding here where there was just one way in and out? His feelings for the woman had him so mixed up he'd made the same asinine mistake twice now. At this rate he wouldn't last much longer.

Talbot's footsteps came closer, like he knew exactly where to find Connor.

Well, there wasn't much Connor could do now but face his stepbrother like a man. Standing, he left the sanctity of the shadows and met Talbot's gaze.

Hugh hadn't changed much. The corners of his thin mouth seemed to be perpetually curling down and the long nose in his oval face looked as if he was constantly sneering, giving him an aristocratic air, which epitomized that he was the sole heir to the penniless and quite useless title of Baron Wickfield. But the title had had its advantages; it had served to make him the only acceptable suitor for Gabby. Her parents were eager to attach their name to a title—not to that of a common, albeit rich Irish merchant. In his capacity as governor, Talbot's father-in-law had appointed Hugh Constable of Georgetown.

"I thought I'd find you here." Talbot's eyes gleamed like those of a vulture having spotted a juicy carcass. He flicked his wrist in an effete gesture. His pretty clothes and his foible for fancy wigs had reached new heights, Connor noted. Despite his overall weak and feminine appearance, Connor knew not to underestimate the man. He was even more dangerous because he didn't look like it.

"Not in a very talkative mood?" Talbot crooned, pursing his lips. His whole stance seemed to light up with glee. "I knew when my men came to wake me up this morning that there was only one place you could have run to. Kieran's house was actually first on the list. It's under surveillance, of course. But I knew I'd find you here. You're too smart to hide in the usual places like caves and such."

Connor pressed his lips into a fine, pale line.

"You're probably asking yourself how I knew you were here?" Talbot waited all but two heartbeats for an answer he'd never get. "Don't forget, I had years to find and catalogue each and every place you and your despicable brother played hide-and-seek in.

"Oh, I forgot," he added, waving at the two soldiers behind him that were guarding the door. "Sullivan and Brown. Gentlemen, this is our criminal."

Looking back at Connor, Talbot grinned. It was hard to imagine that Hugh was in fact Connor's stepbrother. "You don't know how long I've waited for this moment. There are several scenarios I played out in my head, but somehow they all end the same way. The one question I always ask in the beginning is: Will you come with me?"

"And hang for the scheme you concocted?" Connor laughed low, the sound lacking any trace of humor. "Never."

"See." Talbot waved his hand in an airy gesture. "I knew you'd say that."

"You know bloody well I've never smuggled contraband." Connor gritted his teeth, his hands balling into fists at his thighs.

"Yes, but we're the only ones."

Connor's eyes darted back and forth between his stepbrother and the young soldiers, who were gawking at Talbot then exchanging puzzled glances. "That's not true. They know now too."

"They?" Talbot turned as though he'd totally forgotten about them. "Oh, yes. Now they know. Let me remedy that."

Drawing the two guns at his front, Talbot fired. One of the guards was hit right in one eye; the other one was hit in the shoulder, stumbled back, and slumped with a groan.

Talbot furrowed his brows as he glared at the pistol in his left hand. "It's a bit off." His eyes wide, the soldier stared at him before he fell facedown and went limp.

Connor sucked in his breath. He hadn't just witnessed that, had he? He knew Talbot was capable of many things—but murder in cold blood? He wouldn't have thought it possible. But it gave him an idea where this encounter with the Constable would lead. Certainly the hangman's noose wasn't the worst of his problems any longer.

"What a pity." Talbot gave a theatrical sigh and turned to Connor. "Say, why did you have to kill them?"

Clenching his teeth, Connor remained rooted to the spot. "*She* knows as well."

"Gabrielle? Don't concern yourself with my wife. I can handle her."

"Handle her? As in 'beat some sense into her'?"

Talbot pursed his lips, nodding with a dreamy smile. "Something like that."

"You're pathetic," Connor spat.

"Says the man who's about to hang from the gallows." Talbot let Connor hear that brassy cackle again, then cupped his chin, his eyes narrowing. "You wouldn't believe it, but as often as I put the cane to her back, you'd think I'd beaten him out of her. No such luck. He, on the other hand, was much easier to be persuaded of her wavering alliances."

Any movement on Connor's part could have Talbot snap and going at his throat. Not that Connor had any problem with that, though somehow he knew Talbot, despite his supposedly blue blood, would fight dirty.

"So, is Gabrielle the reason for the grudge you hold against your own brothers?"

"Why do you care?" For the blink of an eye, Talbot's face twisted, but immediately fell back into his fake geniality. "I have my reasons for needing to destroy you."

Connor didn't let his bafflement show. Instead he feigned interest to keep him talking. "What do you mean?"

"Your father never loved me the way he loved you two, his 'real' sons. And don't you dare call me your brother. You were never anything to me. Mother was a fool to remarry so far beneath her."

That was a blatant lie, and Connor didn't believe one word of it. His mother—her maiden name was Fanny Driscoll—was widow to the late Baron Wickfield, and she remarried an Irish merchant out of love. She was a wonderful woman, and Connor and Kier's father was absolutely devoted to her and tried to treat them all equally, which sometimes meant that he was harder on Connor and Kier than he'd have been on his ward, Hugh Talbot. Being a few years older than his common stepbrothers, Talbot had always looked down upon them. But Connor had a feeling his animosity went much deeper than that.

"If I'm nothing to you, then why bother going through all this trouble?"

Connor noticed that Talbot grew agitated. "All your charm and your good looks and your father's money. And later, when you were older. All that decadence you two indulged in. Despicable. You even more than your brother."

"How so?" So was it envy that had grown into some sort of twisted jealousy?

"You know very well what I'm talking about." Talbot's chin tilted higher, his nostrils drawn in disgust. "Your flexibility

226 / *Chloe Harris*

when it comes to *partners*. What you do is not natural by any stretch of the word. It's an abomination!"

Connor let his eyebrows wander up his forehead. "Why? Because I'm not ashamed to live it as opposed to others?"

Talbot's face alternated between a deep red and a sickly pale color. Connor saw the muscles in his jaw jump, his eyes narrowing considerably. He had definitely hit home with his last remark. That Talbot desperately clung to that reasoning could be exploited. He'd just have to draw him out, make it up the stairs, and run.

"I know all about your dirty little secret, Hugh," Connor bluffed. "You may act the aristocratic, traditional, and unadventurous man, but you feel inferior to us. Taking Gabby, then framing me. It's Kier you're focused on, isn't it? This was all about hurting Kieran. Could it be that you love Kier and you know he'd never have you, so you concentrated all your frustration and hatred on him? You took the love of his life from him and then concocted that scheme that branded me a criminal. But you really hate what you yourself crave, not Kier."

Talbot's face contorted into a mask of pure hatred. "I'll make you bleed and die slowly for that," he pressed out between clenched teeth.

Connor gave a jaded shrug. "I don't suppose you fight like a gentleman rather than the devious scum you are."

With a toothy grin, Talbot shed his coat and wig. His glare darkened to a dangerous gleam just before he hunched, dropped his shoulder, and let out an enraged snarl as he charged Connor.

Bracing himself against the impact, Connor flexed his muscles, ready to pounce himself. But Talbot got to him sooner. Connor grunted as Hugh's fist landed in his stomach with all of Talbot's body weight behind it, driving Connor into the crates behind him.

The pistol at the small of Connor's back bit into flesh and bone, grinding against his spine mercilessly. If Talbot got his hands on it . . .

Oh, this was going to get ugly, Connor thought as he regained his footing.

18

Jaidyn's heart sped up. She could feel Connor was here some-where. All the other hideouts they'd tried had been empty.

She almost crashed into Neil as he suddenly stopped and cocked his head. Muffled grunts traveled toward them from somewhere in front of them, or maybe it was under them. It was the first time they'd actually heard something, and as quickly as they could, they tried to find the source.

With each hasty step forward, the din became louder and Jaidyn realized they were the sounds of a fight. She thought she'd been anxious before, but now her nerves were contorted into a raw, bloody mess as she heard Connor fighting for his life somewhere beneath them. Jaidyn struggled not to throw up.

Around the corner, amidst several stacked crates, Jaidyn saw an open trapdoor. The sounds of the fight were loudest there. Neil tiptoed, one arm stretched behind to keep Jaidyn where she was, stopping her instinct to rush forward into the fray.

Bile rose in her throat when they reached the trapdoor and she saw the two young soldiers lying at the foot of the stairs leading down into the pit. One moved, but only just. With his face down, he tried to reach his musket with the bayonet on it. His fingers, splayed like a spider's legs, dragged his hand toward the weapon. The other soldier couldn't move anymore, Jaidyn realized. All the blood drained from her face.

Once they reached the end of the stairs, they found Connor in the throes of a desperate battle. Jaidyn wanted to howl, tears of pain and despair running down her cheeks. He was trying to ward off a man who seemed bent on killing him, fighting with a determination bordering on madness.

Neil enveloped Jaidyn in his arms. She gripped his upper arms tightly watching the scene before her, helpless to do anything but cling to her father.

Connor grabbed the stranger's arm, spun him around, and slammed him into the stone wall. Dust rained down on them all and it seemed the whole building shook with the impact. The stranger grunted, twisted and kicked, and pulled away with a snarl.

Back on his feet, he spat, blood running from his nose, and charged Connor again. He hooked an arm around Connor's waist and slammed him against the crate behind him so hard it knocked the wind out of Connor. The crate cracked, groaned, and splintered.

Snarling, Connor punched him squarely in the face and sent him sprawling across the filthy ground. The stranger gave a low grunt, then scrambled backward. He stilled for a heartbeat as his eyes fell on something lying on the floor. Jaidyn followed his gaze. A small pistol lay abandoned near both men's feet.

The man gathered some of the grit and dust of the ground in his hand and threw it in Connor's face. Blinking furiously against the dirt that blinded him momentarily, Connor froze. Meanwhile, the stranger bolted for the pistol.

Shaking his head as if it would help him to see clearer, Connor stalked over to the stranger and towered over him. He kicked him in the stomach and the man lost his grip on the pistol.

Connor kicked him again, this time in the ribs, then bent over him and pounded him. The stranger somehow managed to gain a little ground. But suddenly the men were in a heap on the ground, rolling in the dust. It all happened too fast for Jaidyn to see anything but a blur.

Fists flew, punches and grunts followed.

Jaidyn's eyes traveled from the men on the ground to the place where the pistol—

Sucking in her breath, she struggled against Neil's grip. The pistol, it wasn't there anymore. Instead, she could see it in the other man's hand, pointing at Connor, who was trying to fight it off.

A shot was fired and all the fighting stopped.

Jaidyn stared at the tangled bodies of Connor and the stranger lying there, unmoving.

Neil's hold on her tightened as she stopped fighting him. Her knees gave out and she heard herself whimper. Nausea rose in her stomach and she thought she was going to faint.

Connor lay there. Unmoving. The shadows were too hazy to make anything out beyond that.

She needed to get to him. Jaidyn needed to tell him she loved him before it was too late.

Strength came back to her in a heartbeat, something at the end of her spine sent invigorating tingles through her body. She fought Neil's hold, fought as desperate as a greased cat until she broke free, shoved past Neil, and stumbled toward Connor.

Tears blurred her vision as she groped Connor's shoulders and separated him from the other man. She groaned with effort as she turned Connor on his back, dreading the thought of finding his eyes empty.

They were closed. Jaidyn could see a dark blotch on his chest and she burst into tears. She'd seen wounds like that before. She knew what it meant. All her strength left her and her forehead bumped into Connor's ribs. She'd lost him, had lost him before he knew what she felt for him, before she could tell him she loved him and she wanted to be with him, only him, no matter how, no matter where.

"Connor," she sobbed, knowing her heart would never recover from this. "I love you. Oh God, I love you."

Connor's body twitched. Jaidyn jerked her head up and sat back on her heels. She hiccupped, wiping her face with her hands.

Connor gave a low groan. Still not opening his eyes, he gingerly patted his ribs and winced. "Woman, I knew you were going to be the death of me."

"Oh God! You're alive!" Jaidyn let out a relieved sob and threw her arms around him.

Connor cringed and gave a pain-filled grunt. Lifting his head a little, she saw his wonderful dark blue eyes glitter with an emotion that sent warmth and elation through her.

"Of course I am." He smiled and Jaidyn gave another sob.

"I thought I'd lost you."

Cupping her cheeks, Connor held her still, locking his gaze with hers. "I'm not that easy to get rid of."

Jaidyn's lips trembled, the corners curling into a hesitant smile. Oh God, she was so beautiful. And she'd said it—had said that she loved him. His heart did a complete somersault and he wanted to tell her he loved her too, but suddenly the harsh reality crashed down upon him and he caught his breath, blocking the words so that they didn't spill from his lips.

Connor released Jaidyn from his grasp and sat up slowly. She scrambled back to give him room. A sharp pain pierced his chest and for a moment he was dizzy, but somehow he managed to stand.

Jaidyn's probing hands brushed down his arms and chest as

if to make sure he wasn't injured. With another sob, she wrapped her arms around him and buried her nose in the hollow where his shoulders met his throat.

"Jaidyn . . ." Connor struggled to find the right words. He couldn't be so selfish and do that to her. He couldn't accept her love, not now when she'd just found a home. Theirs would be a life on the run, because he'd just piled murder on top of the ugly crimes he'd been charged with in the first place. "I . . . must leave at once and never come back—ever."

"So? I'll come with you." He could hear the smile in her words.

"You can't. You must stay here."

"What?" Jaidyn stepped back, narrowing her eyes at him.

"I can't stay here. But you . . . There's no way we can be together."

Connor could see Jaidyn's nostrils flare. "You're not only stubborn, you're a coward as well."

"Is it cowardice to not want to be hanged?" Connor growled.

Before Jaidyn could reply to that, she was cut off by someone stomping down the stairs. Turning his head, Connor saw Kier coming to a halt, his gaze shocked and unblinking as he took everything in. Connor realized Neil was there also, his chin quivering as he pressed his lips into a fine line. What was he doing here?

"About time you showed up," Connor grumbled in Kier's direction, shaking and flexing his scraped hands.

More footsteps could be heard above, moving toward the trapdoor.

"Stay there." Connor heard the bellowed order before the man who had issued it came down the stairs. Dread enveloped Connor in a frosty grip. The man was wearing an officer's uniform.

What a coincidence. An officer following on Kieran's heels, seeing the two soldiers on the ground and the constable shot as well, and Connor was the only man left standing. It would take a dimwit about two seconds to figure out what had happened here.

The officer squatted between the soldiers, looking at one, then at the other who lay facedown. He placed his hand on the man's shoulder. "Sullivan?" Without waiting for a reply, he barked up the stairs, "He's wounded. Quickly, get him out of here."

"Colonel," the soldier on the ground croaked. "Talbot played us false."

The officer looked up, then squinted at Talbot's body on the ground. His gaze wandered to Connor standing there with Talbot's blood all over him. Connor could see the man's mind working behind keen eyes. The officer then looked at Kier and harrumphed.

Straightening, he righted his uniform and took a step forward, inclining his head in a half-bow to Connor. "Colonel Frederick Banbury, sir. Your brother sent for us. I say the evidence speaks for itself. Please report for a statement later."

With that, the colonel turned and waited until the soldiers finished getting their two comrades out of the basement.

Connor was dumbfounded. "Kier, what's going on?"

His brother shrugged. "A pang of conscience seemed to have finally changed the Baroness Wickfield's mind. She confessed that Talbot produced false evidence against you."

"See," Jaidyn hissed. "So why exactly do you have to"—she spoke in a deep growl to imitate his words earlier—"*leave at once and never come back ever*? I tell you I love you and I want to be with you, and you are frightened like a maiden on her wedding night?" She gave a derisive snort.

"Jaidyn." Connor fought to sound calm. "Be reasonable about this. We can't be together."

She crossed her arms before her chest and took one more step back. "Why not?"

Why . . . wasn't it obvious? "Because you're married!"

"So?" Her chin inched higher. "I'll get an annulment. The marriage has never been consummated."

"Um . . ." Kier stepped forward, his face a self-conscious grimace. "There might be a bit of a problem there."

Jaidyn didn't grace him with more than a brief glance. "Keep out of this."

Taking a deep breath, Connor was certain, so she could rain another tirade on him, she stopped short, blinking back at Kier. "Oh . . . Connor? You never told me your brother was actually your twin."

Kier was daring enough to take one step closer to her; Connor himself kept a safe distance. Jaidyn was deep in a fit of pique, and it was a fine line between courage and stupidity.

"So," Kieran drawled, rubbing his chin to hide an oddly broad grin. "You are the real Jaidyn Donnelly."

"Yes." Jaidyn's glare zeroed in on Kier. "Well . . . never mind. Pleased to meet you, Mr. . . . ?"

"Kieran. Kieran O'Connor."

Jaidyn's mouth went slack. Even her arms seemed to lose all strength and fell limply to her side. She only stood there, gawking at Kieran, blinking every once in a while.

"She's speechless?" Connor would have never thought he'd see her like this. He turned to his brother. "Why?"

Neil spoke up, his words drenched with offense. "I say an annulment is out of the question."

"Neil?" Connor felt his forehead wrinkle. "What do you . . ." He gasped. "Are you her husband?"

"No." He sniffed like he was slighted by the question. "I'm her father."

"But why—" Clearly, Connor was missing something. Could perhaps somebody explain to him why Kieran was amused, Neil snubbed, and Jaidyn perplexed?

Jaidyn was the first to break the heavy silence. "You," she huffed, glaring at Connor. It was difficult for him not to squirm under her stare, which was more perilous than Connor had ever seen. "You. Are. Ronan O'Connor."

"How do you know my real name?" Priceless, wasn't it? The mystery kept on becoming more and more obscure. It seemed everyone knew what was going on but Connor.

"Er . . ." Kier spoke up once more. Both Connor's and Jaidyn's withering glares settled on him, and he duly cringed but stood his ground. "She knows your real name because you both signed the document. But as opposed to you, she apparently read it carefully."

"What document?"

"The proxy."

"What proxy?"

Kier sighed. "Circumstances called for desperate measures, and since you never read anything I give you to sign, I thought it was best this way. So . . . without knowing it . . . you were married . . . to her." Kier breathed deeply. "Felicitations, brother."

Connor had signed a proxy? "What?" He heard his own voice rise in pitch.

"You lied to me," Jaidyn growled.

"No, I didn't. I didn't even know—"

Jaidyn stepped up to him. "You lied to me!"

"Pah!" Connor leaned down until his nose almost brushed the tip of hers. "You lied much more!"

"No-no-no-no-no." Jaidyn shook her head, prodding at his shoulder with each syllable. "All this time I had a bad conscience because of this—and then it turns out you're not such an open book after all!"

What was this about now? "I just went under a different name."

"See?" Those elegant ginger eyebrows wandered up and she gave him a superior look. "I didn't. I didn't lie about who I really was."

Goodness, she was sexy when she was that worked up. "Of course, *Miss Donnelly*."

"Lying, deceiving bastard!"

Her fists pounded his shoulders, but the punches didn't have the intended effect. Instead of backing down, he felt himself grow hard.

"Watch your mouth, *wife*." God, it felt good to say that. "Or I'll stuff it."

"Hah! Anything you put in my mouth you'll lose!"

"Oh yes?"

His mind was roaring, his body tense. Her lips beckoned seductively, the fire in her eyes adding to the allure. Connor dipped his head and closed the distance to her mouth, his tongue stroking deep between her lips. His arms whipped up and wrapped around her, pressing her body into his. There was nothing gentle about his kiss; Connor devoured her, staked his claim on her.

With a moan, Jaidyn melted into him, tilting her head and kissing him back, matching his hunger stroke for teasing silken stroke with her tongue as it swirled around his.

Feeling her melt in his arms, Connor let one hand slide down to her waist. Jaidyn whimpered in pleasure, her hands fisting in his hair. She drew herself closer to him, rubbing her feminine softness against his engorged rod.

Their greedy kiss went from desperate hunger to sweet, slow enjoyment, and when it finally ended, both Connor and Jaidyn were panting against each other's lips.

"We're married," Connor whispered.

Jaidyn nodded and smiled. "We are."

"All right now. That's quite enough." Neil peeled Jaidyn off him, but she never broke eye contact with Connor.

Out of the corner of his eyes, Connor saw Neil and Keir murmur, then Jaidyn was being dragged up the stairs and out of sight.

With a dreamy smile on his lips, Connor stared at where he'd seen Jaidyn last.

"She's got a temper." Kier was at his side now.

"Yes."

"You are aware she's going to give you hell for the rest of your life?"

"Yes." And he was looking forward to it.

"God!" Kier exclaimed. "Look at you. Smiling like a half-wit."

"Mm-hmm." Then suddenly it dawned on him. "Wait, where's she going?"

"Home. With Neil."

Connor jumped into motion without thinking. Kier clasped him by the elbow and held him back. "Calm yourself. You'll see her tonight for dinner. Come on. Let's get that statement down now and then go home."

With a friendly pat on Connor's shoulder, Kier started up the stairs. "Did you ever sleep on your way here or just fornicate? You look like you could use some rest."

Connor grumbled under his breath as he shuffled after Kieran.

19

Restless, Connor paced the parlor. Where the hell was she? He stopped and looked out the window from behind the curtain. Still no coach in sight. What the hell could possibly be keeping her? He paced some more, stopped to check his pocket watch. Connor frowned. Not even a minute had passed?

This was torture, pure and simple, and Connor hung on to his sanity by a thread.

He sighed, his eyes rolling skyward, trying to ignore the prickling feeling at his nape. Impatience sizzled through his veins and a dark hunger nagged him. Purgatory couldn't feel much different.

"Anxious to meet your wife, brother?" Kieran patted him on the shoulder. For the blink of an eye, Connor was tempted to wipe that smirk off his face.

"Here, maybe that'll calm your nerves a bit." He held up a glass of brandy for him. Connor downed it in one gulp.

Kier's eyes narrowed on Connor's necktie before he fiddled with it. Next, he righted the lapels of Connor's coat and brushed some lint off his left shoulder. "There now. That's better."

Hooking a finger into the necktie, Connor tried to loosen it a bit. "That's much too tight."

Kier shook his head, playfully slapping his hand away. "No. You just think it's too tight because you haven't dressed up like this in years. Which, I might add, would have never happened if you'd stayed here instead of running away because you couldn't stand being near me."

Connor felt his eyes bulge. "Is that what you think?"

All this time he'd thought Kier couldn't bear that on top of everything his brother was a criminal. He'd been convinced that not even Kier believed he was innocent. Fleeing from Georgetown had been one of the hardest decisions in Connor's life. Leaving his brother had felt like his soul had been torn in two.

Kier's face sobered. "It doesn't matter anymore, does it? It's in the past."

His voice was almost devoid of emotion. Kier had become so cold. That Connor had stayed away so long had probably added loneliness to the bitterness. But Connor was convinced there was still a scrap of Kier's former self left. If only he could help him find it again.

Kier poured himself another glass and sat down on the settee facing the window that Connor had been staring out of for the last half hour at least.

"Care to tell me how you met her? Or where?"

Connor reluctantly wrenched himself away from the window and forced himself to sit down next to Kier, setting his empty glass on the table in front of him. "I sort of ran into her on Grenada. She needed a passage north and I told her I'd get her wherever she needed to go. That's it."

"A remarkable coincidence. This sounds, dare I say it, beyond belief especially considering the fact that you normally frequent places where she wouldn't likely be." Kier gave a knowing chuckle.

Connor refused to elaborate. Kier didn't need to know all the details. After all, this was Connor's wife they were talking about.

His *wife* . . . It still felt surreal. Good, but it would feel even better if she were here.

Connor had never thought he'd marry, ever, not after all that happened to his brother and to him—that is, until he met that feisty woman. She'd drawn him in immediately with her fabulous beauty and fiery hair to match her temper. Her eyes could burn with fury, but they burned even brighter with passion.

"And all this time she didn't tell you who she was or why she needed to get here?"

Shaking his head, Connor admitted, "I lost my heart to a woman with secrets. It seems to be a pattern with the O'Connors."

As soon as the words were out, Connor saw Kier look down to hide the sudden scowl on his face before he stood and re-filled their glasses.

After all these years, he still refused to talk about it. But Connor didn't back down. "What still strikes me as strange is that Gabby suddenly found the courage to defy Talbot."

Kieran shot him a warning glance. "The Baroness Wickfield surely had her reasons. And now she'll rot in prison for covering for her husband." His mouth twisted in a humorless smile, flashing white teeth.

Careful to hide his thoughts behind an impenetrable mask, Connor leaned back, cradling the glass of brandy in his hands. "Do you think that's wise? A mother belongs with her child, no?"

"Her parents can look after the boy." Kier shrugged with an air of total detachment, but Connor knew it was just an act.

"Oh yes, I forgot about her loving parents, who were so devoted to her that they traded her off to a title rather than to—"

"No, she'd said herself it was her desire to marry Talbot."

"I wonder, though . . ."

Setting his glass down with a loud clank, Kier whirled around. If looks could kill, Connor would at least be maimed. "What?"

"Oh, nothing." Walking around the table, Connor leaned against the window again, capturing the curtain between his index and middle fingers to pull it aside just a little and glimpse at the driveway. Still no coach anywhere in sight.

Silence stretched between them and Connor had a rising feeling that this gamble was about to explode in his face.

Kier sighed. "We both know you won't let it rest until you've said what's on your mind. So, what is it you wonder about?"

With a one-sided shrug, Connor tried to appear casual. "Knowing her parents, they'll ship her off without hesitation. But if Gabby were put under someone's supervision until the authorities decide what to do with her—someone who'd make sure she didn't flee. Could she spend some more time with her son before going to prison then?"

Looking back over his shoulder, Connor saw Kier had drawn his eyebrows together. The muscles in his cheeks jumped, his mind working overtime. Then some dark, merciless thought flickered in his eyes.

Maybe it hadn't been a good idea to tell Kier that. After what Gabby must have been through with Talbot, a man as bent on revenge as Kieran was probably the last thing she needed.

But before he could devise a plan to remedy his mistake, movement caught his eye. A coach halted just outside and Connor felt his heartbeat pitch to a deafening staccato.

"Ahh," he heard Kier say behind him. "There they are. Well, now is your last chance to run, Ronan."

Connor jumped as Kier addressed him by his real name. He'd almost forgotten it, having used the other name for so long. It was strange, yet when Kier said it, it felt like he'd come home for real.

As for his last chance to run . . . No. His last chance to run was three weeks ago, before he ever met Jaidyn. Even if he'd wanted to, it was completely out of the question now. She'd snatched his heart away and without her he was nothing but a miserable man greedy for her presence, starving for her touch. Only Jaidyn made him complete.

The butler, Malory, if Connor remembered correctly, led them in, announcing them formally as "Mr. Flaherty and," after a brief hesitation in which he seemed to have lost his voice, he introduced Jaidyn as "Mrs. Ronan O'Connor."

When she stepped into the room, Connor's mouth went dry as if someone had just poured a bucket of sand down his throat.

Her beauty was not merely stunning. Jaidyn was as blinding as the sun.

Head bent in modesty, her shoulders squared, her back straight, she demurely folded her hands in front of her as she stood just one step behind Neil, who seemed to burst with pride, his nose high up in the air.

Connor was rooted to the spot. He couldn't move, couldn't breathe, couldn't blink. All he could do was take in her appearance in stunned silence. Jaidyn wore her hair up. It was unusually tamed and a few strands had been forced into locks that played over her neck, evoking an immediate reaction in Connor. He asked himself what it would be like if it were his fingers and not those curls that skimmed her neck.

His gaze wandered down lower. Her sky-blue gown was open at the front. The slightly squared neckline was rimmed with white lace, as were the edges. The same frills lined the split sleeves at her elbow. Connor could see each one of those coquettish freckles he'd already kissed, but right that moment he was sure he must have missed one or two. Or more.

A matching dark blue ribbon, the same darker shade of blue

as her petticoat, was laced over her stomacher. A choker with a sapphire-studded bow bobbed at her neck when she swallowed.

Jaidyn met his gaze and a blush crept up her décolletage. When it reached her cheeks, she broke eye contact and looked down, and her fingers played with the lace over her petticoat.

Realization struck him. She'd shed the role of the impetuous, wild, and bold woman as she'd slipped into the garments of this refined lady. Despite her sudden fussing, probably born out of irrational worries that Connor wouldn't like what he saw, he knew right this moment he looked at the real Jaidyn. With every pore she exuded she was versed in society, probably used to soirees and balls every night.

Connor also knew her playful side, her illogical whims and her delicious sensuality. As far as he was concerned, his seafaring days were over if he could just see her like this all the time. Afterward, when they'd come home, tired from dancing and drunk from entertainment, she'd let her other side show. Just for him. And they'd seek amusement of an entirely different sort.

After a brief greeting, Kier took it upon himself to show them into the dining room. Connor could only follow, like a puppet whose limbs were attached to her. Jaidyn moved smoothly, elegantly, her hips swaying. She threw a coy smile back over her shoulder at him. Connor was too aroused to gawk.

Sweat beaded on his brow. He wanted her. Right here. Right now.

Well, maybe not with her father watching. Would it be rude if he just rushed up the stairs with Jaidyn in tow?

Dammit. For the first time since Kier's manservant had talked him into it, Connor was glad for the hip-length waistcoat that hid his raging erection. How was he ever going to get through dinner? He hoped he wasn't expected to participate in small talk because, quite honestly, he didn't know if he was capable of more than monosyllabic replies. Or more likely subdued groans, because his hard cock was already incessantly throbbing like a bad tooth.

For Jaidyn it was utterly fascinating that Connor and his brother looked so much alike. At first she thought she would never be able to tell them apart, but gradually the differences between them showed. When Connor would laugh—well, tonight he seemed to be in an odd mood, but what she knew of him in general—Kieran would smirk at best, if he gave away any reaction at all. Jaidyn had a feeling that Kieran had just as much emotion boiling under the surface as his brother. He just disguised it well and preferred to draw his lips down into a constant, slight frown.

Kieran's eyes were brighter too. Where Connor's were a rich sapphire, Kieran's were more a stormy light blue. He also wore his hair longer than Connor. But the easiest way to distinguish them was the small, thin scar on Kieran's brow. Not for the first time that evening Jaidyn wondered where he'd got it.

When dessert was served in small ramekins, Kieran eyed the dish in front of him and gave an exaggerated gasp. "Cook has outdone himself, I see."

"I'll say!" Neil exclaimed, apparently totally enraptured. "*Crème Anglaise*. My, your French cook is truly exceptional." Her father dug into the dessert as if there was no tomorrow.

Her father and Kieran were the only ones who spoke more than one sentence at a time. Out of politeness, Jaidyn tried her best to participate in the conversation, but it wasn't easy for her. She didn't know the men well, and the heavy silence wafting toward her from Connor, seated opposite of her, was rather depressing.

Connor seemed to not want to participate in the conversation at all. He only replied when spoken to directly and then he said very little—if he spoke at all. Mostly he only uttered a snort, or a grunt, for variation, she supposed.

Nervousness caused Jaidyn to feel a little queasy, but the aroma of caramelized sugar teased her nose no end. Well, the thing in the ramekin looked like burnt cream. It smelled like it and now, as she let the cold, vanilla-flavored cream melt on her tongue, she found it even tasted like burnt cream. Maybe the French name made it special.

She dared to glance in Connor's direction. He stared into his ramekin, gripping the spoon so hard his knuckles paled. She grimaced as she saw the scrapes that marred his attractive hands.

His silence couldn't distract from how exceptionally good-looking he was tonight. It wasn't only the dark bistre coat with deep cuffs he wore over a mulberry- or cordovan-colored waistcoat. They were both lined with bands of the same gold embroidery. Clearly they had been tailored to match. Contrary to what she'd expected, Connor wore a white shirt tonight, lace ruffles spilling out at his wrists. His hair was mercilessly tied back with a black ribbon, and the formal ensemble, as she remembered from before they sat down at the table, was perfected with black breeches, white stockings, and black shoes with elaborate buckles.

His brother, Jaidyn thought as she threw another brief glance his way, liked lighter tones. He was mostly clad in gray. But Connor was ruggedly handsome in those dark tones that looked so excellent on him.

More often than not she did have difficulty following the conversation dominated by Kieran and her father. Her attention kept straying to when she'd finally be alone with Connor. The most shocking images kept popping up in her mind, so that sometimes she found it difficult to breathe.

Had he even noticed she'd taken so much care with her attire this evening? It was a special occasion. Very special. For Jaidyn, it was, in a way, her wedding night.

Maybe something had him worried. Perhaps he'd changed his mind and would rather be on his way? As bitter as it was, the proxy stated clearly that he wasn't expected to be her husband but on paper. Those were the terms she'd insisted upon, as much as it pained her to admit it.

Maybe he finally read through the proxy and didn't like what he'd gotten into. But she'd insisted on those terms when she hadn't known who he was. Now each and every one of those terms was up for negotiation—for the fun of it. Frankly, Jaidyn thought they were null and void now that she had married the man of her dreams.

She'd said she loved him, but he hadn't said it back. Although he'd wanted to marry her . . . it didn't really count when he'd said it. His mind must have been addled. Jaidyn felt a pleasant shiver down her back and only just held back a low moan as she felt herself become moist just thinking of what they'd shared the moments before he'd proposed.

Jaidyn was torn out of her mulling when Kieran stood and bowed to her. "I'm afraid I have no sherry for the lady."

Blinking a few times, Jaidyn forced her mind to start working again. "That's quite all right. I should withdraw to the drawing room now."

"Whatever for?" Kieran looked intrigued. Her father gaped at her. Connor's features were arranged into an expression of boredom.

Jaidyn stood, checking her gown for wrinkles. "So that you gentlemen can be alone."

Where could the drawing room be? She hated that she'd be confined in there and could only twiddle her thumbs until the men were done drinking and whatever it was they'd do.

"A laudable show of manners, indeed." Kieran laughed. "Alas, there is no drawing room here in this house yet. So sit with us and have a glass of port."

Under those circumstances she could hardly decline the offer. It would be impolite. Jaidyn gave him a smiling nod and they all made it to a room at the back that looked like a peculiar mix between a study and a sunroom.

Because of her wide skirts, Jaidyn could only sit sideways on the edge of one of the two leather armchairs. Her father sat in the other. When Kieran offered him a cigar from the box on the board next to the glasses and decanter, Neil gladly accepted.

Connor leaned casually against the wall opposite her, a little in the shadows. But Jaidyn could see the look of strained forbearance on his face.

Kieran held a glass of the garnet-colored wine out for her. She took it from him and sipped it. The port's sweet aroma covered her tongue and throat like delicious, velvety honey. It didn't take long until she felt a peculiar tingle spread from her fingertips and toes up into her body. The cloying smoke of Neil's cigar started a buzz in her head. Jaidyn had to fight the strange impulse to giggle.

She didn't think it was the port that affected her that much. Or not only. The looks Connor threw her way made her head light. His gaze was like a tender whisper over her skin at first. Soon Connor's eyes turned smoldering, like the look a hungry predator would have. Jaidyn swallowed hard and tried to suppress her body's instinctual response, but it was hard staving off the secret longing coursing through her veins. Her face flamed and Jaidyn coughed slightly to cover her telltale reaction.

"Would you like one more?"

Jaidyn's ragged breathing pitched. She looked up to see Kieran waiting for a reply and she held up her glass to him. "Y—"

Connor stalked around Kieran and took the glass from her

hand. Without taking his searing gaze off her, he handed the glass to his brother and took her hand in his. "I think she's had enough."

He pulled her hand close to his chest until her knuckles brushed the lapels of his coat. She thought she could feel his erratic heartbeat even through the layers of garments.

Automatically, Jaidyn stood on wobbly knees as the blood rushed through her veins. She forgot to breathe when his alluring scent and the entrancing heat he seemed to radiate sneaked under her skin, doubling the thrum of yearning in her core that was already too hard to ignore.

"Gentlemen, if you'll excuse us, my wife and I shall retire for the evening."

Jaidyn sucked in a deep breath and held it. All of a sudden she was nervous beyond reason.

She was about to exchange a few unnecessary, yet in polite society customary, phrases with her father and Kieran, but she never got a chance to. Not releasing her hand from his, Connor wrapped his other arm around her, his fingers splayed at the small of her back. He herded her out, up the stairs, and, Jaidyn supposed, into his room.

Well, *their* room now.

20

Behind her, Jaidyn heard Connor close the door. When she looked back, she saw he was leaning against it, taking her in with the same devouring look he'd had downstairs. Anticipation had her tingling inside. All through dinner she'd thought about what was to come now.

Reaching for the ribbon at the front of her gown, she opened it as she turned to face him. His eyes were riveted to her hands as they worked to slowly reveal the corset underneath. Remaining where she stood, she let the gown gape, hooked her fingers into the edges of its neckline, and pulled it down. Catching the blue dress in her left hand, she placed it over the chair next to her.

Reaching back, she opened her petticoat and let it slip from her waist, all the while aware that the look she gave Connor was an unconcealed challenge.

His gaze darkened dangerously, but the hardness around his mouth spoke of his arousal. He seemed rooted to the spot, unable to tear himself away from the door. By the way his jaw ticked, Jaidyn knew he was gritting his teeth, holding back.

"What is it? Don't you want to . . . you know?"

Connor swallowed hard, but his voice still came out as a hoarse croak. "I—I don't want to ruin that beautiful dress. Or your beautiful hair. Or . . . hurt you."

"I see," Jaidyn purred, letting her fingertips travel over her bosom, which was ruthlessly pushed up by the corset. Connor's eyes hungrily followed their advance. She fought the knowing smile tugging at the corners of her mouth.

Turning her back, she displayed the laces of the corset and sent him a deliberately coy glance over her shoulder. "Would you?"

At first she thought he hadn't heard her or had simply chosen to ignore her. Then he took one hesitant step forward, and another, and another. When he was close enough to start working the laces, a battalion of butterflies started to buffet in her stomach.

Jaidyn was pushing him hard to his limit. The knowledge made her head light and the desire coiling in her belly pitch to a heavy pulsing.

When she felt the corset give way, she inhaled deeply. Connor took a step back again and moved around to face her. The way he watched her made her feel so very feminine and so very powerful that she felt like she was on the edge of falling.

Standing there in just her chemise, she reached for the lapels of his coat and went around him as he shrugged out of the garment. He had his hands balled into fists.

When she'd helped him out of his coat, she held it up in front of her like a shield so he wouldn't see through the sheer shift. "Why don't you just sit on the bed, then?"

Bringing her lips closer to his until Connor's head dipped, she evaded his mouth and gave him a teasing, sensual smile instead. She shoved him back with her hand on his chest right over his heart, her fingers splayed. When his calves met the end of the bed, his knees buckled and Connor sat unceremoniously on the bed.

Kneeling before him, she helped him out of his shoes. Then she let her hands travel up his calves until her fingers arrived at the small buttons of his breeches at his knees. She slipped them through the holes, then hooked her fingers into the rim of his stockings and pulled them down.

Jaidyn reached up and began to unbutton his waistcoat. She noticed her hands were shaking with the craving that had her body aching and burning inside.

First Connor didn't help her with the task at all; all he did was lean back, bracing himself against the mattress, never releasing her from his intense stare. But finally he shrugged out of his waistcoat and pulled the shirt over his head.

As he sat with his delicious, naked torso before her, Jaidyn let her chemise fall down her shoulders, pooling around her waist. When she wiggled her hips a little, the shift fell down to her knees.

Connor cupped her cheek in his palm, his thumb caressing her lips. Her core clenched with need. She had to swallow the lump of choking hunger that changed her breaths into gusty pants.

Her nether muscles quivered and tightened with longing again when she saw the bulge in his breeches. Her tongue traced her lips and she lifted her gaze back up to his.

"What do you want?" Her voice was unusually gravelly. "Talk to me."

Jaidyn dug her fingers into Connor's thighs, hands wandering up his thighs. Her deft fingers freed him in no time. His hard member was, it seemed, darker and larger than usual.

Entranced by the glorious sight, she wrapped a fist around his cock. Just touching him, her fingers trailing over him, brought bliss to her senses. His muscled torso twitched, as did his rod. Was he as starved for her touch as she was for his?

Pumping him slowly, Jaidyn let the pad of her thumb tickle his head, spreading the moisture leaking forth. "What do you want? Do you want me to . . ." Jaidyn had to clear her throat. "Suck your cock?"

She should feel ashamed, but those stark, carnal words caused a shiver of lust to rake her body. All she could think about was how much she wanted to taste him on her lips, feel him push deep into her mouth.

Without waiting for a reply that she had a feeling wouldn't come anyway, she lowered her head and let her tongue explore his head, snaking over the tip and tickling the tiny hole. She moaned as his seductive taste detonated in her mouth and her desire spiked to an aching want.

"Is that what you want?" Jaidyn met his gaze, reveling in the hunger darkening his eyes.

Wrapping her lips around his head, she used the flat of her tongue to massage the tiny, sensitive spot on the underside. He gave a sensual rumble from deep in his chest and she sucked more of him into her mouth.

Looking up, Jaidyn saw his lids lower over eyes that glittered like heated sapphires. That she could give him so much joy made her heart flutter and her sheath spasm yet again. Implacable desire swamped her, hunger so demanding that she wanted to shove him back, straddle his thighs, and ride him right now.

But she held back. Jaidyn wanted to draw the pleasure out until it was almost beyond bearing.

Connor's elbows must have become too weak to hold him up any longer because he fell onto his back, his head digging into the mattress. He arched under her with a gasp, his hands fisting in the sheet. She slowly bobbed her head, let him slip from her lips, gave the tiny hole another quick tickle with a flick of her tongue before she took him deeper.

The urge to please him, to show him just how much she enjoyed this, had her thinking of all the other things he liked. There was something else she hadn't tried yet. But with what she knew of him, Jaidyn had a feeling he'd like it.

Letting go of him, she tugged at his breeches. Connor lifted his hips to help her get them off, then scrambled to lie in the middle of the bed. Jaidyn crawled up and took his engorged member into her mouth again, pumping him with one hand while she sucked at him and let her tongue massage him.

With her free hand, she touched herself and let out a low moan as she felt how wet she was already. She bathed her fingers in her cream, giving in to the need to rub over her swollen nub every now and then, all the while licking and sucking him, lavishing attention on him. She had to stop arousing herself or she'd crest right about now. She wanted it to last.

Her hand left her moist lips and as she took him deep down her throat, she brought her wet fingers up to massage his tight entrance. Connor starting to pant made her smile around his member. She hadn't been wrong.

One lubricated finger slid in bit by bit and Connor arched off the bed. A hoarse cry ripped from his throat. His hands wrapped around her head and brought her down on him faster.

She could taste a small spurt of his salty juice at the back of her throat and, knowing it wouldn't be long now, Jaidyn continued to tease him, sucking him hard, lavishing him with her tongue, her finger massaging him gently, pumping in and out in the same slow, steady rhythm her mouth traveled over him.

He thrust hard into her mouth as she moved her finger in deeper just to let it slip out again. She continued to work him like this, weaving a net of mind-blowing lust around him. He tasted fantastic, felt so marvelous, and those tiny pants and moans he uttered caught her in the spell. Jaidyn increased her efforts to please and pleasure him. Her teeth grazed his head gently before she swallowed almost all of him once more. She thrust into him, feeling his muscles constrict around her finger when she met that one spot, that tiny lump, and concentrated on it exclusively.

Connor shivered under her ministrations, groaned, and the response of his hips turned urgent. Jaidyn took him deep faster, swallowed and massaged him relentlessly, teasing him to the brink of orgasm. When she felt his member twitch, she let go of him and sat back on her heels.

"Uh-uh," she uttered, but her voice came out as just a husky purr. "No coming yet."

With a throaty laugh, Connor threw one arm over his eyes, probably to find his focus again and get his ragged breathing under control. His wide, muscular chest was shiny with perspiration.

Jaidyn crawled up his body, straddling his hips. Her wet folds gyrated against his hard rod. Throwing her head back with a gasp, she brought her hands to her breasts and cupped them. Pleasure had tingles start in her belly.

Squeezing her hard peaks between thumb and forefinger, she felt a fresh gush of moisture surge from her, wetting his engorged member. When she pinched her nipples and twisted them slightly, pleasure darted from her breasts down between her legs. Jaidyn sank her teeth into her lower lip, but a low moan ripped from her regardless. Release was so close, reeling and boiling under her skin just out of reach, but so ferocious she could actually taste it.

Jaidyn felt Connor's hard grip on her hips and threw her head forward again. She felt him lifting her off his member just long enough that his head was tightly pressed against her moist entrance as if probing the warm, wet passage for a comfy place to snuggle into.

"Do you want me to ride you? Is that what you want?" Jaidyn croaked and impaled herself with deliberation. She caught her breath when she felt him stretching and filling her so completely. Joy made her head spin. His heat, his thickness, his strength in her. It felt so good. Nothing could have prepared her for this perfect, supremely intense moment.

Rising off him, she let him ease out of her only to press down again, taking him back inside. She chose a slow pace on purpose. Each circle she drew with her hips heightened her enjoyment.

Simultaneously, Connor rolled his hips upward, driving his member even deeper into her slick core. A shower of hot sparks washed over her and she felt her nether muscles clutching him tighter with tiny pre-orgasmic spasms.

A hoarse scream ripped from her throat when his thumb stroked her already too sensitized nub, lighting a bonfire in every fiber of her body. Jaidyn was about to fall over the precipice, give in to the sizzling pleasure, but she forced herself to open her eyes and lock her gaze with his while pushing the coiling and impatiently snarling climax back just a little longer. Bending, she leaned forward and by doing so stopped his hand from stimulating her further.

Connor grasped her waist to hold her in place. While she ground on his hard member, he took one of her stiff nipples into his mouth and sucked it against the roof of his mouth, his teeth biting hard into the soft flesh. Her mind was about to shatter into so many pieces she was sure she was going insane.

Connor pumped into her from below and Jaidyn couldn't help but move with him, meeting him stroke for delicious stroke. Their ride turned into something different, something wild, desperate, both seeking abandonment in the delicious friction they created with each stroke. The faster he pumped, the harder she ground against him.

But suddenly Connor lifted her nearly off his member. Jaidyn froze, her whole body stiffening with a guttural sound of protest toppling from her lips.

Connor let her hear a deep, almost growling chuckle and smacked her left buttock hard. Jaidyn wheezed in a breath, her gaze zeroing in on him and that cunning smirk on his luscious lips.

"You're tightening on my cock," he chastised. "Remember: no coming yet. You said so yourself."

Jaidyn felt the soft skin on her buttock pulsate. At first the pain helped her focus, but then the pricking ache turned to a sweet, fiery pulsing that had her leap toward the precipice.

Aware that he was watching her struggle to get her rapidly approaching climax back under control, she found the strength to hold on for just a little longer.

Connor lowered her on his thick rod again and began to thrust into her with a heady, steady rhythm that made her body burn, her head spin.

She couldn't fight it off any longer, simply couldn't. It was too much. Her conscious began to dissolve with the merciless onslaught. Raking her hands through his dark hair, she stopped moving altogether, forcing him to cease his strokes into her core as well.

"What do you want, then?" Her voice was more a breathy whisper than a croak.

As fast as lightning, Connor snagged her around the waist and lifted her off completely. Jaidyn gave a shocked gasp and gripped the headboard hard for balance. His arms snaked around her thighs and pulled her down. Her mind was submerged in a thick, syrupy layer and was reluctant to work.

Next thing she knew, his mouth was on her core, lapping at her swollen and aching folds in long, slow strokes. Too addled to do anything but sit on his face, Jaidyn threw her head back, mewling and whimpering.

Pleasure lashed inside her with every pass of his clever tongue. Hot, forceful lust steamed through her. She cried out and her hips jerked, slamming her core against his lips.

Jaidyn feared she'd crest hard and fast no matter how much she wanted to hold it back and make this night last forever. Fighting against the rising tide of desire that was about to crash over her, she shook her head, gripping the headboard harder. It was the only thing still anchoring her to the here and now.

Connor pressed his teeth into her folds until her nub pouted up for his twirling tongue. While nipping it gently, he flicked his tongue over it, tender, but fast. Her vision dimmed, small golden spots dancing and jostling before her eyes.

Fire trails streamed through her body and mind. The pressure built hard and fast and, rolling her hips, she begged him for more. And then she drowned in the fire, unable to hold back any longer. Her climax crashed over her with the force of a riptide, sucking her under and spitting her out, his name a hoarse scream on her lips.

Taking her tight little ass in his hands to keep her just where she was, Connor continued to lick and swirl leisurely strokes with the flat of his tongue over her folds, careful to avoid her clit. He felt her squirm over him and his grip tightened to hold her in place. His mouth sucked, his tongue lapped slowly, and he rumbled deep in his throat.

He wasn't ready to end this just yet. Quite the contrary. Connor was eager, starving actually, to lap up every drop of the sweet female cream that flowed from her pussy now that she'd finally come. The more he could draw out her climax, the better for him.

Her every breath came out as a gusty pant. Moaning himself as her rich syrup tickled down his throat, he contemplated if he shouldn't bring her again. Her taste had him completely enraptured. He'd never tasted a cunny as sweet as hers. And he never would now that he had the sweetest the world could offer right there, in his arms.

True, he could make her come again. And again. As often as he wanted. He had his whole life to dedicate himself to the task.

But he hadn't really claimed her yet. His weeping, abandoned cock throbbed viciously. Connor ached to cover her, fill her, make her his forever. That's what he wanted, what she'd asked him for repeatedly.

Jaidyn jerked her hips, squirmed and sobbed above him, and he felt her body slowly become pliant. Oh no, he wouldn't have any of that.

Reluctantly, he ended his very pleasurable task and lifted her off him. Licking the taste of her musky honey from his lips, he drowned in the need for more.

She landed on her back next to him, her limbs splayed, her breathing nothing more but shallow gasps. Her eyes were closed, a dreamy smile on her slightly open lips. He saw tears dotting her lashes. Pride exploded in his chest that he could make his woman weep in pleasure.

Sliding his thigh between her legs to spread her even more, he settled down on top of her. Her sex was so hot, so wet for him and he entered her with no effort at all. She moaned and her hips bucked as she welcomed him. Sensation and emotion had shivers explode within him and with one quick thrust, his cock was buried deep in her slick passage.

Jaidyn blinked her eyes open and smiled at him, her hand cupping his cheek. He latched onto her lips and his tongue thrust deep. Connor let his hungry kiss give her an idea of the need to possess her roiling in him, the hunger to take everything he wanted, craved, needed to breathe, to feel alive.

"You," he finally answered her question.

With a moan, she arched her body under his, opening herself completely to his touch.

"It's you I want," he rasped against her throat, then nuzzled his way up to nip at her earlobe.

She sobbed, then let out a breathy laugh, the sound more arousing than anything he'd ever seen her do or had done to her.

"Only you," he whispered and then began to make love to her with unhurried, steady thrusts.

Her arms snaked around his shoulders and he felt her fingers rake down to the small of his back. Rolling his hips, he slid in and eased out of her, taking her in slow, deep thrusts that had her whimpering mindlessly.

Connor burned to take her harder, his cock itching to slide faster into her hot, tight, slick sheath, but still he rocked gently against her. He didn't know if he could keep up this slow pace for long. Squeezing his eyes shut, Connor tried to focus, but the little whimpers that left her throat eventually crushed his will.

His rhythm escalated and he stroked her with long, hard thrusts. Feverish with passion, Jaidyn gave a throaty sound of pure pleasure, opened her legs even wider, and thrust her hips up faster, demanding without words he give her more. Connor obliged her, gritting his teeth as he served her, lunged in and out of her heat.

She panted. She moaned. She arched under him, her fingernails digging deep. Connor growled as he felt her need for more and deepened his rolling thrusts until he pistoned away in her, thrusting hard and deep.

Her blazing moans turned to searing little cries of passion as she met his every stroke, and Connor felt the scorching pleasure in him expand dangerously fast. It threatened to swallow him, steal his control, his sanity, and never return it.

Twisting under him, she caught her breath and Connor could feel her tighten around his cock, gripping him as if she never wanted to let him go. He propped himself up on his arms

262 / *Chloe Harris*

for better leverage. He thrust into her harder and faster still, sliding his cock almost completely out of her only to slam it back into her, rapid, harsh, relentless, sending her toward the orgasm he could feel was closing in on her swiftly.

"Come, Jaidyn," he croaked and the next instant, she was there, her cunny contracting and rippling.

The pleasure he gave her ricocheted and spiraled down his spine. Connor continued to ride her hard, even though her sheath clamped down on him. The friction was too delicious to ignore and he shoved into her sex and retreated only to thrust into her again.

Connor shuddered at the devastating ecstasy, his body taut and trembling. He knew he couldn't deny himself for much longer. She was going to shatter him with the orgasm that he felt rushing toward him. Rapture slammed into him like a hot poker, starting an earth-shattering prickle at the base of his spine that raced through his balls up to his cock—

Flaming and violent, his climax hit and he burst into so many shards of glittering light he thought he was going to faint. Pleasure ripped her name from his lips. The jagged bliss seemed to last forever and he found himself going helplessly limp.

Collapsing on top of her, his heart roaring in his chest, Connor tried to gather his scattered wits while at the same time fighting to pump air into his lungs.

Through the haze fogging his mind, he felt her move and lifted himself off her to give her room to at least breathe.

Closing his eyes, Connor reveled in the stillness spreading through him. Part of it was because he felt contented. Oh, his body craved hers, still did. But there was the peacefulness that stilled all his worries and doubts, bliss he experienced in her arms only.

Lifting his head and propping it on his arm, Connor looked at her. She was so beautiful. He could look an eternity at her, could kiss each one of those stirring freckles, could remain there as he was with her beneath him, and not tire of it ever.

"I love you."

She inhaled deeply, turning her head to gape at him. Then her features softened. Her eyes turned misty. After a breathy snivel, she cupped his cheek in her palm. "I love you, too, Connor."

Suddenly, her ginger brows wrinkled. "Or Ronan." Pursing her lips, she whispered, "What should I call you? Connor? Or Ronan?"

"Whatever you like. I've gone under the other name so long I don't even remember my given name."

"Ronan is your given name. Should I call you that?"

"I'd like 'husband.' "

A smile broke out on her face and she lifted one leg to entwine it with his, letting her toes tickle up and down his calf.

"Don't move."

"I'm not moving!"

Connor let his brows wander up on his forehead, stating quite clearly that she *was* moving her leg.

Jaidyn rolled her eyes. "Well, I'm not moving the important parts. I like you just where you—ohh!" She moaned and pressed her head back into the mattress, a clear sign that she must have felt him harden in her again.

Connor chuckled at her immediate response.

Licking her lips, she let her thumb caress his cheekbone. Connor thought he saw something like mirth flicker in her eyes for a moment.

"Hm . . ." Her smile turned to an impish grin. "I still think I could have done better than a rich merchant like you."

Naughty, playful little pixie. Connor had no idea where this was supposed to lead, but he played along, interested in what was on her mind now. "How so?"

Her fingers ran through his hair, massaging the back of his head. "You see, I do believe I attracted a dashing, wicked sea captain's attention."

"Really? A dashing, wicked sea captain?"

"Yes." She gave a jerky nod. "He always expected me to address him as 'sir.' And he had a treasure chest too."

Connor felt his slowly hardening cock promptly stand to attention. "That sounds wicked, indeed."

She hummed as she must have felt him stretching her again, her eyes fluttering closed for a moment. "Oh yes, very wicked."

Connor rolled his hips, starting to stroke her deliciously slowly yet again. "All this talk about wickedness . . ."

With a moan, Jaidyn arched her body into him, whispering, "Gives you ideas?"

"Wicked ideas," Connor confirmed.

Biting her lower lip, Jaidyn apparently struggled to keep her mind on the conversation. "How wicked?"

Reaching up, Connor grasped the velvet rope hanging from one bedpost to hold the brocade curtain back. Swiftly capturing her wrist in it, he pulled the rope tight and grinned. "Very wicked."